BLOOD
AND
ROSES

BLOOD
AND
ROSES

A HOLLY JENNINGS THRILLER

A. K. ALEXANDER

BLOOD AND ROSES

fTHOMAS & MERCER

Text copyright © 2013 A. K. Alexander

Published by Thomas & Mercer

PO Box 400818

Las Vegas, NV 89140

ISBN-13: 9781611099638

ISBN-10: 1611099633

Library of Congress Control Number: 2012922333

DEDICATION

For my dad, who helped me with the plotline before he passed away, and I believe he helped me write the book from the other side. He was a true and dedicated horseman his entire life who aimed to improve the lives of all horses. He was my biggest fan, and a true inspiration.

PROLOGUE

Tommy Lyons was on a high.

And a roll.

He strolled through the jockey locker room, sweat, anxiety, irritation, celebration all culminating in the air as each jockey relived his high and low of the day. Exhausted jockeys tossed bright-colored silks into gray metal lockers to land amid religious relics. These guys typically prayed. At any given second while riding a thundering thousand-pound animal traveling at 40 mph in only 2.5 seconds, life could be ripped away or changed drastically with one fall, one mistake.

Just one.

And it happened—all the time.

So, they prayed.

The scent of leather and horse also remained on their clothes and skin, smells they all relished. They were jockeys, and this was Del Mar, California, where the surf meets the turf and the track's backdrop of the Pacific Ocean just to the west made everything a little bit sweeter and brighter.

Except when you lost.

No ocean blue or land of the beautiful could take away the sting of a loss. But losses came with the job.

Except for Tommy Lyons these days.

Nope. Tommy was on that roll.

A nice, tasty winning streak.

"That mare another Zenyatta, hombre." Juan Perez slapped him hard on the shoulder. Tommy winced, but even an ass like Perez wasn't going to get to him today.

"Oh, you don't know the half of it, man. That mare is going all the way. I say she's gonna win the Infinity Invitational." Tommy set his helmet inside his locker.

"You think, Tommy?" It was Pete O'Leary, an old-timer in this business. He'd won more races over the years than anyone else in the jock locker room. He had become something of an icon. And in most everyone's opinion, he should've retired by now. His age was showing. He was losing the better mounts. He had a bit of a drinking problem, and rumor was he did his fair share of drugs to keep his weight under control. No shock there. It wasn't beneath any of the men and women in the sport to use a little help to stay in the game.

"Yeah, man. I think. I definitely think." Tommy clasped his hands, folding his fingers out and raising them over his head, stretching.

Everyone was talking about the Infinity Invitational. This race was going to be huge, and it was a first. A first in many ways.

The racing commission had changed the bylaws. Horse racing could take place in the state of Nevada—after a lot of politics and an exchange of cash.

The sport needed a face-lift. Bad press, a seediness that had seeped in over time, had torn at the walls of a great tradition, and an honorable sport had suffered a loss in spectators. There was ridicule, and for several years now there had been talk about how to make changes. Owners, trainers, and other industry professionals had come together and used that old adage "Money talks."

Some big-time investors swooped in and big money was set down. Horse racing could take place in Nevada again—specifically in Las Vegas. And although racing was tried back in the sixties in Vegas and failed badly—due in part to Mafia corruption—everyone agreed that there was no better time to bring the sport back to the glitz and glamour with which it had once been associated. Bring it back to the days when horse racing was America's favorite pastime and the biggest spectator sport out there.

A grand track had been built on some land just outside the strip.

A major casino had gone up with Edwin Hodges's name behind it. Hodges was a billionaire who loved the ponies, and of all the investors involved, he'd contributed the largest sum.

The stage had been set.

The biggest purse ever to be offered in the world was being offered at the Infinity Invitational.

Fifty million dollars.

The theme of the race was eighteen. Edwin Hodges was an interesting guy and he had a thing about the number eight, being that it was the sign of infinity. They'd named the track the Infinity, Las Vegas. And eighteen horses would be invited. Eighteen three-year-olds. The race and speculation about who would be invited were all anyone and everyone was talking about these days.

Tommy Lyons laughed with joy at the prospect of being headed to the Infinity at only twenty-two years old. It was good to be alive.

God, this was fun. Winning was so much fun.

"She got some gas, that's for sure." O'Leary palmed his thinning hair and looked up at him from the bench on which he sat in front of his open locker. He smiled weakly at Tommy, tiny fine lines around his stark blue eyes crinkled up on the side of his face. "Beautiful animal."

"Like her owner. Man, I gotta say, I'd like to ride *her*," Perez said.

O'Leary gave him a dirty look. "Don't disrespect Elena Purdue around me."

Perez shook his head and ignored O'Leary.

"Yeah, man. Elena is good people. Good trainer. Good owner," Tommy said. "And an awesome horse. Fast." He shook his head. "Real fast. Unbelievable fast."

"Rode a horse like that once. Man, that colt was one fast son of a bitch. Nobody's Business. Amazing animal."

"Yeah, *cabrón*. No one could forget that horse," Perez chimed in. "Fast horse. Too bad what happened though." He shook his head and tsk-tsked under his breath.

O'Leary sat there for a second. The air settled in thick as some of the guys stopped and waited.

They got what they were waiting for.

O'Leary slammed his locker and jumped up. He was in Perez's face as quickly as a fly discovers a pile of horse shit. He shoved the younger jockey hard. "What you sayin', Perez?"

"Nothing, hombre." He raised his arms halfway up, palms out, shoving his chest toward O'Leary in a gesture that said *fuck you* rather than *nothing, hombre.*

The jocks in the room did nothing to stop the spectacle they were witnessing.

Everyone knew what Perez was saying.

Back in the day, Nobody's Business was the first horse in over a decade expected to win the Triple Crown. The colt and O'Leary had it, but in the final turn O'Leary got aggressive with the horse and jockey next to him. Nobody's Business gave them a good bump. Nobody's Business tripped, and he came down hard, fractured a proximal sesamoid bone in his front right leg. Two other horses crashed as a result, one of the jocks badly injured—paralyzed from the waist down. Nobody's Business had to be euthanized on the track. An investigation ensued and O'Leary was acquitted, but the horse was dead, and many in the business blamed O'Leary. Not only did the jockey lose his reputation that day, but also much of his career. The hall of famer had gone down in disgrace, but Tommy liked him.

Mistakes get made.

It was a tough business they were all in, and they didn't always make good choices.

Shit happened.

Horses died.

They died a lot on the track.

Tommy walked over to them. "Hey guys, come on. Not here. There's no reason for this. The past is the past, Perez. O'Leary, everyone knows you're good people and one of the best jocks ever. Relax."

O'Leary took a step back, his face purple with rage. "Watch your fucking self, Perez. Watch your fucking back." His hands were shaking as he retreated a couple of steps.

"Fuck you, O'Leary." Perez smiled.

O'Leary looked as if he might pounce again. "I'm warning you."

"Fuck off, Perez," Tommy said. "Why don't you go get a beer and chill out? No one needs your bullshit today. You're a blowhard, man." Tommy was feeling just a tad more confident than usual. Normally, he would have bitten his tongue when it came to talking smack to a colleague—especially someone like Perez, who was one helluva rider and also a bit shady. That was the word anyway. But today, Tommy was on that roll and talking smack came easy.

"You know what? You just made my shit list, too, Lyons." Perez walked past his locker and slammed the door, leaving the jock's room and the tension inside.

Low chuckles and some indifference wafted through the room. It didn't take long for high fives to resume, guys thinking ahead to their evenings, back to business as usual.

"Don't listen to that guy," Tommy said to O'Leary. "Everyone knows you can ride, man. You have to ignore guys like him. You're too good a man to allow someone like Perez to light you up. Like I said, you can ride, and that's what matters. Get your mojo back, and you'll be in the winner's circle again."

O'Leary gave him a sad smile. "My days are about done, kid. Just done." He shook his head. "But yours...yours are just beginning. Be smart. I like you. Look, I've gotta go. Things to do. Have a good one." He patted Tommy on the shoulder, and with his head down, walked out—a beaten man. The industry did that to some guys.

Tommy watched O'Leary leave the locker room, feeling sorry for the guy. A legend like that shouldn't have to put up with this shit from the likes of Perez. Maybe he should take the guy for a drink, try to pump him up. Not let him give up like that.

But he had plans with Katarina.

His girl.

O'Leary would have to wait.

No one knew about Katarina—that she was his girl. Katarina was another jockey, and she was a real good one, too. She'd requested they keep things between them quiet. There was enough politicking she had to deal with, being a female jock, and she was afraid that if any of the other jockeys caught wind of their affair, she'd be harassed. But dammit, he was falling in love with the girl, and he wanted to shout it from the rooftops.

Tommy checked his watch. They would meet at their favorite bar in an hour and then go back to her place. It was nicer than his place—but not for long.

If the filly...

If that sweet, beautiful filly Karma's Revenge kept going as she was, surely the owner and trainer, Elena Purdue, would let him continue riding her. He was forming a connection to the horse. She loved running for him. She wanted to make him happy. He could feel it with every stride on which she lengthened herself out.

The adrenaline.

The energy.

God, it was pure bliss. That horse was opening some doors for him!

Tommy bowed his head in front of Jesus Christ hanging on a cross inside his locker. He touched the small picture of the Virgin Mary taped to his locker door as well. He said a prayer and crossed himself, not forgetting *who* had gotten him here and *who* was in charge.

He shut the locker and wove through the locker room, receiving a few more congrats on the day's big win. He hoped Katarina would be as happy for him. He knew she would likely be pouty, since he and Karma had left her and her horse in the dust just out of the starting gate. His girl was as competitive as any of the guys, and she did not like to get beat. He would make it up to her. They had agreed business was business and best left on the track.

He headed to his jeep, sure to be upgraded to a sports car—soon! He dialed Katarina's cell to see if she was on her way, too. She didn't answer. He left a message and headed out, but first he drove over to the barns. He parked the jeep in front of barn four, took a carrot from his bag, and walked over to Karma's stall. Everyone had gone home for the day, and the sounds of horses chomping on their feed echoed up and down the aisle. Tommy spotted one of the security guards pacing the barn aisles. They gave each other a cursory nod and a brief "Good evening" and went about their business.

Tommy walked up to the lovely bay mare. She lifted her head from the feeder and stuck her nose out at him, expecting the treat. A perfect white snip adorned her face as her delicate ears flitted forward, attentive, waiting. Out of her nostrils came a warm breath of anticipation. A thick line of lashes added femininity to the horse's bright and kind eyes. What a gem.

The jockey made this a daily ritual with the mare. Not only did he like speed and adrenaline, but he loved the horses. He had respect for them, and especially for this filly, which he knew was his meal ticket to better days.

Karma took the carrot from the palm of his hand. Tommy gave her a pat on her dark neck, which shone like satin in the dim lighting of the barn row. "You done good today, filly. You done good. We're going places. We are going places, girl." Karma took her perfectly sculpted head and nudged him. He laughed. "Nope. I don't have no more. Tomorrow." He kissed the warm nose and headed back to the jeep to meet up with his other girl.

Life was so very sweet for twenty-two-year-old Tommy Lyons.

At the bar, Tommy ordered a beer and waited for Katarina. And waited. He thought about Karma. He thought about O'Leary and Perez. He wished he could have helped O'Leary, and he was anxious to get out there and kick Perez's ass on the track. Pompous jerk! And he waited some more—for nearly an hour he waited and kept calling her cell phone. Panic set in because just the night before she had insisted that he agree to her rules. "We don't fall in love. We don't tell no one. We are having fun and that's it. No relationship. Deal? I don't have time for a relationship, Lyons," Katarina had said in her Irish lilt, shaking a finger at him, "and neither do you."

He'd agreed, but he wasn't feeling that way at all. In fact, Tommy was already in love with the just-under-five-feet, blue-eyed, redheaded freckle face from the Emerald Isle. His hope was that over time she would come around.

Maybe she had sensed his hesitation to truly agree to her stipulations. Maybe he had freaked her out. He called and left her one more message, saying that he was headed home and for her to please call because he was worried. He knew she wouldn't like that, but dammit, it was true.

Tommy paid his tab and headed to the jeep. He got behind the wheel a little buzzed and definitely on a high from the day's win with the filly. As he started the engine, he spotted something on the passenger seat that had not been there before.

Or had it been?

No. It had not.

A racing form from that day. He picked it up. What the hell? He could see in the dim light that a typed sticky note was on top. It read, *Sacrificial Lambs. That's all. Point to make. Bigger fish to fry.* "What the he—?" Before Tommy could finish the sentence, something struck him hard on the head from behind. He had no time to defend himself before he blacked out.

🌹 🌹 🌹

He called himself Joque.

It was a pun.

"French for jockey, huh, boy? Pretty fucking smart, aren't I?" He winked at Tommy Lyons who was bound, tied, and gagged, seated in a folding chair across from his pretty little girlfriend, Katarina. Tears sparkled in her eyes.

Ahhh. So sad.

Pitiful. Yeah.

Whatever.

Lyons eyed him. Fear. Pure, unadulterated fear. Good. He should be scared.

"Do you have any idea how many horses break their legs on the track each year, Tommy boy?"

Lyons just stared at him.

He'd brought them to a warehouse. The smell of rubber was thick, or maybe it was oil. The lighting was dim, but the warehouse looked to be empty. A light buzzing sound rang through the air, almost like a mosquito but continual.

"How about you?" He turned to Katarina. "You are two up-and-coming superstars. Do you know what you've gotten yourself into? Do you have any fucking clue?" he screamed. "Let me tell you how many horses break their goddamned legs on racetracks each year. Eight hundred horses. Eight hundred! Oh, and lest we forget how many suffer heart attacks. Two- and three-year-olds having heart attacks!" Joque wiped the sweat off the back of his neck. A ski mask still covered his face. He couldn't take any chance of being spotted. He knew that wouldn't happen. Plans had been carefully constructed and were now being executed. And this here with these two jockeys was only the beginning.

Joque walked to the corner of the room of the industrial building off Interstate 15 near Poway. He had taken Katarina first when she'd gotten into her car at Del Mar. It had been a little too easy, and he'd hoped the boy would be more of a challenge. He was sad because he had not been.

He picked up the metal baseball bat and brought it over to the kids.

The *jockeys*.

He looked from one to the other, smiling. Katarina's eyes widened and she began to shake her head. She was the smart one. Lyons looked stupefied.

Joque brought the bat up and swung as hard as he could, connecting directly with Katarina's shin. He heard the snap. He heard what probably was some kind of gasp from Lyons. A strange sound emitted from the girl jock. Her eyelids fluttered.

"Oh no, no. We don't pass out. You think when a horse you're on top of snaps his leg that he gets to stop? He doesn't stop. He keeps going because that's what he's been trained to do. Trained against nature. Or shot up with so many drugs that he can't feel a thing for the first few minutes." He placed a hand under her chin and shook her head from side to side. "Noooo. You are not allowed sleepy time. Not yet."

Such a shame.

Such a waste.

A pretty girl.

And all she'd had to do to live in this life was something different from racing horses.

That was it.

Tears now fell down the girl's face. Joque looked at Lyons. The kid was white as a sheet. "Hey, cowboy, how do you like seeing someone you care about being hurt like that? Not so fun, is it?"

"Here, let's make it even." Joque wrapped his palms tightly around the bat, brought it up, and swung. This time he connected with Tommy's leg. He didn't hear a snap, so he brought the bat up and swung again. He did that four more times. He wanted to be sure he broke both the boy's legs. When he stopped, Tommy's head hung. "You can't fall asleep either." He cupped Lyons's chin and looked into his eyes—eyes filled with pain. "I am sorry about this. You are simply sacrificial lambs to this thing. You're pawns. Kind of like the horses. You're stupid. I know your stories."

He faced Katarina. "You're a poor girl from Ireland who grew up on a farm. You worked the tracks there and then came here. Some fuckwad—what is his name—brought you here." Joque tapped his chin with his forefinger, pretending to think. "Oh yeah—Geremiah Laugherty. That guy. Big mistake, you coming on board with him." He turned to Tommy. "Too bad you won't get a chance to ask her anything about Mr. Geremiah Laugherty there, Tommy. Seems the two of you have something in common. Like getting into her pants." Joque laughed. He took note of the look in Tommy's eyes. Even in pain, those eyes were now searching Katarina's, as if to say *how could you?* "It's all right, jock. Love hurts. And I can't blame you for wanting to make a better life, sweetheart." Joque tickled Katarina's exposed arm with his free hand. "But you should have known. You both should have. You both know what goes on. It makes you as bad as the rest of them! You say you love the horses?!"

He now faced Tommy. "You don't give a rat's ass what happens to them. How about that colt just last week, Lyons? Cannon bone fracture. Do you know how painful that is? You know, the one in the third race? Do you even remember the horse's name? I do. Stand by Me.

"Did you stand by him when they put the needle in him and killed him after you had run him into the ground? A goddamn three-year-old!" He was screaming again. His face burned underneath the mask and tears stung his eyes. "You're a whore! You are both whores! Sellouts!"

He pulled the 9 mm Glock from his waistband, his rage taking over, and he pointed it at Katarina. He didn't think. He aimed. He fired. The bullet struck between her shocked blue eyes.

"One down." He turned back to Lyons, who was now crying. "Fucking baby! Do you think that colt cried? How much pain do you think he felt?" He shot Lyons in the stomach, where he knew it would take the jockey a few hours to bleed to death. "I'm not going to give you the mercy your girlfriend got. You should have known better!" he growled. He picked up his bat, raised it one more time, and struck Lyons in the legs again—for good measure.

With his gloved hands he pulled a couple of carrots out of his pockets. He removed the gag from Katarina's mouth and shoved in a carrot. He did the same with the dying Lyons. "Good race, jock. Here's your treat."

He left the building.

Small fish.

Big pond.

Much to do.

He had much bigger plans and many, many people were going to die at his hands.

He was seeking justice and he aimed to get it.

CHAPTER

1

Three weeks later

The news came in many forms that Monday morning. Television, newspapers, radio, the Internet, and *by invitation only.*

Eighteen three-year-old Thoroughbreds had been invited to the biggest event in horse racing history. The Infinity Invitational, to be held Friday, October 12, 2012.

On the list, fifteen colts and three fillies.

A fifty-million-dollar purse.

Only the finest, fastest animals in the world would be running.

And the world waited.

CHAPTER

2

"Lunch in backpack?" Holly Jennings asked her ten-year-old daughter, Chloe.

"Yes," the blue-eyed, dark-haired girl replied.

"Homework in there, too?" Holly hurriedly wiped down the kitchen counter.

"Oh wait. My science. It's um, it's uh…"

"Chloe. Think. We have to get Maddie, too, and we'll be late. This is why I tell you to pack up your things the night before." She shook her head, rinsed her coffee cup, and turned off the coffee-maker, tempted to pour herself a to-go cup; but time was short. She did grab her hazelnut creamer, though—the coffee at the station left a lot to be desired.

"I'm sorry. I just…oh wait, it's in Petie's crate."

"Petie's crate?" Holly asked. She started to ask why and then thought better of it. "Hurry up. Go get it." Petie, their Yorkshire terrier, had come into their life through a brutal case Holly had worked on a couple of years back. The dog's owners had been murdered and Holly took the poor thing in. She had to crate him while at work, until her older soon-to-be stepdaughter, Megan, could come by after school and let him out. Petie had an issue with chewing anything left out that looked remotely chewable, including a leather ottoman in her living room. Countless shoes had also gone by the wayside, thanks to Petie. Who would have thought a five-pound dog could eat his way through an ottoman in a few hours, not to mention a TV remote or two? Petie could.

While Chloe fetched her homework, Holly headed for her room. She needed to get a sweater. The offices at the station were kept so cold that even in eighty-degree weather, as Indian summer settled in like clockwork around Southern California, it was frigid inside her office.

She searched through her closet and found a sweater she actually hadn't worn in about a year. She liked it for the big pockets.

As she swung it over her arm, something dropped out of one of the pockets. She bent to pick it up. A charm—a plumeria flower charm.

From Hawaii.

From her honeymoon.

With Jack.

She remembered why she had the charm in the sweater. Last winter, she'd slipped it on after an argument that she and Brendan had about her work, which did seem to be the source of most of their arguments. She'd come home from his place, put the sweater on, and then gone to her jewelry box and taken out the charm, remembering when Jack had given it to her.

That night a lot changed.

"Mom!" Chloe yelled. "I'm gonna be late!"

Holly put the charm back in the pocket and donned the sweater. The pressures of the ten-year-old being late to school made her decide that she would put the charm away when she came home.

"Got my homework." Chloe ran into her room. "Come on, Mom. Let's go."

Holly shook her head, put the dog in his house, closed the plantation blinds in the front room that faced the street, locked the doors, and headed out.

A few blocks away she picked up her younger soon-to-be stepdaughter, who was also Chloe's best friend, Madeline. Holly's fiancé, Brendan, was a small-animal vet and already at his office, so Holly handled the morning pickups, while Brendan was in charge of getting the girls from school in the afternoon. They would all eat dinner together if Holly was available. There were many nights when her job as a crime scene investigator/homicide detective required her to work late into the evening, which meant Chloe stayed at Brendan's. They had been together now going on two years and had discussed cohabiting, but mutually decided that it wasn't the best example for their girls. Only a few more months and they would all be under the same roof. Poor Brendan was going to be bombarded with what Holly had started referring to as the estrogen O-zone. Holly hoped he knew what he was getting into. She smiled thinking about him as they pulled up in front of his older, Spanish-style home, similar to hers, in the Point Loma area of San Diego.

Chloe jumped out and ran up the cement stairs to get Maddie. The two came flying back down the stairs a moment later. Maddie's strawberry-blonde hair streamed behind her. She was as gorgeous as her father and her older sister Megan. They were indeed a pretty family, and before long they would be hers.

The girls chatted wildly in the backseat of the jeep—something about Justin Bieber. Their school was only a couple of miles away, and once they were out of the car and the energy had settled, Holly dialed her partner, Chad Euwing. Chad was one of the good guys, and he watched her back. When she was running a little bit late, like this morning, he'd cover for her.

"Hey you," she said cheerily when she heard his voice come over her Bluetooth.

"Jennings." He sounded alarmed. "I was just picking up the phone to call you."

"Everything okay?" She knew by the tone in his voice that it wasn't.

"We've got a long day ahead of us."

"Talk to me," she said.

"You know our case? The two jockeys...Del Mar...last month? The ones found in that defunct dive-suit manufacturing warehouse?"

"Yes. How can I forget?" They had been working on it now for a few weeks, with no leads. Nothing. They'd hit a wall and she was as frustrated as Chad. To make matters worse, they'd caught another homicide case since the jockeys' and, because the newer case had been tied to a local judge, the pressure had been on. Their boss, Chief Greenfield, was a great boss and well respected, but like most people, he caved under pressure from higher-ups. That was what had happened when Judge Winchester's niece had been found murdered behind a nightclub in downtown San Diego. Holly and Chad had spent a couple of weeks with the case and had come to the sad answer. The twenty-three-year-old girl had gotten herself messed up with the wrong guy, who had connections within the drug world. A seedy, scandalous story, and the girl's family had suffered a great deal. In the meantime, their jockey case had grown cold.

"Ever hear of Marvin Tieg?"

"The movie producer? I think everyone has. I mean, at least if you either watch *Entertainment Tonight* or read the sports page on occasion. Wasn't his most recent movie *The Guilty*?"

"That's him. And aside from his movies, he's the guy whose horse was expected to win the Triple Crown last year, right? But then there were all those accusations and something about illegal drugs found in the horse's system. Big story. The guy liked the ponies."

"Liked?" Holly asked.

"Liked. Good thing we solved the judge's case, because the story on the jockeys is going to get bigger. Tieg is dead. Murdered in his home in Hollywood Hills."

"Okay. Not our jurisdiction." Her stomach sank. This was not going to be good.

"Yeah, well, the detective on the case just called for you. Tieg was tortured and left for dead with a carrot stuck in his mouth."

CHAPTER

3

Holly and Chad ran the lights on top of the car while working their way toward Tinseltown.

He drove and she went over the notes regarding Tommy Lyons's and Katarina Erickson's murders. "This guy, this detective, did he say anything else about the victim, other than the carrot in the mouth?" Holly asked. She tucked her short auburn hair behind her ears. Holly had worked CSI for several years following her years as a detective for San Diego PD. Most CSI were not trained police officers. They didn't have to be, but she had chosen that route, and after working a case with Jack ten years ago—the case that had resulted in his death—she'd taken the schooling needed to be a CSI. She'd been pregnant at the time, and she hadn't wanted to risk her child's life. Then, after Chloe was born, Holly didn't want to risk Chloe becoming an orphan due to a dangerous case.

With the economic downturn and cuts in the department, Greenfield had asked her if she would be willing to come back on as a detective. She'd agreed, with a few stipulations. One—she would not work narcotics, as those cases posed a lot of threat to an officer's safety. Two—Greenfield had to pair her with her partner, Chad, and he had to allow them to work their cases in the best way they saw fit, affording them flexibility and the freedom of not having Big Brother over their shoulder at every turn. They were good cops who knew how to do their jobs. Greenfield had agreed, and for the past few years now, she and Chad had made a good team, solved some solid cases, and kept costs down within the department because of her proficiency as both a detective and a CSI.

"No. The Hollywood Hills detective was very discreet. His name is Devraj Amar, I believe. Had just a hint of an Indian accent. Nice guy, from what I gathered."

"Interesting that he would go so far as to ask us to come up and view the crime scene."

Chad nodded and glanced over at her. His hazel eyes darkened with a knowing that she recognized.

"Yeah. I know what you're thinking, and I am going to agree here. Either we have ourselves a serial killer, or a copycat." A text came through on her cell. *Love you. Dinner at eight? Just us? Megan will babysit.* "Shit," Holly muttered.

"What?"

"Nothing. Brendan. You know the drill. Trying to split my time between job and family."

"I do," he said. "I know that drill well." He glanced at Holly. "Brooke's due date is getting closer. I wonder how the baby will change things."

Holly smiled at her partner and decided not to respond to Brendan's text. Maybe, just maybe, she would be able to make an eight o'clock date with her beloved. The next few hours would dictate if that was a possibility, or not.

Chad cleared his throat, back to business. "A copycat, though?" Chad said. "I don't think that's as viable as a serial killer. Unless the carrot bit has been leaked to the press, but we've kept tight lips on this thing. I think we got one and the same guy here. The obvious connection is that these vics were involved with horse racing."

"I think you're probably right, partner. Here we have two young, up-and-coming jockeys. Now an owner. As far as what we know about the jockeys, it seemed that everyone we spoke to thought the world of them. Trainers liked them, owners liked them, other jockeys. I did have one red flag but couldn't take it anywhere."

"What was that?"

"The guy training the horse Katarina had ridden that afternoon." Holly read back over the extensive notes on her tablet. "Geremiah Laugherty. He was a charmer for sure, but something went off in my gut when we spoke. I could never put a finger on it."

"I didn't get that. Tall guy, right? Kind of looked like Clint Eastwood back in the day?"

Holly laughed. "Right. Before he shouted at an empty chair."

"Don't get me started."

"I'm just saying...You brought up the gunslinger. But as far as good-looking and seemingly genuine, then yes, that is the guy," Holly said. "Nothing stands out in my notes from the investigation, though. Everything has been a dead end. The killer was clean, no prints, nothing but the dead kids and the note in the racing form. I'll be interested to see if maybe Geremiah Laugherty had any association at all with Marvin Tieg."

"Your gut is usually decent. As far as that note left by the killer goes, I've played out every puzzle I could with it. Sorry, but nothing. Until now..."

"Until now. Maybe," she replied.

They exited the freeway and followed the GPS, making the turn off Sunset onto Laurel Canyon and winding on up the palm-tree-lined street—serene, clean, and speaking volumes of wealth.

"Wow," Holly said as they pulled up into the driveway. The place was a monstrosity of glass—truly a glass house, built to take in the views of Los Angeles below.

LAPD had a line of vehicles parked up top in the circular drive, along with the coroner's van. As odd as she had felt asking the detective who had called her to see if they could hold off moving the body until she arrived, he had agreed. This wasn't her case, and she didn't know if the dead producer was related to her case with the two dead jockeys. But if this was the same perp, and from the sounds of the carrot-in-the-mouth move it might be, then Holly was hoping to discover some answers.

Anything.

She wanted to be able to call poor Katarina Erickson's family back in Ireland and let them know that the devil who had destroyed their beautiful daughter was locked away. And Tommy Lyons's father, who had been crushed by the news, would possibly be able to move on in some small way.

The families of murder victims never really moved on completely, but when the perp was caught—or better still, dead—there did seem to be closure and some small sense of peace. If Holly could in any way provide that for the families, then she would. Even if that meant going out on a limb and asking a colleague from a different jurisdiction to do this favor for her.

Chad ran his hand through his sandy-colored hair. He gave her a grim smirk and a nod as they got out of the car. The temperature was warm under the sunny LA sky, the smog lighter than usual as a westward breeze pushed the pollution out over the Pacific. Even with the clarity of midmorning, a heaviness hung in the air—the kind of heaviness that seemed to always accompany death, especially as dark a type of death as murder.

The twelve-foot-high, double-wide wooden doors stood open. Holly and Chad flashed their badges at the cop standing guard. He gave them a funny look, and Holly knew he had made the badge from outside of LA. "Detective Amar requested us. I'm Detective Jennings. This is Detective Euwing."

"Let them through."

The officer stood out of the way, and Holly could see a thin man in his midthirties, with dark hair, dressed in khakis and a white polo, standing in the massive foyer. He approached them and took off his rubber gloves to shake their hands. "Good morning, Detectives. I am Devraj Amar, detective in charge on this case. I am the one who phoned you." He smiled. "Thank you for taking the time to come up."

"Holly Jennings and Chad Euwing. Of course. We appreciate your asking us. We have been at a loss with the jockey case in San Diego, and if this is tied in, we're more than happy to cruise up the coast and see what we have."

"Why don't I show you?" Amar replied. He spun on his heels and led them to the back of the house, his shoes clapping against the cream-colored marble floors. They passed through glass-walled hallways and through a bachelor-chic interior—a lot of beige, shades of browns and grays, leather and suede furniture with interesting artwork that ranged from nude women to movie posters, and photos of different horses either in racing mode on the track, or in the winner's circle.

Staleness and the smell of copper and death wafted throughout. It was all too familiar. A cross between burned rubber, melting iron, and decay. The kind of smell that came with violent death.

The family room where they wound up looked out over an infinity pool and the canyon. Houses were sporadically fanned out along the hillside, and depending on what time of the day the killer had come into the home, it was doubtful anyone would have been able to see what had taken place.

The first image to catch Holly's eye inside the large living space was a massive flat screen mounted onto a wall. Amar began speaking almost as quickly as he walked. "Marvin Tieg. Hollywood producer, lived alone after a divorce three years ago, liked lots of women and parties. No kids. Forty-three years of age. Made a lot of money in the entertainment industry. He also liked the ponies and owned a half a dozen, from what I can figure out at this point, but I will be digging deeper into that. I present Mr. Tieg to you."

Amar took a new pair of latex gloves out from a case he carried and slid them on. Placing his hand on the leather revolving recliner, he turned the chair around.

There sat the dead Marvin Tieg with a carrot in his mouth. His pants were rolled up past his knees. Dried blood had caked on his legs over what appeared to be pinholes, as if made from a needle. Around the blood, his legs were badly bruised. Rigor mortis had set in, and the stiffened body looked more like something at one of those creepy haunted mansions on Halloween that Holly refused to take Chloe to, than what was once, probably less than twelve hours earlier, a living human being.

Holly stood speechless for a few seconds as she tried to make sense of the sight in front of her. She crossed her arms and cocked her head. "What in hell are we looking at, Detective? What was done to his legs?"

CHAPTER

4

The first time Elena Purdue uttered the name "Karma's Revenge," the words carried just a tad of bitter sweetness. Elena loved the filly in a way she hadn't loved many horses. She'd always loved horses, always had them from the time she was a little girl, but she didn't love them all equally, and Karma was the horse she loved above all.

For more than one reason.

Elena had nine horses in training at Purdue & Co. Stables out in her own quiet corner of the world: Ramona, California. The "Co." had at one time been her longtime lover, Carter, but then Carter decided that he *was not* the marrying kind. So he left and married someone else—the ex-wife of one of the owners with a horse in Elena's stable. Elena in turn screwed the owner, as if that was going to make anything better. The owner—a guy named Raymond Scarborough—decided that mixing sex and business was a bad plan. Elena agreed. Bedsides, the guy sucked in bed, and all he wanted to do was talk about how his wife, Patty, had run off with Carter.

The thing that hurt the most for Elena was that Carter had a little girl—Sophia. Elena adored the child, whom Carter, of course, had out of wedlock—because he *was not* the marrying kind. Six years spent with Sophia and Carter because Mom was in and out of the picture. And then, Carter left and took Sophia, who at the time had been seven. Elena's heart had nearly broken.

The filly had saved her from total despair.

Karma had been born on one of the colder nights in January three years ago to one of Elena's favorite mares—a daughter of the ever-controversial Big Brown. The night of the filly's birth something went very wrong, and the mare died. Karma had not had an easy beginning, to say the least. Because the filly had been orphaned, Elena had to work quickly and diligently to supply the foal with the mare's colostrum. Born without any antibodies—and without that vital colostrum to provide the necessary antibodies—her chances for survival were slim from the get-go.

However, Elena had poured everything into the filly. Because foals nurse up to seventeen times per hour during the first week of life, Elena jacked herself up on caffeine and vigilantly nursed her when others told her it was likely to no avail. But there was grit in Karma's eyes. There was desire—desire to live, desire to race. These animals were born to run—running was what they knew. Elena had grown up around racehorses and she understood them. And Elena sensed that Karma knew it was her destiny to fly on the track.

She was going to see that the horse fulfilled her destiny.

The "Co." in the stable's name now stood for the horses. Especially her girl Karma, whom Carter had the gall to call about one night after hearing that Elena was working herself to the bone to see that the filly survived. "It's a waste, Elena. Look, I still care about you. It just wasn't meant to be between us, but I certainly don't want to see you make yourself sick over some horse."

All Elena had said back was, "Can I see Sophia?"

"I don't think that's a good idea. She's finally bonding with Patty."

"Don't ever call me again. I'm fine." She'd hung up the phone, wiped the tears that had sprung to her eyes with the memory of Sophia's sweet face and the times spent with her. That was the night when she cemented her determination to see her filly become one of the greats.

And the night she gave the filly her name.

Karma was rapidly becoming America's sweetheart. Her story was the kind that people loved. Made them feel good. The only dark cloud in Elena's and Karma's lives had been the horrendous murder of Karma's jockey, Tommy Lyons. The kid had been a bright and shining star. A good guy. A good rider. A jockey who loved his job and the horses. Elena missed him. She'd thought of him as a little brother. Tommy had been so grateful when she'd given him the ride on Karma at her maiden race a year ago. They continued on together after that, until Tommy was murdered a month ago in San Diego. Karma was burning up the tracks up and down the West Coast, and had been back east twice now—all successful meets.

Both Tommy and Elena had agreed that the filly had more talent than any animal they'd seen in a long time. Whispers of the next Zenyatta were springing up across tracks around the country, and the fact that they had been invited to the Infinity—with a good chance of crossing the finish line first—was causing a lot of interest in her once-sickly girl. But the void Tommy had left remained deep in Elena's heart, and she prayed daily that his and Katarina's killer be caught. Tommy should have been the one to ride Karma in the big race.

Elena had to find a quick replacement for Karma's jockey— painful as it had been, it had been necessary. She'd hired Juan Perez. Perez had come into the picture right after the murders, and Juan and Karma seemed to have a connection that was making them a winning team. Juan was a pro. He'd been around for a long time and knew how to get horses across the finish line in top placements.

Elena could hear Juan coming down through the barn aisle before she could she see him. Perez was a whistler. The Oakwood meet would finish up that week, and then they were headed to Vegas for the Infinity. Today was Karma's last go at Oakwood.

"Morning, Señorita Purdue." Juan approached her, stick in hand. He twirled it around like an acrobat.

Elena stood outside Karma's stall forking over the carrots and drinking down her third coffee of the morning, and it was not quite ten o'clock. She ran on caffeine. "Juan. You ready for today?" Today they would be running in a stakes race. Nice purse. All eyes were on her horse.

"I am. I am." He ran his hand down the bay filly's snip. Her big brown eyes shone softly in the light of the morning.

"Natalie took her out for a short exercise at daybreak."

"Good. Good. Big stuff, this filly. And I like the bug," he replied, referring to Karma's exercise rider.

"Be careful with the *bug*. Those young, pretty girl jockeys can get someone like you into a heap of trouble. I've seen the way she looks at you. Don't go robbing any cradles." Elena raised her eyebrows.

Juan waved his hand dismissively. "Nah. I'm her mentor. That's it. Natalie...she's just a bug to me with a lot to learn, but the horse likes her, which makes me like her. I like the filly better." He winked at her. "Besides, you know I like you, Elena."

Elena shook her head. "Juan. That was one night, and we'd both had too much to drink, and I'm sorry. As I told you after, we need to be strictly business. I don't want to mix that up with something we don't need to be mixing it up with."

Damn. How could she have been so stupid? Not long after she'd hired Perez, they'd wound up having dinner at her place to go over some things. They drank too much, and she'd been lonely. Perez was smooth and handsome. And now she felt like a slut, but what was done was done. She didn't want to change jockeys again. He was doing a great job with the horse, and he was one of the best.

She'd been trying to remain mature about the entire thing, but he wasn't letting it go. "Just ride my horse, Perez. Let's leave it at that."

"Okay, señorita. As you wish. I love the filly. Don't doubt that."

"Yeah. She's a good mare." Elena smiled. "Did you see this morning's paper?" Switching the topic to focus on the horse made her happy.

"No." He shook his head.

"Sports section. Tells our story. And they're betting that Karma will be first across the finish line at the Infinity." Elena smiled broadly. "She's making a name for herself."

"That colt of Farooq's, he's nice, too. And with Laugherty training..." He shrugged and flipped the crop in the air. "We got some competition, lady."

Elena now frowned. "Of course he's nice. The sheikh has a lot of nice horses. The colt is fast, I'm not going to argue that. Laugherty is one of the best trainers out there, but don't discount my efforts." She swallowed more caffeine and regretted her words. In this sport, a lot of money spent on a horse didn't necessarily mean much, but sometimes a thousand dollars spent on a horse with so-so breeding could mean the world. It was a bit of a crapshoot.

"Sorry," Perez said. "I would never discount your efforts. It's gonna be a good race."

Elena shook her head. "It will be. But the girl and I here aren't feeling threatened. Are we?" She ran her long manicured nails—her one real indulgence for herself—through the mare's wiry, black mane. "I'd better get on with it. I'll see you in a couple of hours. I have a few more rides to watch right now." She held her coffee cup up high, first to Karma. "Looks like a good day for the winner's circle, sweet girl." Then she held it up to Perez. "Ready to kick some ass out there?"

"Always, señorita."

Elena smiled and headed down the row and out toward the track, where the morning workouts were almost finished.

On her way she passed an old friend. Pete O'Leary. He'd actually been more than a friend at one time, over a dozen years ago when she had been barely twenty-one and he'd been thirty. The romance had been short but oh so sweet, until O'Leary had decided she was too young for him and that his schedule running all over the country wasn't fair to her.

Of course, there'd been a lot more to it than that.

Elena had always suspected her father had his hand in making sure the romance didn't go any further. Dillion Purdue never admitted it, and O'Leary had denied it, but one thing Elena knew about her father: if he didn't want you around either of his daughters, then you weren't going to be around his daughters. Dillion Purdue had been a respected big-time attorney out of Los Angeles back in the day and also owned some of the finest horses on the track. Elena felt traded in when O'Leary began riding some of her dad's top horses. She knew exactly what deal had been cut.

She'd cried to her sister Leann, who tried to help, but she was living in the UK at the time, and didn't want to get between Elena and their father. That was understandable. Most people never got in Dillion Purdue's way. Their dad was gone now. He'd passed away two years ago, and their mother had moved down to Florida to be near some of her longtime friends.

The funny thing about O'Leary was—unlike Carter, whom Elena could never forgive—her heart still skipped a beat every time she saw him. Even though his life had taken a dark turn. He'd been her first love, and that was something one didn't ever forget.

"Hey, El." He was obviously headed back to the barns, atop a horse.

"O'Leary." God damn! Why did her stomach sink and fill with butterflies when she looked into his crystal-blue eyes? "How are things?"

"Oh you know. Comme ci, comme ça," he replied.

"Right." She looked down at her feet, hiding her smile from him, and shook her head. "Good luck today."

"You, too, El."

She continued to walk past him and the dappled gray horse he rode.

"Hey, El?"

She turned around. He'd stopped the horse, who danced in place anxiously. "Yeah?"

"We should grab a beer sometime."

She thought about it for a minute. "How about coffee?"

He smiled that old familiar smile—the one that had convinced her to go to bed with him when she was a girl. "Okay. Coffee it is. When?"

"Oh God. You're serious?" she said.

"Yeah."

She looked toward the track, seeing dirt fly through the air behind a horse, clipping the time away. She tucked a loose piece of her auburn-colored hair into her ponytail. "I don't know. I've got to get ready for the Invitational. We're traveling in two days. "

"Good. We can have coffee tomorrow morning and dinner in Vegas."

"You're going to Vegas?" she asked.

"I am. I may not be riding, but I will be watching. I wouldn't miss the biggest race in the world now, would I?"

"I guess you wouldn't."

"Coffee tomorrow, then dinner in Vegas." He smiled.

"I didn't say anything to you about dinner," she replied. "I'll see you in the morning."

"Yes you will. See you in the morning."

Elena turned back around, trying to force the smile off her face. How was it that O'Leary could still do that to her after a dozen years?

CHAPTER

5

*"There is something about the outside of a horse that is
good for the inside of a man."*
— Winston Churchill

What goes on behind the eyes of a horse? Is it all a lot of nothing in
the brain? Eat, sleep, respond nicely to good care, suck it up when
humans don't care? Is there feeling, emotion? Is there a thought
process there?

Maybe the language is different, but the words are there.

The feelings are there.

The emotions are there. A horse responds to care and love more
than anything else put in its path.

Except fear.

Horses can differentiate good people from bad.

CHAPTER

6

Amar raised his eyebrows and then glanced down at the victim's legs. "I have just learned that it is called pin firing," he said. "Apparently a treatment for an injury to a horse's leg. The vet, or trainer, I guess, does it by burning, freezing, or dousing the leg with acid or caustic chemicals."

"Why in the hell would they do that to an animal?" Chad asked.

"Good question. I was told that it's supposed to induce a counter-irritation and speed and improve healing. A small blowtorch with a needle attachment is used. The needle and blowtorch flame are applied directly through the skin and down to the bone."

"And that is what was done to Tieg. Good lord. Who told you this?" Holly asked.

"Guy named Jim Gershon—he trains Tieg's horses. He's the one who found the body. Guy was really shaken up. I spent some time with him. One of the other detectives took him back to the station to speak further. Just talked with my guy not too long before you arrived, and they let him go."

"Do you mind if we speak with him?" Holly asked. "Do you think he's a suspect?" She glanced at Chad. "We need to see if he had any connection to the jockeys." Chad nodded, making a note.

Amar looked down at his feet for a second and then shook his head. "Too early to say if he's a suspect, but isn't everyone a suspect in the beginning?" He smiled. "And no. I don't mind if you speak with him. I read about your case down south. Then when this came in, I knew I needed to contact you. I know you have been careful not to let the carrot detail out in the media, but word has a way of traveling police lines with cases like what you two have down south. Then after your partner here vetted me over the phone..." He winked at Chad. "...he realized I was the real deal and that tidbit of information came out after I told him what we had found. Maybe if we put our heads together, it can help. More minds, you know..."

Holly nodded and appreciated the fact that Amar was open-minded enough to think this way. A lot of cops wouldn't be so open and willing.

"Okay, so this Jim Gershon can give us some more info on pin firing and anything else horse related here. I think we have to look at a few distinct possibilities for the type of killer we've got on our hands," Holly said. Chad gave her one of his eyebrow-raised, quizzical looks, and Amar smiled in a way that said he was on the same wavelength. "If I had to guess, I'd say that this guy is out for revenge. How the three victims tie in together likely goes beyond them just being in the racing industry. There may be some association among all of them, but I could be jumping the gun."

"This is sadistic and full of hate," Chad commented as he stared at the corpse. "What about the neighbors? Anyone see anything?"

"I've got some people canvassing the area and talking to folks, but so far we haven't come up with anything. This guy is possibly a pro. I don't know. Too early to tell. But there is something else here that I believe you also found at your scene." Amar walked over to a granite island in the kitchen and handed Holly a piece of paper.

"Racing form," she said.

"Open it," Amar replied.

She did. One of the horse's names was circled from a race out at Arlington Park in Chicago. "*El Chicano.*"

"There is something else. Turn it over." A small piece of paper with the words *In the Mouth of Madness* typed on it was glued to the back side of the form.

"What do you think this all means? I mean, the note he left last time with the jockeys referred to them being sacrificial lambs. The message was more direct. But this?" Holly gestured with her palms outward.

"He *knows* what it means and he wants us to find out," Amar said.

CHAPTER

7

Sheikh Mahfuz Farooq loved his colt, Whiskey Sour. He named almost all of his horses after alcoholic beverages, which was funny to him because he didn't drink. His brother and son thought it was stupid that he named them this way. But he didn't care. He found the names humorous, and Whiskey here was his boy. His favorite boy. He was a winning colt. Farooq had paid half a million US dollars for the colt at the Keeneland yearling sale almost two years ago. Not the most expensive colt. Not the cheapest. He came from good stock, but not the best.

Farooq was interesting that way. He could afford any horse he wanted. He did not usually listen to anyone else, study the stats, pore over every bloodline—though much of that type of knowledge swirled in his brain. When buying a horse, Farooq relied on his sixth sense. When he spotted a horse he liked, he looked the animal in the eye. As with people, he believed, the soul of a horse could be seen through his eyes, and when he looked into Whiskey's eyes, he spotted a winner, a warrior, but not the kind of warrior that is a savage. There were some of those horses out there, just as in people. Farooq didn't like savage people, or savage horses. No. This warrior had heart.

The sheikh stroked the glimmering neck of his chestnut colt, bent down to breathe into his nostrils, and then took in his own deep breath. Breathing in and out with the horse—a spiritual exchange. He cooed to the colt, who in turn licked his hand as if it were a salt block. Whiskey's strong jowls and fine-looking head spoke of elegance and confidence. A white blaze decorated his face. The only other white on the near-perfect animal was a stocking on his left hind leg. Farooq liked to rub that stocking. He felt it was lucky.

The sheikh had been a horseman from the time he could walk. Raised in Saudi Arabia as a royal, he had plenty of access to the finest horses in the world. His grandfather had given him this strong love for the animals and taught him everything he knew. If Farooq was not a sheikh with the weight of the world on his shoulders, he would have been what the Americans refer to as a horse whisperer. He liked the sound of that. The horses were his sense of peace. His soul. They understood him as no woman or man could. His favorite place in the world was the exquisite and immaculate barns he owned in Versailles, Kentucky. Walking through the barns, smelling the sweetness of the earth and the majestic animals he paid millions for eased him, pampered him. There was no better way to spend his time, especially when the grooms were gone for the day, and everything quieted as the horses ate their dinners. The routine sounds of slight shifts of weight atop straw piled high, and the rhythmic eating with an occasional sneeze or nicker echoing off stall walls, were the sounds of joyful respite for Farooq.

Although Farooq knew that he was never truly away from the eyes of humans, he could at least pretend here. He could go back to a time when life was simpler, or so he thought. When he was a boy and his cares were small, and he had a constant access to the horses with no watchful eyes. Someone had always been watching, but when he was a child they were much easier to ignore.

Bodyguards who stood in the recessed shadows of the barn were not as easily ignored as childhood babysitters. Security cameras scanned up and down the aisle to be certain no intruders passed through intending harm to the sixteen animals in this section of the barn and farm. These sixteen were special beasts—either former champions who now stood stud or horses who were currently winning out there. The special ones.

"Father?"

Farooq turned around to see his daughter standing behind him. "Ayda? You never come to the stables. Is there a problem?"

"No." She tossed back her long black hair. "I thought maybe that since we do not talk much or do anything together, that I would come here, and you could show me your horses. They are what you love."

The sheikh frowned. "I love you, too, Ayda. You know that."

She didn't respond. "What are their names?" she asked.

Ayda had ridden a horse only once in her twenty-eight years, and it had gone badly. She'd take a decent spill and had never gotten back on, although the sheikh had tried. He had encouraged her for many years after, but she had no interest. Neither did his son, Muhammad.

He nodded and smiled. "All right. I will show you. This is my colt—Whiskey—he will prove to be the most special of all. He is destined for greatness."

"Why do you say that?"

"Because I know these things, and he is fast. He wins races, Ayda, and he wins them because he loves to run."

"How do you know he loves to run? How does anyone know what an animal loves? Animals can't speak."

The sheikh laughed. "You are wrong. They do speak, only in a different language. There is something in the racehorse, in all horses, called heart. And heart is what they speak with. The heart of a horse is four times larger than its brain. Contrary to what many believe, this does not mean they are dumb animals. Not so.

However, I will say that if their brains were as big as their hearts, they would not do the things they do for man."

"Your horse has heart, then? This is how you know he likes to run?" she asked, staring at the colt, her hazel eyes narrowing into thin lines.

Farooq was unclear about what his daughter really wanted from him, but she was here and he would indulge her. That was what she enjoyed the best—to be indulged. "He does, and that is why he wins races. There are horses on the track who don't like to run. You can see it in the eyes. You can tell their heart is not in it. This does not make them bad animals. It makes them animals that would rather do something else with their time. Some enjoy to jump. Some enjoy to prance and dance as in dressage, and some enjoy to chase a cow. They are as diverse as people."

Ayda rolled her eyes.

"Make fun of me, but it is true. I tell you that if I am right and my dreams are correct, then this horse will race in and win the most prestigious distinction in the world of horse racing."

She smiled. "Yes. I've heard of this race. The Infinity Invitational. In Las Vegas."

"It is good for the sport. I am not a fan of Las Vegas, but because there is a need to boost interest again in horse racing, it makes sense to hold the event there. The last few years as the economy around the world has not been so positive, the sport has been hit hard as well." He shrugged. "But I do not like to dwell on the negative of anything."

Ayda looked bored at his rhetoric.

"My horses—*our* horses—have the finest care, the best feeds, attention, exercise, respect, and love. Not all horses have this. Bush tracks across this country are turning up every month on reservations. They are called racinos—racing casinos." Farooq did not like this one bit. It left a foul taste in his mouth—of American greed, and that was something he despised. He loved these animals whether or not they were as majestic and worthy as his colt. To Farooq, the horse, in all its glory, was one spiritual energy, one essence shared among the creatures no matter how great or small. "It is bad business, these racinos. It is like taking a beautiful woman and turning her into a whore."

Ayda yawned. "This horse is racing in the Infinity, no?"

"He is."

"Can I go to the race?"

"Of course you can come. That would make me very happy, Ayda. Yes. Yes. Of course. That would be wonderful. I've put much into the investment in the Infinity. It is going to be exciting. A very good time."

A lot of money had gone into building the track, which had been built in record time—only two and a half years. Marvin Tieg, whom the sheikh didn't think much of as a person, had actually done something pretty decent by rounding up major investors from film studios to a huge software company and the financial wizard Edwin Hodges, as well as himself. Most of the investors were doing it for the money. Farooq was doing it for the sport and the horses.

Tieg also made a film documenting the building of the track, and about horse racing. Then the idiot was looked at for drugging his horses. Blind eyes were turned, a few payoffs were made, and the next thing you knew, his hands were clean.

Enough money and interest had been poured into the race to keep people excited about the Infinity Invitational. Even more money than the World Cup in Dubai.

"A fifty-million-dollar purse! Yes, that has people talking, Ayda. This will be grand!"

"Good. I will go. I have an appointment now." Ayda kissed him on his cheek and walked away.

Farooq was perplexed by her sudden interest, but he was not going to question it. He wanted a relationship with at least one of his children. His relationship with his son was so strained that it was a lost cause. He was pleased his only daughter might be having a change of heart toward him.

"Sheikh Farooq." One of the guards approached him. The sheikh glared at him. "I am sorry, Your Highness, but it is time. Your plane is waiting."

The sheikh nodded, kissed his colt on his face, and quietly left the barn and his horses to finish their meals in silence. He prepared for his trip back New York City, where he would have to take his mind off his horse and his daughter, and pray that he could help save the world.

CHAPTER

8

Joque took a sip from his coffee and finished his eggs.

Good stuff.

All of it.

Room service and last night's memory. Not all of Joque's memories were good ones. But last night—last night was good.

And he had not had any nightmares. That was a change.

He couldn't help but laugh out loud at the thought of chickenshit Marvin Tieg squealing like a little piggy through the gag.

Look, the fucker deserved it. Tieg was the one who signed checks to trainers and vets. He knew a lot more than he pretended. It was all about signed checks, man. Who signed them and for how much. Guess the check written on Joque's life ten years ago wasn't quite large enough.

Because he wasn't dead.

He was very much alive.

Joque chuckled again recalling the scene from the night before. So fitting that the guy was so arrogant that he thought he was safe in his own house on the hill. How stupid. How ignorant. Those same bastards who had signed an amount on Joque's head had actually sent him to school. They just didn't know it.

The University of Kentucky State Penitentiary.

And, he learned a lot there—like how to break and enter anything. Boy, that surprised Mr. Supersize Ego, seeing him in his big
glass house.

"You know what pin firing is, Tieg?"

*Marvin stared at him—like Tommy Lyons had. It wasn't as if
the guy could answer. Joque kept him gagged and bound. "Do you? It
doesn't matter. I'm going to show you."*

*Joque had been around. He knew things. He knew a lot of things.
He knew how security cams worked. He knew how to break into places.
He knew how to hide and then become an element of surprise. He knew
that the bastard Tieg liked to have his first drink around five-ish, when
he got home. He knew things because he'd been a good study.*

And he knew how to pin fire a leg.

*Joque had also known there was a risk to what he had planned
last night, because Tieg liked companionship. But in a way, that idea
made the hunt a little more fun. Challenging. He liked that. But he
got lucky. Tieg had no companion. After Tieg had sucked down his
scotch—the bottle had been spiked with a little sedative—and settled
in for the evening in his chair in front of his big, fucking, obnoxious
TV, Joque surprised him by simply entering the room. The groggy Tieg
tried to stand and confront his intruder, who thought it would be
ironic to dress in a copycat of the silks worn by Juan Perez, the jock
who was once supposed to ride Tieg's horse, Cayman's Cult, to stardom
in the Triple Crown. That certainly didn't happen, and it was Tieg's
fault.*

*So, whether or not fuckface Tieg had ever even heard of pin fir-
ing didn't really matter. He was still a culprit in the whole scheme of
things. The guy wrote the check to the bastards who had administered
the treatment. He deserved to die.*

*That Tieg was the moneyman made him liable and made it just
easy-peasy to go on into that ridiculous mansion, sedate the moron with*

*some Acepromazine, and fire away. The Ace didn't kill the pain. Joque
didn't want the pain killed by any means. He just wanted the guy to
stay still.*

*"Do you think that the sedatives that were given to those horses
that were pin fired—your horses—do you think those poor beasts
didn't feel it? Even with sedation, you know they felt it!" He had
scolded the wide-eyed Tieg, who after just the first round had tears
flowing down his red, fat fuckwad face. "No. They felt it. Every time.
Just like this." He'd knelt down, and with the needle attached to the
blowtorch, stuck it through the skin, watched the blood drip then
slither down the bastard's pale white legs, and he pin fired away.
"How is that? Healing, huh? Healing tendons for greed?! You think
that heals? No, motherfucker. It doesn't. In reality it broke your horses
down faster. And then, once they were all good and broken down,
what do you and your disgusting entourage do? Get rid of them. That
is what you do! By the way, Tieg, do you remember me? Remember
me at all?" Joque stopped and took a step back, looking down at Tieg
in the chair.*

Tieg opened his eyes, but there was no real recognition there.

*"That's what I thought." Joque shook his head. "Just like with the
horses. Once you're done with them, that's it. The thing is, Mr. Tieg,
horses can't come back and get even. People can. You have plenty time
to remember me." He bent down and whispered in the man's ear, "An
eternity in hell might jog the memory."*

*Joque then kneeled again and pin fired Tieg's legs up and down
until Tieg had given up the ghost and passed out. Joque gave up then,
too, and shot him full of the rest of the Ace. He waited until he was
good and dead. No taking chances. Then he'd stuffed the carrot into
Tieg's mouth and left the doctored racing form, as planned, for the
police.*

He turned on the shower in the hotel bathroom. Had to start
his day. Yep. Had to get packed and start his day—a day in a life

of who he *really* was, or wasn't. Well, a day in the life of who others thought he really was.

Joque knew damn good and well who he was.

A protector of horses.

A killer of men.

CHAPTER
9

"What are your thoughts on pin firing, Mr. Gershon?" Holly walked down the barn row to the right of the man, who was built like a Brahma bull. Curious horses stuck their heads out and took note of the newcomers. Grooms came and went with various buckets, saddles, and horses in tow. A horseshoer's truck was parked next to the barn. The shoer pounded away on steel, shaping the shoe of a horse before taking it into the barn row and placing it on a horse's hoof. The horse stood with his groom in what Holly had learned was called cross-ties. The smell of hot metal wafted through the air. Gershon had dark hair, nice brown eyes, and wore a black baseball cap that read *Tieg Farms*.

"If you think sticking a few red-hot pokers into an extremely sore portion of your own anatomy several times and then slapping on a substance that causes a severe burning sensation is a decent idea, then okay, fine. I personally think it's archaic and brutal. Pin firing is not a practice I use on my horses."

"Why do you think someone did this to your boss?" she asked.

Gershon shrugged. Amar stood on the other side of him. He said, "Do you know if Mr. Tieg ever allowed anyone else to use this practice on his horses?"

Gershon looked down at his folded hands. He didn't speak for a moment. "Look, I've only been training for Tieg for about a year. He fired Rafael Torres last year after that debacle with Cayman's

Cult. The fact is that a lot of these guys—these owners—they don't know much about the animals. They're in it for the sport and the money. They don't pay attention. They write checks or their wives, accountants, or assistants do."

"Now you've only been training for Tieg for a year, but you obviously knew him well enough to go to his home, which isn't exactly close by."

"Tieg owed me a paycheck. And I owed my guys here a paycheck. He was a week late in getting me paid. I can't run a barn like that. He told me to stop by his house this morning after the horses were exercised and I could pick up the check. He also said he needed to speak with me about something."

"Do you know what?" Amar asked.

Gershon shrugged. A horse whinnied from another barn, setting off an echo of whinnies and nickers. A Spanish music station played loudly on the radio in the barn aisle. The place reverberated with high energy. "No idea. Tieg was one of those guys who liked to be in control. He kinda seemed to enjoy messing with people."

"Did that bother you?" Holly asked. "His controlling behavior?"

Gershon stopped and crossed his arms. A horse in the next stall banged his hooves loudly against the wooden door. "Manny, stop it!" The horse complied, turning his big brown eyes on them with a look of innocence. Holly had to admit they were beautiful animals. "I don't let owners get to me, Detective. I don't allow much to get to me. Life hasn't always been kind, and I take everything with a grain of salt."

"Ah. I suppose that's why you were able to come back to work today," Holly replied.

"I'm not sure what you mean," he said.

"I think she means that typically when someone discovers a dead body, they're shaken up," Chad interjected. "Especially when the body looks like Tieg's. But you don't seem all that fazed." He gave Holly a sideways glance.

Chad typically played bad cop to her good cop. They'd agreed that at times it was the best way to go. On occasion they'd switch it up. But Chad had read Gershon correctly. He was one of those men who would be more intimidated by another guy than a woman. Holly noticed Amar watching them and wondered if he'd figured out how they played the game together. She also wondered if Amar had a partner, and if so, where was he or she?

"I spent all morning talking to cops," Gershon replied. "I have an alibi for what you people believe is his time of death. It was checked out. Your guys let me go. I am here because this is my job. I don't know what will happen with Tieg's horses, but there are other horses here under my care. Plus some of Tieg's horses are syndicated—he invested in the horse with a small group of people—and I still have to answer to those other investors in the syndicate. Tieg was not the only owner I train for. What good am I at home all spooked, when I have a job to do? My wife likes to say that I'm practical. I would say she is accurate, and for the record, she and my sons were with me all evening last night. The only involvement I have in Tieg's death is that I found him."

Holly switched her tactic. She had a feeling about this guy, but she couldn't put her finger on it. "What kind of owner would you say Tieg was, other than controlling?"

"Tieg was a decent guy. He thought of himself as much more of a horseman than he was. I mean, sure, the guy did know a horse's ass from his head, but he acted like a know-it-all, and sometimes he didn't know much at all."

"Did that ever rub you the wrong way?"

Gershon laughed. "As I just told you…I'm practical. I'm used to dealing with inflated egos. Goes along with the paycheck. If Tieg told me to do something, I would tell him that I would, and if I didn't think it was a good plan, then I wouldn't."

"You would lie to your boss?" Amar asked.

"Yeah. I guess so, but most of the guys on this side of things lie to their bosses. We know what we're doing. They don't. We let them think they do. It works. For most of these guys, the horse on the track is an investment, pure and simple, and they want a quick return on their investments. I know how to do that better than they do, I believe. End of story." The horse started banging against his door again. Gershon reached into his pocket and handed him half a carrot. "Horse is a beggar, and I spoil him."

"If Tieg had told you to pin fire a horse and you didn't, would he have had someone else do it?" Holly asked.

"Look, Detective, if someone did that to one of my horses here, I'd know it. It's not something you can hide. I think you saw that on Tieg. Right?" She didn't answer. "It's extremely painful and their legs have to be wrapped tightly afterward. When those wraps need to come off to rewrap, it's like tearing a Band-Aid off open skin. It hurts like hell, and the scabs come with it. It's wrong. I don't know why some sicko did this to Tieg. I don't. Tieg was decent enough. He was a bit of a blowhard. I'm sure he had some people who didn't much care for him. But I certainly didn't do it."

"Does anyone stand out in your mind? Any enemies you can think of, off the top of your head, that Tieg may have had?" Holly asked.

"Maybe. There's a guy who owns a company called Equine Health Systems. They make a variety of wraps, supports, that kind of thing for horses. Anyway, this guy, his name is—let me think... Scott Christiansen."

Holly shot Chad a look. They recognized the name, but she didn't let on to Gershon.

"He invented this medicine boot of sorts that he claims absorbs a shitload of negative hoof concussion," Gershon continued. "I don't know. He'd been after Tieg for some investment opportunity with the company. They had a connection. Tieg had made some kind of deal with this guy, and then pulled out a few months ago. It got ugly. Not sure what happened. I keep my nose out of stuff like that. Drama. You know. I think his company is down south, maybe around San Diego."

Holly glanced at Chad, and then at Amar. Holly and Chad both knew exactly where Scott Christiansen's company was located.

"What about Tommy Lyons and Katarina Erickson?" Chad asked. "Did you know them?"

"Sure. I knew them. Just enough to say hello."

"Do you know if they knew Tieg? Any tie-in there?" Amar pressed.

"I don't know. I guess it's possible. Uh, you know Tieg was making a documentary that's scheduled for primetime TV the week of the Infinity. I was interviewed, but I don't know who else. I didn't get much involved. Did it because Tieg basically said I had to. It's kind of a promo thing—you know, highlight the good stuff about this sport. Too much negative talk out there, and half of it lies."

"Do you know what the documentary is called? Was it finished?"

He shrugged. "Do you guys watch TV at all?"

Holly looked at the other two detectives. No one responded.

"I've seen some commercials. It's called *The Infinity Invitational.* There's some subtitle to it that I can't think of off the top of my head, but yeah…the spots are airing. The Infinity is not far away. One of Tieg's horses, Skeedaddle, was invited, but I got bad news for the other owner. Horse pulled up lame in a workout yesterday. I planned to tell Tieg and then let him tell his partner."

"Who is the other owner?" Holly asked.

"None other than Edwin Hodges," Gershon replied. "Mr. Financial Wizard. I am sure you know the guy. Wrote books on wealth, big real-estate magnate."

"Pretty sure everyone knows who Edwin Hodges is." Holly shook her head and tried not to show her aggravation. Interviewing guys like Hodges was never easy. They had assistants up the yin-yang and avoidance tactics on par with politicians. The über wealthy could easily dodge a police interview. They would have to try to speak with him, though. Any connection to Tieg, especially one that involved the sport, had to be looked into.

"And the documentary?" Chad asked. "Was it finished?"

"I don't think so. I think he was making two parts. One followed the setup of the event up until a few days before race day, and that would air the day before the race. The second piece was going to be a post piece from what I had heard. Showing the winner. That kind of thing. Talk to Hodges. I know he put a lot of cash behind the track out there, and he was Tieg's partner on a lot of things."

They thanked Gershon for his time and headed to their cars. "Guess we're going to pay another visit to Scott Christiansen," Chad said.

"Another visit?" Amar asked.

"Scott Christiansen's equine sports medicine company is located within yards of the building—a dive shop to be exact—where the jockeys were found murdered. At the time we found it interesting that an equine company would be in such close proximity to where the victims were found, considering Katarina Erickson and Tommy Lyons made their living on the track. When we interviewed Christiansen, everything checked out and looked to be coincidence. His primary business is focused directly on the western riding world, not much to do with anyone on the track."

"Interesting, then," Amar replied. "Looks like this Mr. Christiansen did have some stake in horse racing."

"It does," Chad replied.

"We will be speaking with him again," Holly said. "Then we can get back with you and see what we have."

"Good. Thank you," Amar said. "And I believe we will need to visit Edwin Hodges as well."

"We will, but I'm not done checking Gershon out either," Holly replied. "Trust me, he's lying about something—perhaps about not knowing what Tieg wanted to discuss with him. We need to push him harder next time. I want to check his story out further."

"Why do you think that he's being deceitful?" Amar asked.

Holly glanced back and saw that Gershon was watching them walk away. "Trust me, he's hiding a secret. And also trust me, boys, we have stumbled onto a tangled mess. Woman's intuition."

CHAPTER

10

The drive back to San Diego late that afternoon took a bit more time than the drive up. Holly hoped they would get to where they wanted to go before five and that they would find Scott Christiansen at his offices. She was hoping for an element of surprise. They were going to be pushing it. They had interviewed Mr. Christiansen at his place of business, Equine Health Systems, days after the jockeys had been discovered. Upon learning that there was an equestrian-focused company in such close proximity to where the jockeys had been murdered, Holly knew it was a good idea to question Christiansen and his employees. Everyone had checked out.

"Now why do you think Christiansen didn't mention when we interviewed him that he had dealings in the racehorse world? He indicated to us at the time that his primary source of sales came from within the western world, didn't he? Like cow horses and stuff," Chad said.

Holly nodded. "It's certainly strange, and now Tieg is dead. Guess we're going to find out." While they continued down the Golden State Freeway, Holly looked up on her iPhone information regarding Edwin Hodges and Marvin Tieg's documentary. The documentary angle could lead nowhere, or it could lead somewhere. Hopefully, that somewhere would point them to a killer. When dealing with big personalities like Hodges and Tieg, public scrutiny would be high. This case was big and likely to get even bigger. Holly wasn't intimidated by a big case—she would work until they found justice for the victims.

She also looked into anything she could find concerning connections between Tieg and Christiansen. Scott Christiansen had created some kind of wrap that went on the leg of a horse in order to absorb energy. He claimed the wrap would help keep a horse sound and could prevent injury, as well as aid in recovery from existing injury. From all that Holly had learned from the initial interviews at Equine Health Systems and what she read subsequently, the wrap appeared to be a reasonably successful venture, and independent studies at top universities had also been conducted to prove Christiansen's claims. That was all fine and dandy, but it was not what was interesting to Holly at this point.

What interested her were the mentions of Scott Christiansen that popped up on a few equestrian blogs specific to horse racing. Apparently he had pissed a few people off. This was news to her.

"So these guys in the racing industry appear to be pretty traditional when it comes to how they deal with horses," Holly said.

"What do you mean?" Chad asked.

"Well, you have Christiansen, who has created a wrap that he likens to putting good running shoes on your horse, which seems smart, but the guys in the racing world are saying that the way the wraps are designed, they would slow a horse down."

"And that would be the last thing those guys would want."

"Exactly. But Christiansen was out to get them to buy and invest in the product. I can't figure out how he was connected to Tieg yet, but I will. I've also been able to find where Christiansen filed a lawsuit against Tieg just last month, around the time the jockeys were murdered. I don't know the details, but maybe Mr. Christiansen can fill us in."

"Maybe he can," Chad replied.

They turned into the industrial complex just after four thirty and located the Equine Health Systems building. Heading to the parking stalls in front of Equine Health Systems, they passed the building where the jockeys had been discovered. The detectives had never been able to find any kind of link between the dive shop and the jockeys. The shop had moved to a new location only a week prior to the deaths. Everyone who worked for Ocean Experience came out clean and so had everyone at Equine Health Systems, including Scott Christiansen. Holly and Chad had come to the conclusion that the killer had seen opportunity in an empty warehouse. How the murderer knew about it being vacant had plagued them. The proximity to Christiansen's place of business just seemed to be pure coincidence. They weren't so sure now.

Holly and Chad had toyed with the idea that the killer's choice of warehouse had been random, although they both knew there was hardly any randomness where killers were concerned. Most sophisticated kills, which these indeed were, were conducted by highly methodical, well-organized, and intelligent individuals.

Now there was a possible link.

The Equine Health Systems building was quite a bit larger than the former dive shop's.

"Not sure what to think," Chad said.

"Don't think anything yet. Let's see what we can find out. Life is strange, my friend."

"True." Chad shrugged.

"Come on. Let's see what we got."

A receptionist sat behind the front desk. She looked to be readying to leave. "Hi. Is Mr. Christiansen in?" Holly asked the attractive blonde.

"I believe he's gone for the day."

Holly flashed her badge. "I believe you should check. Let him know that Detectives Euwing and Jennings are here. He should remember us."

The woman's eyes widened as she picked up the phone and punched in a few numbers. "Hi, Lisa, is Mr. Christiansen still here? Okay. Um…there are some police officers here to see him. Okay." She hung up the phone. "Someone will be here in a moment to take you to his office."

A minute later another attractive blonde appeared. Holly saw Chad take note.

The woman led them through the open door to Christiansen's office. Scott Christiansen stood up. He was of average height and build, with nice blue eyes and light brown hair. He looked to be in his fifties. He wore a button-down shirt and a pair of jeans. Holly spotted the cowboy boots and large silver belt buckle as he came around his desk to shake their hands. She'd also noticed the cowboy hat on the corner of his desk when they'd been by before. The guy was a bit of a cowboy, or at least fancied himself one.

He smiled and looked a bit quizzically at them. "Detectives? How are you? What brings you by here today? I thought we'd already gone over what happened last month."

"We thought so, too, but there has been an interesting turn of events and we think maybe you left out some information when we interviewed you previously. We're here to ask you a few questions about Marvin Tieg."

Christiansen's smile faded.

"Mr. Tieg was found murdered this morning. Would you know anything about that?"

The man sat back down in his leather chair behind the large oak desk, his face now ashen. "What?" He shook his head vehemently. "No. No! Of course not."

Holly nodded. "What can you tell us about Mr. Tieg and your business dealings with him? And why didn't you tell us about them previously?"

Christiansen first picked his phone up and dialed. "Lisa, do you still have that bourbon I brought back from Lexington? Good. Can you make me a drink?" He hung up and looked at the detectives. "When the jockeys were killed last month, I was already on my way out from trying to do business with Tieg. You didn't ask me if I did business with Tieg at the time."

"No, but we did ask if you had any affiliations with anyone in the sport."

"And I told you that we sell some product to people on the track, but very little. Very little."

"The thing is, you were doing business with Marvin Tieg, and he is highly affiliated with the track."

Christiansen sighed. "Fine. Here's the deal. My business dealings with Tieg turned ugly when the man decided to rip me off. As if he needed to do such a thing. And I also realized I was dealing with someone with no ethics where either business or the animals was concerned. My wife has incredible instincts, and she warned me not to do business with him. She was afraid that if I worked with him it could ruin who we are on principle. She didn't want to be associated with Tieg, and she didn't want our company associated with him. She didn't trust him. So I lied to her and told her I wasn't trying to work any deals with him. I thought if she was wrong, which I should know better, then we would make a lot of money in a business venture with Tieg. The money would likely outweigh her personal feelings. I never told her. When you guys showed up after those poor kids were killed and were asking all sorts of questions, I was afraid word would get out and back to her if I let on that I had any business with anyone on the track, especially Tieg. My marriage has been a bit shaky lately. I never thought those jockey killings would be related to Tieg. I would have never expected this. With Tieg."

Holly looked at Chad. She was usually really good at spotting a con job from a hundred miles away, but as crazy and convoluted as this guy's story sounded, something about it rang true.

"What about Tieg's ethics had your wife, and later you, so concerned?" Chad asked.

Christiansen shook his head. "Look, I'm a horseman. I love the animals and I have spent years trying to come up with a product that works in keeping them sound, meaning their legs stay fit—no lameness issues. Horses are all bone and tendon from the shoulder on down. You can imagine what carrying that kind of body on those thin legs can do to them. Many of them wind up with a lot of leg issues resulting in lameness. It's been my goal to prevent that in as many horses as possible. I have that product now, and it does quite well, but the horses that can really benefit are the ones who are racing. These are thousand-pound animals that at three years old and younger, before they have even fully matured, are pounding down tracks at forty-plus miles an hour. These horses need protection. I have been at the tracks talking to trainers, owners, grooms, anyone who will listen. And Tieg actually listened. I thought it was great. Here's a guy with clout and money. Get his horses into the product and we're off. Right? The guy was even going to talk about it in the big documentary he was doing to coincide with the Infinity Invitational. And, it was all good, until Tieg saw the potential to take this product, *that I have created,* and have it made under his name."

"So, he was getting into the equestrian health care market?" Holly asked. There was a lot here to tear apart. But she would take it one step at a time.

"It would seem so." Christiansen picked up a magazine on his desk and tossed it across to her. It was an equestrian magazine specific to racehorses and a page was marked with a sticky note. Christiansen nodded at her. "Take a look. Money was no object to Tieg, and it scared me to think he could run me out of business by plunking down his cash and using his name."

Holly opened up the magazine, and he was right. There was a full-page, glossy ad for a product that looked just like the one Christiansen had created, but bearing the Tieg logo. "Do you have a patent on your product?"

"Sure I do. But do you know how many knockoffs are out there, and cheap ones? I try to beat them in the marketplace, but this really ticked me off. I filed a lawsuit against Tieg last month. I realize now that I should have told you all of this initially. I was trying to save my ass at home."

Holly and Chad didn't let on that they already knew about the lawsuit, and Holly didn't voice it, but she did think that he might need to be saving his ass in more places than just home, if he still wasn't being completely forthright. "Tell us what angered you so much about Tieg's copy."

Christiansen shrugged. "I think that's self-explanatory. The guy made a deal with me, said he'd endorse the product, put it on his animals, talk it up on a documentary scheduled for primetime TV, all of that, and then he turns around and stabs me in the back."

"Where were you last night?" Chad asked.

"I worked late. I was here, and then I went home. I had dinner around eight with my wife and daughter."

"What time did you leave the office then?"

"About seven thirty."

"Was anyone else here?" Chad asked.

"No. I set the alarm. I'm sure you can somehow validate that, as only two managers and I have access to the security system, and we each have our own code."

"Can you give us the name for the security company and the code?" Holly asked.

Silence ensued momentarily. Tension settled in among each of them. Finally, Christiansen said, "You guys think I could have killed Tieg?" His eyes widened. He shook his head.

"This is our job, Mr. Christiansen. We aren't accusing you of anything. We are simply investigating and to do so we have to ask questions and check out stories," Holly responded.

"Understood. It's a little surreal, though." Christiansen grabbed a notebook off his desk and wrote down the information.

"You mentioned that Tieg didn't have ethics when it came to the horses. What exactly do you mean by that?" Chad asked.

"You know, I believed him when we started talking and planning to do business together. I believed that he wouldn't harm the horses. His trainer, Rafael Torres—former trainer, that is—was implicated in using dermorphin in Cayman's Cult and likely other horses that Tieg had with him. I now have to wonder if Tieg really wasn't aware, or if he was involved at a whole other level than his trainer administering the drug. Torres was never officially sanctioned or anything. At the time, the drug was hard to detect, and nothing could be proved. But just recently a lab in Denver developed some new procedures for detection. Torres is out of the limelight on this now, but there are some trainers and folks likely going down because of this drug—it's also being termed frog juice."

"Frog juice?" Holly said.

Scott nodded. "Pretty exotic, huh? Dermorphin is a performance enhancer. It comes from the back of some South American frog. They say it's forty times more powerful than morphine and hard to detect. The fact is, if a horse can't feel his injury, he's likely to run harder and faster. Rumor has it that a week before the Belmont last year, Cayman's Cult had a tendon injury, but Tieg insisted they find a way to race him. I think they believed they'd found a way. The drug would have made the horse hyper—full of euphoria and excitation. Can't ask for more in a talented racehorse, right? And you know the public attention was on the horse and his jockey, Juan Perez. Big-time jockey. People were itching for a winner after thirty-four years. That horse was a big deal. The sad thing is that if my product had been used on the colt even just during workouts, it could have prevented an injury. Instead these people choose drugs to mask the pain, and when they're done with the horse, they're done with him."

"Brutal," Chad said.

"That is the world of horse racing."

"You said that you thought Tieg could somehow be connected to the, uh, frog juice?" Holly asked.

"The guy was wealthy." Christiansen's hands shook as he picked up a pen and weaved it through his fingers. "With connections. He traveled a lot, and he'd told me of a recent trip to South America. That's where this stuff is being produced. You have chemists out of work. I think Tieg expanded his business ventures beyond producing movies. Look, he tried to rip me off because he saw money. If he thought there was money to be made by doping his horses…racing regulators know fighting illegal drugs in horses' systems is an uphill battle. If not frog juice, it's cobra venom…there is a plethora of stuff tried out on these animals. A lot of these drugs go undetected, and a lot of these trainers and owners are willing to take that risk to get a horse across the finish line. Big business. And, I believe if Tieg thought he could make a dime by producing performance-enhancing drugs, both in legal and illegal form, then I think he would have. My invention would have been legit for him and maybe opened up the door to create supplements and give him credibility. The supplement business is a huge market in the equestrian world. I have no idea if that's what he was up to. I wouldn't have put it past him, though. What I can tell you for certain is that I think he was unethical and somewhat dangerous—but I didn't kill him."

Holly nodded. "You also mentioned a documentary that Tieg was making about the Infinity. We've heard of it, too. Can you tell us anything more about it?"

Christiansen set down the pen. "Not really. I know he'd been involved in having that facility built out in Vegas. His pal Hodges built the adjoining casino and put a lot into the grandstand. Tieg and his friends fronted a ton of cash, and as you have probably read, the purse at the race is going to be the largest one in history. Fifty million. I suppose that's chump change to people like Hodges and Tieg. As I said, Tieg had connections, and he promised to get my product out there. He lied and tried to steal from me, but I repeat, I'm not a murderer."

"Did you know either Tommy Lyons or Katarina Erickson? The jockeys who were killed?"

"No. I told you that last month. I didn't know them." He shook his head. "I didn't." He made a face as if he realized what she was thinking. "Remember you questioned me about where I had been when the jockeys were murdered? On a cruise with my family through the Panama Canal."

She did remember. And his story had checked out, but for a man who hadn't given up much on their first visit, he sure knew a lot about horse racing and was involved far more deeply than the few products he sold to the racing world.

Holly stood to go, and Chad followed suit. "Thank you for your time, sir. I hope you understand that we will need to question your employees again. I am certain you'll cooperate with us. I am also certain that if anything else comes to mind, you won't hold back that information."

"Of course. I do apologize. Obviously this is Friday, so my employees won't be back until Monday."

Cases grew cold, and it had taken another man's murder to breathe life into her month-long investigation. Holly wondered if, had Christiansen filled them in on all of these details the first time they spoke, a murder could have been prevented. "We will be back on Monday then, Mr. Christiansen."

He nodded, shook their hands, and showed them out of his office as his assistant came down the hall with the drink he'd requested in hand. Holly was sure he would down all of it.

"What do you think?" Chad asked, once back in the car.

"I think the guy had motive. I think he was pretty damn angry at Tieg, and he admitted as much to us. I think his reasons for not telling us the whole truth earlier seem shady, but he was convincing, and if his wife is in charge...well, we all know husbands don't like to piss off their wives. Husbands have been known to lie—or in his case, not be forthright—in order to stay out of trouble, even to the police."

"No doubt."

"You have to admit, partner, that this is strange, and even if Christiansen has nothing to do with these murders, my gut says there is some kind of connection. Let's check his employees again. And I think we also need to find this Rafael Torres. Frog juice, cobra venom? What the hell?"

CHAPTER
11

Leann Purdue brought two cups of tea to bed. Dan was already tucked between the sheets, their German shepherd, Rascal, at his feet.

She walked around to his side of the bed and set the cup on the oak nightstand. "I bet you're tired."

"A little." He took her hand. "Thank you."

"Of course." She winced when she saw the scars on his hands. She'd thought, after nine months of being together, that she'd gotten used to the scars, but she hadn't. Dan had been badly burned by boiling water as a child.

He picked up the mug and took a sip of the tea. "It was good, though. I'm excited to think we're going to expand this business." He smiled. True happiness was reflected in his green eyes.

"I don't know if that's going to happen." She crawled into bed and tucked her blonde hair back behind her ears.

"What do you mean? I just signed the deal yesterday in Virginia for the land. I thought we agreed we wanted to open another rescue facility. I've already put some ads out there for volunteers and someone who can manage the place." Dan set the cup back down.

"We did agree, but I think Cay is shooting blanks. I had another mare's owner call today, furious that his horse didn't take." Leann picked up the lavender-scented lotion off her nightstand and put some on the palms of her hands.

"Shit. I knew we shouldn't have trusted Tieg."

"You haven't heard," she said.

"Heard what?" he asked.

"Tieg. He was found murdered this morning in LA." She replaced the lotion on the nightstand and rubbed her hands together.

"What?" Dan said. "You're joking."

"I'm not at all. Pretty graphic, too. I saw it on the racing blog. There's not many details yet, but it's scary."

Dan shook his head and patted the side of the striped duvet cover, indicating for her to scoot in next to him. "Dammit. That's not good. I hate to see the guy dead, and we certainly won't get any money back on the horse now."

"Danny." She moved over and leaned her head on his shoulder.

"I'm just saying the truth, love."

"Right, but it also means…" she whispered.

"I know what it means, sweetie. It means the funds could dry up. We all put up a lot of cash to buy that horse, expecting the stud fees would help supplement the needs here." He put his arm around her and pulled her in closer.

She tried to fight back the tears. Leann Purdue, like her sister Elena, had been raised on the track, but they had been raised to be compassionate. They worked hard, and they invested wisely in horses, and when those horses were off the track, they brought them back to Leann's farm in Kentucky where they could live out their days in peace. They also took in other horses that needed rescuing. Between her fiancé, Dan, and another friend, Ian, they had two trailers running across the country to pick up horses in need. All the workers on their place, Golden Hearts, were volunteers. But feeding fifty head and counting and running an operation like theirs wasn't easy. Elena, Dan, and she had banked on the purchase of Cayman's Cult last year when the horse was pulled out of his last race with rumors of drugs in his system, and then a suspensory branch issue. But they figured he could stand stud, so they'd made Tieg an offer he couldn't refuse, especially considering he really wanted the bad press behind him.

Dan shook his head. "Man, whatever they were shooting that animal with caused this. I know it."

"I need to call Elena."

"No, babe. Not yet. We'll figure it out. I promise." He took her hands and then kissed her. "I promise you. I know this is your dream, and we won't let it fail. Okay?"

She nodded.

Dan reached to scratch Rascal between his ears. "I will say, though, that it's a good thing Tieg is dead, or I'd probably go kill him myself for this."

"Dan!"

"You reap what you sow, and I don't think Tieg was too great a guy."

"That doesn't mean he deserved to be murdered."

"I suppose not, but life has a funny way of getting even sometimes."

"I guess it does."

"Let's not worry about it anymore tonight. It will all work out. I know it will," he assured her. She tried to be comforted by his words, his strong arms around her, the familiar scent of the spicy cologne he wore.

Leann wished she could be as sure as Dan that it would all work out, because at the moment, she wasn't certain about how they were going to save the farm.

CHAPTER

12

Brendan leaned across the table where he and Holly sat outside on his upstairs balcony drinking a glass of wine, and he gave her one helluva kiss. He leaned back with a mischievous look in his eyes. She was happy that she had made it in time for their eight o'clock "date," which they'd decided to have at home.

The downtown skyline spread out before them to the right, bright city lights blinking, and they watched airplanes land at Lindbergh Field, the brakes of the planes screaming across the tarmac as the flights touched down and slowed to a stop. Orange blossoms on the large tree in Brendan's backyard scented the air.

She smiled. "What was that for?"

"Because I love you." He sipped the cabernet.

"I love you, too." She reached across the table and took his hand. His warmth and familiarity eased the ugliness of the day. As corny as it sounded, she referred to Brendan as her soft place to fall. He'd come into her life at the right time, when she had finally been willing to let go of the ghost she had been hanging onto for over eight years—her husband Jack who, like her, had been a cop. He'd died in a huge warehouse explosion during a drug bust. Holly had clung to the fact that his body had not been recovered. The fire had been too hot, and two other officers had died that day as well. There had been no remains. For so long she held out hope that Jack would come walking through the door and tell her that he was alive.

Her mind played tricks on her, allowing her to convince herself that Jack was on a work trip. But that fantasy only lasted so long. On top of everything, she had been pregnant with Chloe at the time. Depression had set in, but the birth of their daughter helped, as did years of therapy. And then the fateful day when she'd met Brendan at their daughters' school. It had taken some time, but she'd finally given over her heart, and although the demands of her job were grueling, her personal life finally seemed in order. She'd met a man she could love, one who wholeheartedly loved her back.

"How was your day?" Brendan asked. "You were late. Something happen?"

"I'm a cop. Something always happens. But yes, today was one of those days. Hard case. Very difficult, and with some ugly aspects." She tried to keep her mind focused on him, but there were notes that she wanted to go over from Tommy and Katarina's murders. She knew she needed to see what she could do about speaking with Edwin Hodges, and there were so many other details of the case that needed picking apart.

"Ah, well, why don't I help you take your mind off of it?" He winked at her. "The girls won't be home for another hour."

Brendan's oldest, Megan, now almost eighteen, had been good enough to take Chloe and Maddie to a movie. Granted, the kid was bucking for her own car, so they were certain there was an ulterior motive to her babysitting generosity, but they did have the house to themselves for a little while on a Friday night. "Hmm. I think that can be arranged." Holly stood and grabbed his hand, and they headed into the bedroom.

Holly took off her sweater and set it over one of two leather chairs that Brendan had arranged in front of the fireplace in the master. As she did, she remembered that morning and the plumeria charm. She felt a slight sting in her heart. She really did need to put the charm away. She needed to close all doors to her former life with Jack. Although she had given her heart to Brendan, an occasional fleeting moment still reminded her of her deceased husband.

The night that they'd had their argument over her work hours and seeming lack of commitment to their relationship and she had raced home to sulk, things had changed. She'd sat in the family room with a glass of wine, holding the charm. Chloe and Maddie were together at a slumber party for another friend's birthday. Two hours into her sulkfest as she walked down memory lane, the doorbell rang. She put the charm in the pocket of the sweater.

It was Brendan.

She opened the door.

"Just listen to me, Holly."

She crossed her arms.

"I love you. I love you with every ounce of my being, and I don't want to lose you."

"I don't want to lose you either," she whispered. "But you have to understand that I am a cop."

He nodded. "I do. And I know what your job means to you. And I know that I have to…no…that I want to accept that, because there is no way I am ever letting you walk out of my life." He took her hand, got down on his knee, and asked her to marry him.

Saying yes had been the best decision she ever made.

The right decision.

And now, in this moment with Brendan, his every touch, kiss, whisper in her ear did indeed take her mind off her work. It didn't take long for Holly to remember that she was still a woman with needs and also very much in love with Brendan.

After their lovemaking, lying in his arms, she felt protected and completely loved. These moments had become too few and far between as of late, and she thought about how she needed to pay attention—more attention—to her family and to her love for this man.

She sat up and gazed down at him. "I really do love you very much."

Brendan stroked the curve of her cheekbone. "I know, and I love you."

Holly put her head down on Brendan's chest and sighed, knowing that soon enough she would have to get up and dress before the girls came in. Life as a parent. He kissed the top of her head and as she closed her eyes, taking it all in—the serenity and the comfort—her phone rang. And she recognized the ringtone: the Pink Panther theme song. Chad's.

"Ah, really?" Brendan knew Chad's ringtone as well, and he also knew that if her partner was calling at this time of night, then it wasn't a social call.

"I'm sorry," she said. "I am."

"No, no. It's your job. I understand."

He said the words, but Holly recognized the terseness in his voice. Job or not, she was afraid Brendan was becoming irritated again at competing for her attention. "What's up?" she asked as she answered the phone and sat up.

"I've been doing some research on that racing form today. First, the date the horse El Chicano won that race in Arlington was last year. September eleventh. I don't know if that is a coincidence, but we can't discount it."

"Of course not. You said that was first. What else?"

"The horse's name, El Chicano. I didn't get too far with that, as you can imagine. Got a lot on a band by that name, though."

"Okay." Holly shifted uneasily.

"It ties in to what I think I found from the note on the back of the form," he said. "The note read, *In the Mouth of Madness*, which is the name of a movie created by John Carpenter. A horror movie, to be exact."

"I'm following."

"Yeah, well, John Carpenter used the song 'We've Only Just Begun' in the movie. The song by the duo Richard and Karen Carpenter. No relation, but he did use their song. You know the song, don't you? 'We've Only Just Begun'?"

"I do." She didn't add that the reason she remembered was because that song had been her wedding song with Jack.

"The group El Chicano made a rendition of that song as well."

Holly sucked in a deep breath, her brain going right where Chad had been leading. "I get it. Oh my God. *We* have only just begun," she uttered the words. "We may be looking for two killers, not one."

CHAPTER

13

Bradley Quentin was a good guy gone bad. He knew that was how many would think of him, but it was far from the truth. Quentin was a good guy. Always had been. Always would be. Quentin knew right from wrong. He knew he'd been wrongly discharged from the military. He had once been so high that the president would have had to look up to him.

That's how high.

And one little mistake. One little mistake sent them all into a tailspin. So much so, they discharged him and did not even listen to the intel he had. Did not care. Did not believe him.

Quentin knew the truth. He knew the facts on the ground and was prepared to use that knowledge to make the situation right. He knew the intel, and he was prepared to use it and make it right. He had begun masterminding this thing four years ago, shortly after they had "let him go."

It all began at a horse race at Gulfstream Park while he was enjoying some R & R in Hallandale Beach. In reality, it had all begun long before that, when he'd come back from the Middle East and changed his name from Darren to Quentin (he had a thing for Tarantino films), and changed his complete identity. Fortunately for him, he knew some good plastic surgeons in places like Brazil, and he knew how to become someone he had not been before.

It had to be done that way. No matter what the government had assured him with their *we won't rock the boat, if you don't rock the boat* rhetoric, Quentin knew that he trusted no one and no entity. His former employers would come after him eventually, because they knew just as well as he did that sooner or later he would rock the boat.

And he was rocking it now. His official plan started taking form that day in Florida. He hadn't expected the ideas to come from there. Who would have? He'd been invited to the races by some blonde bimbo he'd met at a bar the night before. She'd given good head and had some serious cash. He wasn't short on money. Not even close. But coming from money, he liked to hang around other people with money, when he hung around people. Most people—in fact, *all* people—were assholes and cretins. But he was still a human being. Money + blonde + a blow job. That was worth a day at the races. And then his brain started to spin when he heard the name Farooq and the name of a horse. Sheikh Farooq was the owner. Farooq was one of the world's *peacemakers*. What a joke! He couldn't ditch the blonde fast enough.

He raced back to his hotel, turned on his laptop, and could not believe he had forgotten some of the details of the sheikh's life, especially the one about him owning racehorses and those horses being his passion. And that is when things started to really take shape.

That was when Quentin knew that he would have to find himself a partner. One fucked-up partner. It took some time. But that was okay. Quentin was a patient man. In his line of work, patience really mattered.

What that poor bastard who liked to call himself Joque didn't know was that there was no equality in their relationship. This was no partnership. Let the guy believe they were equal. Let the guy believe whatever he wanted, as long as he carried out Quentin's orders.

Quentin sat down behind his desk at Bradley Security Systems. He had turned his bad fortune from being "let go" by the US government into something good, something profitable, and into something that would work to not only his benefit, but to the benefit of mankind.

And, his boy, Joque, was going to carry out the perfect plan.

CHAPTER

14

O'Leary scribbled on his legal pad, then squinted at the computer screen. Things were a little blurry. He probably shouldn't have had that last rum and Coke. The first couple got his mind going, the last couple turned his brain to mush, and he didn't want that. His career as a jockey was on the downhill slope, but he was doing something now that maybe he should have done a decade ago.

He got up and turned down the radio on his kitchen counter inside his small apartment. O'Leary knew he'd had a fall from grace. He'd once owned a sweet condo at the beach in Santa Monica and a nice house out in Lexington. He'd driven some great cars, worn some expensive clothes, lived the rock-star lifestyle there for a bit. Then a few years ago, after the horse Nobody's Business had a bad accident on the track and one of the jocks in the race wound up living out his days in a wheelchair, trainers lost faith in O'Leary. Owners lost faith in him.

Worst of all…he lost faith in himself.

He glanced at the bottle of rum next to the radio and thought about it.

No.

He wasn't going there again. There was something pushing him toward something better, toward a course of action he'd long delayed. Maybe it was his crash from fame, maybe it was Elena accepting his invite for coffee.

Or, maybe, it was time to do the right thing and expose what he figured were certain to be lies.

He knew that if he had looked into the lies of the past when he was riding high, he would have never enjoyed the career he'd had in racing. It would have been over a lot sooner than it had been. He would have been ostracized.

Had it been the right choice?

He didn't know, and he also didn't know if what he was chasing now was the truth, but he had positive suspicions.

Twelve years ago.

Twelve years ago, O'Leary was at the peak of his game. Elena was his girl. He was in the winner's circle more often than not.

His home base was in Lexington, but he was all over the country on horses. And he'd ridden a horse trained by Geremiah Laugherty, who was starting to make a name for himself, but there was word that Laugherty liked women and gambling as much as he enjoyed training horses. And at times, O'Leary questioned the man's training practices. But he was training winners, and O'Leary had won some races on this horse named Dirty Games. How ironic, that colt's name.

The horse was owned by Marvin Tieg, who had just barely gotten on the map in Hollywood. Back then, Tieg was putting as much cash as he could into producing whatever he could. He started out with a money-making slasher film and things went on from there.

The problem was that Tieg had a habit of spending money faster than he could recoup it. He and Laugherty seemed to go hand in hand in that department. Tieg had bought himself a string of horses and a decent estate in Versailles, Kentucky.

Tieg also liked to buy people, and when Hollywood (which is what O'Leary called him) came to town and started spreading the cash around wining and dining folks, no one complained. O'Leary certainly didn't.

This horse, Dirty Games, was a real nice horse that was winning and had a real nice future in front of him. Tieg had some great animals at his place that were insured to the hilt. Millions of dollars in insurance money.

Even drunk, O'Leary remembered it all like yesterday because of what happened. And news of Tieg's murder had dragged all his memories to the surface. He thought about Elena's filly, Karma's Revenge, and wondered if there was truly such a thing as karma. If so, was Tieg's murder karma or was it revenge?

O'Leary didn't know what to think at this point as he tried to compose all of his memories onto the notepad and computer.

Back in the day, when in Lexington, O'Leary had agreed to exercise some of Tieg's horses. The pay to exercise horses wasn't great considering the purses he was winning, but O'Leary knew enough at the time to understand that relationships in any business were what really counted. He figured that maintaining a good relationship with Hollywood could be to his advantage. He never imagined that it would take the twist that it did.

O'Leary started realizing that things weren't so kosher after a few weeks had gone by and he hadn't been paid.

He'd asked one of the grooms about it. A guy he had sort of befriended.

Ted Ivy.

Ted was an odd cat in some ways. But he seemed to really love the horses. He was good with them. Had good instincts.

But the others around Tieg's place treated the poor guy shitty, so O'Leary took pity on him. They had shared some beers here and there and talked shit.

The day that everything changed at Tieg's farm, O'Leary remembered handing Dirty Games—he had nicknamed him Sucio, meaning dirty in Spanish—over to Ivy, who put the horse in the wash rack and started rinsing him. "Want to wash Sucio up, man?"

Ivy nodded. "I got him. Love this horse. You're a lucky bastard. He's a real good boy."

"That he is, and that I am." O'Leary grabbed a couple of Coronas, which he'd noticed was Ivy's drink of choice, from the stocked fridge in the barn office. He waited to give the guy the beer until he put the horse up. It was only noon, but the horses were done for the day, and neither Tieg nor Laugherty was in town.

A spring breeze blew through the aisle, carrying with it the scents of fresh-cut grass and earth. O'Leary handed Ivy the beer as he closed the horse up in the stall. "Oh man, I don't know if I should take this now," he'd said. "It's only lunchtime and since Laugherty fired the security guards last week, I'm taking the night shift."

O'Leary laughed. "Come on, no one is here to give you shit. I certainly won't say a word. Take a nap in a bit and then you'll be good as new."

"Gershon is still here."

"Who's that?"

"The other guy who exercises the horses."

"That pissant. Come on, Ivy, don't worry about it. I'll take the heat if there's an issue."

Ivy took the beer and smiled. "Thanks."

They talked for a while about how great the horse was, and how Tieg had no idea of the caliber of animals inside his barn. And how Laugherty was kind of an asshole.

"I don't like him very much," Ivy said after sucking down the beer. O'Leary had been accommodating and grabbed two more from the office.

"He's kind of brusque. I don't think he's always fair with the animals," O'Leary commented.

Ivy nodded. "That bugs me. I seen him beat one or two around here."

"Right." O'Leary's stomach tightened. He'd grown up around horses. His family had always had a backyard horse. And one thing he

knew was that although an animal needed to understand boundaries, it was very, very rare that one ever needed to be beaten. Beating was for a horse who aimed to kill you. Those horses were out there, for sure, but they were few and far between. And O'Leary's take on that kind of horse was that it was far more humane to put a needle in his neck than beat the shit out of him and hope for the best.

As far as he was concerned, there was no need to beat any of the animals in Laugherty's care.

"I don't mean to get into anyone's business, but have you been paid lately?"

Ivy shook his head. "No man. I haven't been paid in almost two months."

That had been longer than O'Leary had seen a check. He whistled. "No shit? What? Have you said anything?"

"Yeah. I got into it with Laugherty."

"You did?"

"Yes. I did. He told me I was an ungrateful son of a bitch. He then got Tieg on the phone, who basically said that if I didn't want the job, I could leave. They reminded me that I was living on the property."

"Assholes."

"Yep. I think maybe they have some cash flow problems. They both throw money around like it grows on trees. Then they let the security people go the other day and asked me to check the horses at night. That was partly why I got so pissed off at them, but I need a place to live, and I like it here. I like the horses. But I don't like those two. I'd get back at them if I could." He laughed. "But money rules the world and the racing capital of the world is no exception."

Sitting at his computer, O'Leary thought he understood why the two power players, Tieg and Laugherty, hadn't fired Ivy during that phone conversation. Being who they were, no one would have questioned their decision. And no one would have cared what Ivy said.

Ted Ivy was just a groom.

But O'Leary now thought he knew why they hadn't fired Ivy then. In his gut, ten years ago, he figured there was a possibility… but he didn't want to believe it. He chose to believe the gossip that spread like wildfire across the bluegrass. As everyone else did.

But now…

Now that O'Leary had experienced his own dark days, and there were those out there who believed the worst of him, his questions begged answers. He'd heard the rumors about himself—he was a druggie. A drunk.

He'd own drunk.

He wouldn't own druggie. O'Leary had snorted coke once in his life and hated it.

Rumors.

But he wondered about what had been said about Ted Ivy. He also thought of his involvement in the whole mess.

He was getting tired.

He'd been involved.

No doubt.

But not by choice.

O'Leary was pretty sure why Ted Ivy hadn't been fired that day by Tieg and Laugherty.

He was pretty sure they'd aimed to set the poor son of a bitch up for what happened next.

CHAPTER
15

Joque had just finished feeding for the morning. It was good to be back home. He'd done his job, and he was good at it. He treated the horses well because he loved them, and they loved him back. He knew they loved him far more than any human.

Except for maybe his dead wife, Carol. Joque knew Carol had loved him, and he'd loved her. But that was another time and place.

And maybe his girl now, maybe she did love him as much as Carol had…

Everyone remembered September 11, but those who lost loved ones that day had a much heavier cross to bear. His Carol had been on the plane that crashed into the Pentagon. To add insult to injury, all the shit that sent him to jail went down soon after. Shit he didn't cause and was not involved in, but the fingers had pointed at him anyway and he now felt he had a right to be pissed off—he was a tad over humankind. Most of humankind was unkind.

And Joque knew who had caused his demise, who had put him in the hell he'd been through. He had the names and faces of those who had done him wrong burned deep, and they would pay. They would pay for the eight years he had spent in hell.

He entered through the sliding door into the office just off the barn at his farm out in Lexington. Racing country. This is where it all went down. The cream of the crop lived in Lexington—the racing industry's high and mighty—and he'd grown up here. He was once on his way to becoming one of the high and mighty himself, but a handful of people had ruined that for him.

The evil that people do.

He opened the fridge, took out a container of orange juice, and poured himself a glass. Good to be home.

The venom they will strike with.

He sat at his desk, reaching over a pile of *Thoroughbred Times*, racing forms from all over, State Line Tack, and other paperwork to turn on his laptop. He entered his password.

The deceit they will spread for power, money, and greed.

He navigated to his public e-mail and logged in. Good. He had a couple more bottles of Ace on the way. That would likely come in handy. He didn't believe his work was finished. In fact, he knew that it wasn't. Not even close.

He logged out.

He logged into his private e-mail account. An address that only one other individual in the world had.

Joque smiled and rubbed his palms together, seeing what he'd hoped for—new instructions. He took a nice big swallow from his glass of juice and clicked the e-mail. As it opened, he smiled.

Yessiree!

His work was far from done.

Looked as though he was headed for New York.

CHAPTER

16

The first telltale signs of the day broke at a few minutes after five. The inky blue of the night sky faded into a lighter shade as the moon began to sink in the Western Hemisphere.

A bird chirped in a tree outside of Janet's Café as Elena opened the door. She spotted O'Leary already seated in the corner. Her stomach growled thinking about bacon, coffee, and eggs. She walked to the booth and sat across from him. He smelled of booze. "Been out?" she asked.

"Nope. Stayed in," he replied. "Have a seat. I got a place here now. Not far. I'm still exercising horses. I get a ride now and then, you know. You? Still got the ranch in Ramona?"

"I do. When I'm up here, I stay at a friend's place. She travels a lot, so I'm usually there on my own. It's nice. Different from being out in the middle of nowhere."

"I bet."

"You smell like a distillery, O'Leary."

"And you look beautiful as always."

"You're still drunk."

"I am not."

She sighed. "Pete…"

"Elena."

A bottle blonde approached and set a coffee cup down in front of her.

"Here I am," Elena said after taking a sip.

"Here you are, and here I am. So, how are you?" he asked. "What's new?"

"I'm good. You know I have a nice filly."

"I do know. Karma's Revenge. I've been watching her. Everyone's watching her. The Infinity is going to be some race. That is going to be insane."

"My fingers are crossed for a win there. Lot of scuttlebutt on the track though, you know. That colt of Farooq's is nice. Then you got that horse Tieg and Hodges own—Skeedaddle. I'm sure Hodges will still run him. Don't know what to think of Tieg's murder."

O'Leary nodded. "Dark stuff. Very cloak and dagger. I heard, though, that horse of Tieg's and Hodges's pulled up lame in work-outs, so he's likely out of the race. Hope they get the son of a bitch who killed Tieg. You think it's the same guy who killed Lyons and Katarina?"

She shrugged. "I don't know. There doesn't seem to be much information available to the public yet. But it is scary."

"I agree. We'll have to wait and see. Here the commissioners and everyone involved are hoping to bring back the glory days, shine a ray of sunshine on our sport. Those murders aren't helping much."

"No, but the stories are all over the news. The murderers coinciding with the big race…that's creating a lot of intrigue. You know how people work. They eat stuff like this up. It's disgusting but true. The race may even get a boost from all this terrible business."

"I suppose so." He took a sip of coffee, then changed the subject. "I don't know what you're thinking, letting Perez ride your filly."

Before she could respond, the waitress returned and took their orders, then left.

"He's a good jock," Elena said.

"He's a snake, El. You've heard the rumors. Lots of people think he was the one who helped get dermorphin into Cayman's Cult."

"Rumors are simply that. Rumors. It was never even proved the horse had that crap in his system."

"That's because they didn't have a lab with the right kind of resources."

"What I can tell you about Perez is that he has a connection with my filly, and it works. They're a winning team." She shook her head. "And I can also tell you that no one shoots anything into my filly. She runs clean."

He sat back in the booth and eyed her, his blue eyes twinkling. She wondered if the twinkle came from the alcohol, or if he was excited to be spending time with her after all these years. "Uh-huh. You got the filly, and that's good. What else is going on? How's your sister?"

"Leann is good. She's got some breeding horses that we're in on together, and she's still running Golden Hearts. And we should start making some money off Cayman's Cult, you know. Once the syndicate gets paid back, though, it cuts a little."

"Yeah. I bet he proves himself. Sort of was surprised to hear you bought that horse, but good for you. *Anything* else going on in your world?"

She ran the tip of her finger around the rim of her cup. "What are you asking, O'Leary? Want to know if I'm seeing someone?"

He leaned closer. "Actually, yes. I know you and that asshole, Carter, split up."

She swallowed hard when he mentioned Carter's name. "Yes. We did. He's married now."

"Word gets around."

She nodded.

"So?"

"No. I'm not seeing anyone, and don't get any ideas, because I won't be seeing you either."

"You're seeing me now. And we are going to have dinner in Vegas." He winked at her and sat back as the waitress set down their breakfast. Eggs for her, pancakes for him.

"You're terrible. I did not agree to dinner. You're lucky we're having breakfast. I said coffee."

"Everyone has to eat, El. You've said that I'm terrible, or maybe it was rotten, before. Probably true." He spread a slab of butter over the cakes. "What happened between us?"

She set her fork down and stared at him. "Really?"

His face turned red, and he smiled sheepishly. "Just trying to walk down memory lane."

"Really?"

"I always liked that about you, El. You got that spunky little hard-ass thing going on."

She put a piece of egg on her fork and flicked it at him. "And you have that total ass thing going on."

"Let's have dinner together. Vegas. Come on."

"No."

"I'll be good."

"Liar," she replied.

"Maybe. Okay, I will *try* to be good."

She took a bite of her toast and poured a little more cream into her coffee, pondering his offer. O'Leary was handsome. Sure he was five three. She was only five feet, so that didn't matter. He was still, at forty-two years old, one of the best-looking men she'd ever seen. His eyes, his smile, the way he carried himself. But more than that, Pete was smart and funny, and damn him, the time they'd spent together was the most alive she'd ever felt. Granted, she'd been twenty. Not too difficult to feel alive at twenty. But lo and behold, as she sat across from him sharing the type of banter they always shared as if twelve years hadn't gone by...

He made her smile.

But a reality check was in order. O'Leary had a drinking problem. He had fallen from grace. He held a few grudges, and a few were held against him—some justified on both sides of the coin.

Plus he had broken her heart.

Well, she had been a girl then.

She was much tougher now.

Broken hearts were for much younger, weaker women.

She had a life now. One that O'Leary couldn't mess up.

"Sure, why not. Let's have dinner," she finally said, stirring the cream in her coffee.

CHAPTER
17

The horses paw and prance and neigh,
Fillies and colts like kittens play,
And dance and toss their rippled manes
Shining and soft as silken skeins;...
— Oliver Wendell Holmes

What does it mean to be a horse? To live on tall green grass and eat and play. To toil on farmland. To thunder down a track.

To be bought and sold, moved from barn to barn, placed inside fences, eating what's provided, benefitting or suffering at the hands of humans.

What does it mean to be a horse?

CHAPTER

18

"Okay, so we might have two killers on our hands," Holly said. It was early Saturday morning. To stay on top of this thing, Holly was resigned to putting in extra hours. She'd given Amar a courtesy call, since he had been decent enough to contact them about Tieg's slaying. Surprisingly, or maybe not so much, Amar had made the trek to San Diego, where he met her and Chad downtown at the main station. They'd been putting their heads together since before nine o'clock.

"And this is based on the note the killer left inside the racing form at Tieg's scene. If what Chad is theorizing is possible—and anything is possible—then the implication that 'we have only just begun' is huge," Holly said.

Chad jumped in. "And if you want to really break it down and get literal, we have to ask ourselves if there *are* two killers involved, are they siblings like the Carpenters were? Are they romantically linked, being that this particular song is a love song? Could it be a husband and wife team? Man and woman? I think we can assume that our actual killer is a male. This guy has some strength to commit these acts. But is it possible that there's someone else calling the shots?"

Amar stood up and made himself a hot tea. "I think that is all possible," he said. "Maybe we look at husband and wife, or romantic links on the track. You know, trainer/trainer, trainer/jockey, owner/ trainer. That kind of thing."

"That's a good idea, Amar. Maybe even Scott Christiansen and his wife, although their alibi is solid for when the jockeys were killed." Holly input the note on her tablet. "Plus I've lined up a couple of our guys to conduct interviews over at Equine Health Systems starting Monday. They'll have to speak to everyone again to see if there might be a chink in the armor. Could someone within the company, who also has the same passion for horses that Christiansen seems to have, have carried out the killings on his own, or at the will of Christiansen?"

"There are a lot of angles to explore yet," Chad said. "This isn't going to be easy. I was able to get a hold of one of Edwin Hodges's assistants. We got lucky, gang. The guy has a beach house here in La Jolla, and guess who is in town tomorrow for a little R & R?"

"Good work. That was fast. Were you able to schedule an appointment with the great Mr. Hodges?" Holly asked.

"Yeah. It was surprisingly easy."

"Good. Looks like we will be heading to the beach tomorrow, guys. Amar, are you able to join us?"

He sighed. "My wife will not like it. But I think, because of what we are dealing with, that we are now a team. It is my job."

Chad nodded.

"Not always easy on our families. So true," Holly said, thinking of how she'd left Chloe with Brendan and his girls that morning. "I have a guest room that you're more than welcome to crash in."

"Yes. That would be nice. Thank you." He took a sip of his tea.

It pleased Holly that the three of them made a good team. It wasn't always so easy, and because Amar was from another jurisdiction, things could have been sticky. But so far, no issues had arisen, and they all seemed to be jelling well. And because Greenfield had agreed to allow Chad and Holly the flexibility they requested in working cases, bringing Amar in wasn't an issue.

"That's settled. Let's set aside the two-killer theory for a bit and focus on the connections that we know for sure."

Holly walked to the white board. She had photos of Tieg, Tommy Lyons, and Katarina Erickson. She'd also pulled photos off the Internet of Scott Christensen and Jim Gershon. She had printed up extra sets of her notes regarding the jockey slayings. She wanted to fill in as many blanks as possible along the timeline.

"We can't deny there are some connections already at play. The key is fitting the right piece with the next piece."

Both men nodded in agreement.

Holly posted the photos up on the board in a square. She wrote *One* next to Katarina's photo. The four eleven, petite redhead had been a beautiful girl, and at twenty-two with a huge future ahead of her, the loss was tragic. All loss was tragic, but there was something about looking at the photo of a once-alive Katarina standing next to a horse that hit Holly right in the gut. Maybe it was because she had a daughter and was soon to have two more. Maybe it was just the pure loss of someone so young, so ready to take on the world, that gave her such a visceral reaction. Holly didn't know exactly what it was—and frankly, she didn't care. She simply wanted to find the bastard who had taken these lives.

"We know from the autopsy that Katarina likely died first and suffered less than Tommy did." She placed Tommy's photo on the board and cringed slightly as she recalled the sobs that escaped from the poor kid's father when she notified him of his son's death. "Katarina was shot at point blank range, but not until after the killer broke her legs with a blunt object, probably a baseball bat.

"We also know that she was taken first, likely outside of the barns at Del Mar, but no one claims to have seen anything, and her car was clean. She may have gone somewhere else first. I'm surprised we have no witnesses. That tells me this guy is good, he's calculating, and I am certain he watches his victims for a bit to get their patterns down."

"Or he knows them," Amar said.

Holly nodded. "Or he knows them. We did find a detailed schedule in Katarina's smart phone, and she had noted that she would be meeting Tommy at Brody's at eight. She never showed. The bartender there remembered serving Tommy a beer and reported that he seemed flustered and kept checking his cell. Tommy finally told the bartender that he'd catch him later and left at around eight forty-five. Again, no one saw him after that. According to the estimated time of death, he was murdered between ten and midnight, along with Katarina."

"So our killer held them for a period," Amar said.

"To torture them, which he seems to enjoy," Chad added as he clicked his pen.

Holly nodded. "Yeah, and I would say he is becoming more sadistic. Breaking legs is one thing, but what he did to Tieg is another step up. Let's talk about Tieg for a minute. Amar, have your guys figured anything that might help?"

"We don't find any forced entry to the home, which makes us think that Tieg may have known the perpetrator. Either that, or our killer is a skilled locksmith—all the security features on the home had been disconnected. But something else came up on my drive here. I received a call from the lab. When Tieg's body was discovered, he had a glass of scotch on the side table next to him. The lab found traces of phenobarbital in the glass. As you saw, Tieg was a pretty big guy and likely would not have gone down without a fight, unless there was no other choice."

"Like being drugged big-time," Chad said.

"Yes," Amar replied. "And we believe he was. Oddly enough, my guys found a vial of a drug called Acepromazine in the trash."

"Acepromazine?" Holly asked.

"Also known as Ace, it is used to sedate dogs and horses. It is quite effective. However, it is also a cheap high for humans these days. Some get a prescription for their animal, then use it for themselves. It's similar to diazepam, also known as Valium, but cheaper. We don't have all of the toxicology reports back yet and as you know it will be some time, but we are rushing it."

"Do you know if Ace would keep Tieg incapacitated but still somewhat alert?" Chad asked.

Holly knew where he was going with this line of questioning. "You're thinking that this guy gave him just enough to keep him awake, keep him feeling the pain. Killers who use torture want to see the reaction of their victims. Maybe this guy is a vet. Or in the medical profession. A scientist, possibly. Those guys would know proper dosages and have a drug like that handy. And a vet may be against some of the practices on the track. Does Equine Health Systems sell this stuff, by chance?"

"They don't. I checked that already. No pharmaceuticals through them," Amar said. "But as I said, this drug is relatively easy to get and appears to be common in the equine world. It can be bought online, and proper dosages would be pretty easy to learn. Or, if the prescription was given by a vet, a fairly smart person could figure out how to dose a human. And we all know this guy is pretty smart. Frightening as it is, this guy may not have cared if he overdosed Tieg. He may have been irritated if Tieg was nonresponsive to his torture, sure, but his end goal was Tieg's death. I believe the killer had some vendetta to satisfy."

Holly liked Amar. He was smart, spoke his mind when he felt it relevant, and he also listened. He was a good cop, and she thought his theories prudent. "I think you're right. There is a vendetta mentality going on here, which if we're dealing with two killers widens things even more for us. Narrowing in on a vet with a grudge and a brain that has gone haywire is likely doable, but finding two people in this category might be like finding a needle in a haystack. No pun intended." She smiled at her colleagues. "Okay, maybe a little."

The men chuckled. Amar asked, "Did anything turn up in the jockeys' systems like this Acepromazine?"

"No. He didn't sedate either of them." She walked over to the two jockeys' files on a table and handed them to Amar. "I think we have to look at the possible connections."

"Looks like Tommy Lyons rode one of Tieg's horses in a race, but that's it," Chad said. "The race didn't go so well. The horse, Stand by Me, fractured his cannon bone…" He glanced up from his notes. "His leg, or a part of it. Horse had to be put down on the track."

"Was that this past meet at Del Mar?" Holly asked.

"Yeah, actually it was. Tommy rode more than one horse in that meet. I've learned it's commonplace for jockeys to ride for more than one owner and trainer at each meet, which tend to last around six weeks or so."

"And we didn't question Tieg after the murders?"

Chad's face flushed. "No. And Gershon was the trainer. We asked him if he knew Tommy and Katarina, and all he said was that he knew them in passing. Why not tell us that Lyons had ridden one of Tieg's horses in a race?"

Holly sighed. "Good question, and one we need to address with Gershon." It wasn't her partner's fault that they had dropped the ball on this one. She remembered the various interviews, but the case with the judge's niece had been hanging over their heads, and they'd been pushed hard to solve that one at whatever cost. "Okay. And how about Katarina? Any connection between her and Tieg?"

"I don't see anything there. Yet."

Holly drew a line between Tommy's and Tieg's photos. She continued with the line and took it down to Jim Gershon's name and photo. "He was pretty open about his feelings on the pin firing technique. He claims it isn't something he advocates or practices on the animals that he trains, but how long had he been working for Tieg?"

"I think he said a year," Amar replied.

Holly nodded. "And we spoke with the trainer who Tommy Lyons had been riding for at the time of his murder. Her name is Elena Purdue. He'd ridden that horse of Tieg's just the one time, and then Elena Purdue also owns and trains a horse that he rode a number of times. But not much turned up when I spoke with her. She seemed very happy with Tommy; didn't know much about Katarina, other than she said that she was a good jockey. Elena Purdue seemed distraught over their murders but didn't shed much light on any of it for us."

"Scott Christiansen had mentioned another trainer," Chad said.

"Right. Rafael Torres. Let's come back to him. I want to look at the possible psychology of the killer first. We suspect he's got an ax to grind. He is one angry son of a bitch. He's using methods to murder that we know harm—or in the case of broken legs, can kill—horses. We could be looking at anyone, guys. An animal advocate gone overboard. A former trainer, jockey, groom, vet, or someone with access to this Ace drug. I think we can consider that he might have a territory, and he may strike again soon. It was a few weeks between the jockeys and Tieg, but the method of madness has escalated. That can be a serial-killer trait and I think our guy qualifies, but he's different from the killer who kills simply for sport. He thinks he has a reason to kill—the notes clue us in there. And, if Chad's theory about a team of killers is correct, then we have double trouble here. We haven't even begun to go down that road yet."

"That two-killer scenario—that could be a ploy to throw us off," Chad said. "It looks like he may enjoy toying with the police."

"It does. Any suggestions, Amar?" Holly glanced over at Amar, who appeared contemplative.

"I think we need to look at both the Del Mar and Santa Anita tracks, since Tieg has some horses racing at the Oakwood Meet now. See how many of the same people go from one track to the other."

"That's a good idea," Holly said. "We can divide these tasks up among ourselves and a few colleagues to try and stay ahead of this guy. We all know he's going to strike again. It's a matter of time."

"Hey, speaking of colleagues, do you have a partner?" Chad asked.

Amar looked away. "Killed a few months ago in the line of duty."

"I'm sorry," Holly and Chad replied simultaneously, then looked at each other, chagrined. Holly had wondered. No one spoke for a few seconds.

Amar cleared his throat. "We look at those tracks to see if we can put together some type of cross list between professionals who may in some capacity attend both. It's a start, but I don't know what else to say, other than…I think the three of us better get to know a bit more about horse racing beyond placing bets."

CHAPTER

19

"What you are doing is wrong. It must come to a stop. This is the last time I will help you. I aim to speak with my son as well."

Sheikh Farooq sat across from a man whom he had considered a brother for many years. The man frightened him—he knew his secret and enjoyed using it against him. Farooq knew Waqqas could get what he wanted from a handful of other men. He could have done it without Farooq. But Farooq knew that Waqqas enjoyed placing the target on his back as a form of revenge.

They were in a circular suite atop one of Manhattan's premier hotels. Dark velvet drapes cloaked the walls. The aroma of jasmine candles—one of the sheikh's favorite scents—hung heavy in the air, as did the tension between the men.

Naqeeb Waqqas straightened his silk tie under the dark pin-striped Armani suit and looked Farooq in the eyes. "Is it? Do you not follow the teachings of Muhammad any longer, brother? Are you so westernized now that you have betrayed your faith? Your son is a believer. Your son understands what needs to be done and why we do what we do."

"Our faith is not about death and killing. Do not be so ignorant as to believe the evil spread by the Taliban and the terrorists of the world." Farooq's stomach ached, his heart beat rapidly against his chest. How could they not understand that what they did was not right? "I do good in the world, Waqqas! I help make treaties between countries. I want peace!"

"Peace? You help provide peace by cooperating with infidels. And evil? Look around you, Sheikh. *This* is evil. Our men suffer while the infidels continue to have more than the rest, continue to fight a war against us and our God. That is evil. That is why we are doing what we do, and you will continue to support us. You will continue to support your son and to support me."

Farooq sighed. A heaviness weighed deep in his spirit. "It is wrong. And are *we* suffering? I think not, *brother*. We have more than most men in the entire world, not simply the men in our own world and culture. The *entire* world."

Naqeeb reached down and placed a large briefcase on the marble table. The case contained hundred-dollar bills, totaling $2.7 million. "I am not so selfish as to only be concerned with myself, unlike my brother, Wallid. You know what his selfish ways got him; it is good that *you* have made the right decision. It is always nice doing business with you." He lowered his voice to a whisper as he said, "It would be shameful for the true evil you participate in to come to light. Wouldn't it?"

Farooq could see his bodyguards standing in the recesses of the draperies, their arms crossed, boredom on their faces. They had not heard what Naqeeb said. The sheikh did not respond. He tried to erase the image of Wallid Waqqas from his mind, sick from the thought of what had been done to him. He swallowed his emotions.

"Shame to your family, if the truth be known," Naqeeb continued.

Farooq took the briefcase and set it on the floor next to him. He then opened his own briefcase and removed his checkbook and deposit slip. He wrote a check for the same amount that had been handed to him, made out to the World Bank, of which Naqeeb Waqqas was the president. The bank's central location was in

Manhattan, with international locations in Switzerland and Saudi Arabia.

But Naqeeb Waqqas was much more than the president of a bank.

Naqeeb stood up. "As I said, it was a pleasure doing business with you. I will be in touch."

Farooq's stomach sank. It took a lot to make the sheikh feel this way, and he did not like it at all. If he could, he would strangle this one-time friend with his bare hands, the way Naqeeb had strangled his very own brother. That was the rumor among an elite few, and Farooq believed it was the truth. He knew the viciousness Naqeeb possessed in his heart. Farooq almost wished that Naqeeb would punish him with death, too. What Naqeeb was doing to Farooq was, in many ways, much worse.

He leaned back in the chair as he watched Naqeeb leave the hotel room. Then he walked over to the heavy drapes and pulled them back, wishing that he could pull his pain back in the same way.

The Manhattan skyline was clear as dusk filtered out over the Hudson River. The Statue of Liberty with the torch of freedom held high in the air reminded him that there was plenty of good still left in the world.

The sheikh sighed. All he wanted to do was get back to Kentucky, spend time with his colt, see that he got safely on the plane headed for Las Vegas and forget this bad business. But he knew this bad business would follow him...until he put an end to it.

The problem he had now was figuring out *how*.

CHAPTER

20

"Last call." Holly held up the coffee carafe. "More tea, Amar?"

Both men shook their heads. Holly and the guys were tired, even after copious amounts of tar that substituted as coffee at the station. Add enough creamer and sugar and it became drinkable. The evening had closed in around them and they were all deciding on what to eat, or if they should just go home. However, duty called, and it was looking more and more like pizza accompanied by more theorizing.

"Okay, we already know that there are some unscrupulous tactics allowed as far as what is done to some horses on the track," Amar said. "We also know there is a seedy side to simply participating in racing horses. There are many addicted gamblers at the track and where addictions breed, bad people doing bad things are not far away. There are bookies. We have money laundering. You know, these cases may be more expansive than we can anticipate."

"I agree," Holly replied. "I think we also need to take a close look at the animal advocate groups. There have to be chat rooms and forums—maybe we'll find something there. It's worth a try."

"I can do that," Amar said. "I'll have to be careful. My captain knows I'm sharing with you guys, but he reminded me that I don't work for SDPD. You probably guessed already that I am a bit of a rebel." He winked at them. "But I am good at what I do. If I don't always follow rules, I have figured out ways to work around them.

I will make some calls and put some of my people to work on the peripheral things we have discussed—the chat rooms, and so on. After we chat with Mr. Hodges, I'll head back home and see what my crew has come up with."

"Good plan," Chad said. "Let's finish what we can for now and order up some sausage and pepperoni."

"Gourmet meals." Holly laughed. "All right, we have a growing list here of who races at all of the Southern California meets. We need to start figuring out who knows whom and who might have motives."

"Do serial killers have motives?" Chad said. Holly frowned. "It's a joke, partner."

"This one does. I think we all agree," Amar said.

"It appears that some racing barns travel with an entourage, some with a handful of help, and then there are those that look to be pretty small operations with only two or three people running their show. Some of these people travel by trucks and trailers, some by planes. At this point it looks like we have at least two hundred people to cross-reference. Is this something you can get your guys to help you with, Amar?"

Amar nodded. "Sure. We can divide it."

"Good. Plus we have horseshoers, vets, exercise riders, and even professional haulers transporting horses from the larger barns and from track to track. Within those groups, let's look at possible husband-and-wife teams, siblings, any type of close relations." Holly sat back down at the boardroom table. "Do this traditional style, I guess, and let's run these names and see if anyone has any priors. We should also check if any of the names on our list are linked to any scandals in the racing world. We've already come across the frog juice thing. What do we think of that?"

"Scott Christiansen brought that to our attention," Chad said.

"I think we should check further into the frog juice. It's scandalous in and of itself. I'm curious because he suggested that Tieg possibly had some involvement in it. And that big deal with Tieg's horse, Cayman's Cult…Christiansen also mentioned the former trainer, Rafael Torres. Told you we'd get back to him. Google him, Chad. See if anything comes up." Holly stood and stretched. She paced back and forth, her heels clicking against the tiled floor.

Chad pounded away at the computer. "Yeah. Big-time trainer. He was suspected of drugging the horse. They couldn't find the proof they needed, so he's back training but obviously not for Tieg. Won a lot of races, this guy. Been around for some time."

"Where's he training?" Amar asked.

"Versailles, Kentucky. He trains for a farm called Donahue-Fields."

Holly nodded. "Interesting. Anything else?"

Chad scrolled down the search page. "Wait, wait, wait a minute. Here's another article. It's about Tommy and Katarina's murders. There is a sentence here that reads, *Katarina Erickson had been looking forward to riding Serenity Jones, owned by Donahue-Fields Farms, in Sunday's race. Erickson would have been the first female jockey to ever ride for the farm.*

"I thought she was working for that trainer we spoke with after the murders. The one I had a vibe about, Geremiah Laugherty," Holly said.

Chad shrugged. "Jockeys can and do ride for more than one owner and trainer."

"I think we need to speak with Mr. Torres. Anyone want to go to Kentucky?" she asked.

CHAPTER

21

Holly stood in the kitchen brewing coffee. Amar was still asleep in the guest room. Usually on Sunday mornings, Holly would wait for Chloe to rise, and they would head over to Brendan's, or Brendan and the girls would come to them. They'd have breakfast together and figure out how to while the day away.

However, this case was going to eat up her Sunday morning. She'd phoned Brendan the night before and explained the situation. He of course had no problem keeping Chloe for the night but was disappointed not to be seeing her. She felt as if lately all she did was disappoint him. Hopefully, they would get this interview with Hodges over with quickly so they could enjoy the rest of the day with their families. Still, there would be a damper on the day no matter what. She was going to have to let her family know that she would be headed to Kentucky, in the morning. That news would not go over well.

She poured herself a cup of morning jump-start and put a piece of bread in the toaster. When she turned around to see Amar standing there in her kitchen, she startled. "Oh my God."

"I'm sorry," he said. "My wife hates that about me. She says that I sneak up on her. Trained cop."

"Me, too. Trained cop, I mean. I should have heard you."

He waved a hand at her, and she took down a mug from the cupboard. "Coffee or tea?"

"Coffee in the morning." He sat on one of the barstools at her kitchen counter. The morning light sliced in through the kitchen blinds. Amar looked as tired as she felt. "Sleep okay?"

He shrugged. "It is hard when I am not at home, and my mind is going in circles thinking on this case."

"I agree on both accounts," she said. "I never sleep well away from home and my mind is trying to fit all of the pieces together here." She handed him the coffee. "Cream and sugar?"

"No, thank you."

"There are so many angles to this case. There are pieces that don't make sense. We're learning a lot about horses and horse racing and what goes on in that world, but are we looking too hard at that?"

"What do you mean?" she asked. Her toast popped up and she asked him if he'd like a slice. He nodded, so she gave him that one and put another piece of bread in the toaster.

"I mean, are we digging too deep into horse racing? Is turning over every leaf prudent? To me, this is a serial killer case. It is about a killer, or even two, targeting people involved with horse racing. Could it be as simple as a fan or fans gone off the deep end?"

"It could. But you know as well as I do, Amar, that we have to look at everything. We have to ask all of these questions and hope that even just one answer will open the doors wide." She wasn't sure what he was getting at. She was beginning to doubt her investigative abilities—both she and Chad had dropped the ball in a few areas. But she wasn't going to let that happen again.

"My partner, Mac, he was a good guy. He was a good father, husband, detective. He was organized, thought everything out, no stone unturned—like you. He was killed in the line of duty. The thing is that he was killed working a case, but the guy who killed him had nothing to do with the perp in our case, it turned out. He was a thread."

"But obviously he was also bad. He may not have been who you were looking for on the case, but he proved dangerous."

"Yes, of course, but my point is that maybe if Mac hadn't been looking all over the place and focused in on one area, he would still be here."

Holly's toast popped up, and she turned around to butter it, pondering his words.

"I'm going to get a shower," he said. "Mind if I take the coffee with me?"

"Not at all. I set some new towels in the guest bath this morning…" She turned back around to see that Amar had left the room as silently as he'd entered.

Petie was at her feet begging for his breakfast, which she promptly fed him. She wasn't sure what to make of Amar's words. He'd caught her off guard. Were they looking in the wrong places? Was she going about this all wrong?

She took her coffee and walked into the family room where she kept an old hutch that had once been her grandmother's. She opened it and found what she was looking for—a photo of Jack. She traced his face in the photo. Although she loved another man now, she would never forget her love for Jack. If he were alive, he would have told her his thoughts, maybe helped her see what she was missing.

She shook her head. Jack wasn't here, and life had moved on in so many ways. She stuck the photo back into the hutch, hoping she was not leading everyone down a dead-end road.

CHAPTER

22

Holly and Amar drove over to Hodges's place in silence.

Another palatial estate, although this one had the backdrop of the bright blue Pacific. "Damn, these people have some serious money," Chad said as he got out of his car. Holly and Amar had beaten him there by a couple of minutes.

"High-stakes horses. Drama. It all equates to lots and lots of cash, my friends," Holly replied.

They walked up to the massive doors. Bright-colored flowers and small palms grew in abundance on either side of the walkway. Holly rang the buzzer. A moment later they were greeted by a surly, pimply teenaged boy. "Yeah?"

"We're here to see Edwin Hodges."

"Dad! Some people are here for you."

The kid then shut the door. Holly, Chad, and Amar gave one another *what the hell* looks.

A moment later the door swung back open and they stood face-to-face with the famous Hodges. "Oh hello, officers. I saw you coming."

"Saw us?" Chad asked.

"Officer, I have the best security systems in the world in my homes and business." He tapped an alarm keypad displaying the words *Bradley Systems* encircled by a logo in the shape of a Q. "I have cameras, alarms, whatever I need to keep me and my family safe. Come in."

Edwin Hodges was indeed self-assured. He was shorter than he looked on TV. Somewhere in his fifties, though Holly guessed he'd had some plastic surgery. He was tan, fit, and his hair looked dyed blond rather than natural.

Holly gave Chad one of her looks like, *Okay...what are we dealing with?* as they were led into what had to be the living room. Floor-to-ceiling windows let in abundant light, and everything in the room was white, except for the dark hardwood floors and the chrome accents on the modern furnishings. Holly fought not to be distracted by the amazing view.

"What can I help you with?" Hodges asked.

Holly quickly made a round of introductions, then said, "We're investigating Marvin Tieg's murder, and we know you had some business dealings with him."

Hodges laughed and waved a hand in the air. He walked over to the windows and turned his back to the officers. Holly decided she didn't like this guy. "Okay. But how can I help you?" he asked again.

"Mr. Hodges, Mr. Tieg was a business partner of yours, and we are attempting to learn what he was involved in. It may help us find who killed him," Amar said, being far more diplomatic than Holly.

Hodges turned back around. "You're here because you think I can help you solve who murdered Tieg? Okay. Sure. I think I can. Some goddamned crazed lunatic is responsible. That's about all I can help you with, Detectives. Let's face it. The guy is a serial killer. He murdered two jockeys in cold blood, and now he's killed my business partner. You surely won't find any serial killers running in my crowd."

"And you know that because...?" Chad asked.

"Because I'm a genius. I know enough to know when a socio-path is in my vicinity. You're going to ask me all the regular bullshit questions, which waste your time and mine. Let me save you the trouble. Did Tieg have any known enemies? I am sure he did. We all do. Rich people typically have enemies. Do I know who they were? No. I don't pay enough attention and don't have time for that nonsense. Was he involved in anything illegal? No clue. Maybe. But what *we* did together was legal."

Holly wanted to kick the crap out of this guy. She started to say something, but Hodges held up a hand. "What we did together? Yes, well, what we did together was…invest in a couple of horses. I am also the major investor in the Infinity track—and the casino—out in Vegas. Tieg put up some cash but was really more the pro-moter than anything. The documentary he was creating is excel-lent, and I plan to see it to fruition. His murder, and the murders of the jockeys, have put a dark cloud over what was supposed to be a rising sun on a new day for the sport of horse racing." He stared at Holly. She stood her ground, but his intensity was unnerving to say the least. "And because I refuse to allow that darkness to ruin a new era and the greatest day the sport will ever see, I have work to do. And you do as well, Detectives. I have nothing left to tell you."

"I assume you have a list of all of the investors who helped in building the Infinity," Holly said.

"That's private information, and I don't see how it can help you find a serial killer," Hodges replied.

Holly walked over closer to Hodges. She crossed her arms and lowered her voice. "I need that list. Either you give it to me, or I get a subpoena and go through your lovely home, possibly your offices if need be. I'm sure that would give your employees something to talk about around the water cooler, wondering what you might have to hide."

Hodges glared at her. "I'll be right back."

"Whoa," Chad said as Hodges left the room.

Holly smiled.

A few minutes later, Hodges came back with a document. "Here you go, Detective."

"Thank you." Chad and Amar glanced at each other and then looked at Holly. Something about this wasn't sitting well with her. Amar's words from that morning echoed in her head. Hadn't Hodges just basically said the same thing to them, although in a major asshole way? Was she wasting time? "You know, Mr. Hodges, I think we may need to speak with you again."

"I don't see why you would need to do that." He crossed his arms.

"Make certain we can reach you." Holly didn't bother to thank the man as she headed out. Chad and Amar followed her.

Outside, they all looked like they had been sucker punched.

Chad exclaimed, "What do you make of that?"

"That man is a jerk," Amar replied.

Holly gave Amar a dirty look. She glanced over the investor list. She recognized a few of the twenty names, but not all of them. She handed the list to Amar. "Check each one of these folks out. I'm sure there isn't anything there that could help us, but you never know." She was still annoyed by Amar's earlier remarks. "I don't care what Hodges says, but I guarantee that when I run that conversation through my brain again, when I revisit this interview, I will find something. I will find something that will help us with this case."

CHAPTER

23

Joque didn't quite get why Quentin had sent him to New York City first, before letting him head out to Saratoga. He'd insisted that Joque stay in Manhattan for two days. It had been hard for Joque to arrange that time away, but not impossible.

He was good at putting on the charm.

He was good at deception.

Quentin's only explanation for wanting Joque in the city for those two days had been that he thought Joque deserved a few days off, some nights out on the town. Though Quentin couldn't be with him, he had urged Joque to celebrate, to do it right, as if the two of them were together. He'd wired him plenty of cash, that was for sure. And Joque did what Quentin told him to do because the guy had saved his life. They were kindred spirits.

So, when Quentin told him to do things a certain way, Joque didn't refuse. Not after everything that guy had done for him.

He didn't even know his benefactor's first name—Quentin told him that he liked to go by his last name only. What he did know is that they both had suffered. They had suffered at the hands of some of the same people. They also both loved the horses, and they were getting even, and in getting even they would bring down the entire industry that had not only ruined Joque but also ruined horses. In some ways it had ruined Quentin, too.

That night the year before when, seated in a bar just outside Tulsa, a few beers downed, Joque looked up to see his kindred soul walk in. He didn't know it at the time. In fact, when the dude first sat down he seemed sort of arrogant.

He seemed rich.

Joque had been around plenty of wealthy people, and he did not think much of them. He had moved to Tulsa in an attempt to keep away from the wealthy he had grown up around. He knew he would have been shunned if he'd gone back to Lexington.

Quentin had sat down right next to Joque, who did not feel like making small talk with a stranger, especially one who dressed like money. The bar was dark and dingy—the way he liked it. He could disappear in a place like that bar, so he'd thought. His skin crawled when Quentin had said to him, "I know you."

"No you don't," he replied.

"I do. I think we have something in common, my friend."

"I doubt that."

That was when Quentin handed him a newspaper from ten years before. The *Lexington Herald* to be exact. There it was. *The story.* "What the fuck?" He started to stand. He was gonna knock this guy from here to tomorrow.

Quentin grabbed his arm and then flashed several hundred-dollar bills in front of his face. "I believe you. I believed it then, Ted. I believe it now. Want to get even?"

That was when Ted Ivy, who now liked to call himself Joque, sat back down…

CHAPTER

24

March 3, 2011

Quentin set the newspaper article on the bar and his man squirmed. Once he saw the money, though, things got easier.

Quentin had his story tightly planned out.

He bought Ted Ivy another drink.

"Here's the thing, man, they did you real wrong, and I have my own reasons for wanting to get even," Quentin said.

"What are they? Why?" Ivy asked.

"My wife and my daughter," Quentin replied, making eye contact to draw Ivy in.

"I don't understand." Ivy ran his fingers over the burns on his hands.

Quentin placed another newspaper article on the bar—a manufactured article. He was taking a risk here. He knew that. But he'd weighed it and decided it was a calculated risk. Hell, just having this conversation with Ted Ivy was a calculated risk. "Marvin Tieg is a man of means as you well know, and my wife, Carol..." He could see the surprise in Ivy's eyes. Naming his fictitious wife after Ivy's dead one—another calculated risk. He cleared his throat. "She was driving our little girl Janie back from ballet lessons. Janie was eight." His eyes welled with tears, and he choked up emotion from his gut. "Read the article."

The article told a sad story about how Carol and Janie were on a rainy road late one afternoon in California—six years ago. Tieg crashed into their car, killing them.

"What?" Ivy looked up from the article. "Why isn't he in jail?"

"Good question. Money. Geremiah Laugherty was with him and two other witnesses claimed my wife ran a red light. I think Tieg and Laugherty had been drinking."

"Then how would they get off?" Ivy asked, taking a swig of his beer.

"You aren't serious, are you? How do you think they set you up?"

Ivy leaned back. "Money."

"That's right. Money."

"Guess who else was involved?"

Ivy looked at him.

"Jim Gershon. He was one of the witnesses. He was pulling a horse trailer behind them. Isn't that convenient?" Quentin knew this was a huge pile of bullshit and he hoped Ivy was too drunk and too pathetic to smell it.

"What the fuck?"

"Yeah."

Ivy shook his head. "How did you find me?"

"After this happened, I about died myself. I even looked down the chamber of my gun one night and told myself to pull the trigger. But I stopped myself, because it made me sick to think these guys were going to get off scot-free. I decided to find out everything that I could about them. I've been learning about the lives of these three assholes for the last four years. I found your story, and I thought that we needed to be friends. So I got you out of jail."

"What?"

Quentin nodded.

"How the hell…? Who are you?"

"I am a man who desires that justice be served. I think you are, too."

"What are you thinking?" Ivy asked.

Quentin could see he'd set the hook. Ivy had bought the bullshit story. The tears had been a nice touch. "I am thinking murder, my friend. Slow, torturous murder."

"Oh no, man. I spent eight years in prison. I ain't going back."

"You won't. You are dead, my friend."

"What?"

"I have some connections, and like Tieg, I have made some money in the past few years. I was able to get you out of jail. Didn't you wonder why you had an early release?"

"Good behavior. That's what I was told."

"Yeah, well, good behavior and me. I also fixed it so that on paper, you're dead."

"Come on. No way. That shit don't happen."

Quentin grabbed the articles, put them back in his briefcase, and stood up.

"Where you going?" Ivy asked.

"I can see this isn't going to work out."

"What do you mean?"

Quentin leaned in and said, "Do you really think you'd be here without a little help from the outside? You're free now. I won't bother you anymore. I thought we might have something in common. A way to settle our scores." Quentin turned and walked away.

What happened next played out just as he expected.

Quentin was a master manipulator and he knew there would come a moment of doubt from Ivy, and when that doubt filtered into the man's simple mind, that was when he got up and walked away.

All orchestrated.

And as planned, Ivy fell right in step.

And followed him out the door.

CHAPTER

25

Sheikh Farooq left the Chanel store on West Fifty-Seventh Street with some nice gifts for his wife and daughter. They should be happy with his purchases. He bought them many things. However, Ayda was never happy with him. At twenty-eight years of age, the girl still acted like a child, and because he had no idea how to deal with her, he simply continued to buy her things. He was still surprised that she wanted to attend the Infinity with him.

One never knows how one's children will turn out. He knew his son and daughter considered him neglectful, even though they had never been in need or want of anything. His wife agreed with the children, accusing him of spending his love on his horses. They were probably right. Horses he understood. Women and children he did not. Therefore, he bought the women in his life many things to keep them satisfied.

As for his son, Farooq was forced to do his bidding as well.

He tried hard to ignore the fact that the gifts for Ayda and his wife had been bought with dirty money. Money he had paid for with clean money to legitimize illegal dealings in another part of the world. The kind of dealings he did not believe in and did not want to have any part of, and it weighed heavily on his heart. But he was trapped, Waqqas held the key, and he wasn't letting Farooq loose.

He ran through every scenario he could grab on to, hoping to find a way to expose the truth and escape the lies and those behind them. However, at the end of each stream of consciousness stood reality. The reality that if the truth—*his* truth—be known, the shame it would cause his family and himself would be unbearable. A door of danger would open that Farooq was certain he would not be able to close. The kind of danger that could easily lead him to his own demise, if his conscience did not do that first.

As he slipped in between the soft leather seats of the limousine, he glanced at a bottle of some dark alcohol and for the first time in many years considered taking a drink. He shook his head and leaned back, a long sigh escaping from his lips, catching the attention of the two bodyguards riding with him. Neither of them spoke.

But one of them knew a secret, too.

The bodyguard remained still and silent like his companion as they made their way back to the airport. They would be headed to the farm very soon where, if the sheikh knew what was going on daily in his colt's stall, there would be more than soft, long sighs escaping from the great man's lips. However, the bodyguard knew that he would not say anything to the sheikh until the timing was right.

CHAPTER
26

"You seem troubled," Brendan said, turning over the chicken he was barbecuing. They sat outside while Brendan fixed their dinner, Holly sipping a glass of wine. The two younger girls were in the house likely wreaking havoc, while Megan was due home soon from the mall.

"That noticeable?"

He walked over and sat down next to her. "I think I know you pretty well. The case?"

"Yes, the case."

"Want to talk about it?" He refilled her wineglass.

"I don't know. It's heavy."

"Aren't they always heavy?"

"Yes."

"Talk to me."

She tensed for a moment, then began to talk. "This guy, this sicko is murdering people involved in horse racing."

"The jockeys from last month?"

She nodded. "And now Marvin Tieg in Los Angeles, he looks to have been done in by the same guy."

"What does your team think?"

"There are a lot of angles in this. It's brutal, the things done to these folks. It's as if this guy has some kind of bone to pick. I really don't know. I think that maybe it's an animal rights activist gone overboard."

"A lot of rotten things go on at the track. I know I work on only small animals, but I've had some exposure and have talked with other vets. If you have a killer who has the inside information about what goes on with some of these horses, then maybe you're right."

"I had no idea that the horses are shot full of crap, and are made to run at so young an age," she said. "Then again, pretty much all I know about horses is that they're big, and I think they're pretty."

Brendan laughed. "True. They are that. You will find differing opinions about how old a horse should be to race, and what is okay for them to have in their system and what isn't. The thing that I doubt will change is that where money is involved in such large quantities, the animal—the living, breathing soul—is second to the power of money. And the sport of horse racing moves a lot of money."

"Does it ever." She picked up her wine. "What do you think of racing?"

"I'm not a fan. But I am a vet. Like you, I see the worst of what humans can be. I see them from the eyes of the animals. Just today I had a kitten brought in that had been stuffed in someone's exhaust pipe. Poor thing may turn out blind and he has a broken leg, but I will do what I can for him."

"Why? Why are humans so cruel?"

"I ask myself that question all the time, Holly. There is good, bad, and ugly in all human beings—maybe not good in all." He paused. "But there is only good in you, baby." He winked and gave her a hard kiss.

Brendan had a way of sending serious tingles through her. Here he was, this big guy who worked out and was stronger than an ox. He had a gorgeous Irish lilt, greenish-blue eyes that sparkled when he smiled. He had a zest for life and a zest for her. If you met him for the first time he would appear rough and tumble, the kind of guy who enjoyed a good whiskey and an occasional cigar. In reality, he adored his family, had a huge place in his heart for the tiniest of beings, and understood people and animals better than anyone she had ever known. All part of why she loved him so much.

Brendan whispered in Holly's ear, "I think maybe there's a little bad in you, too, but there is not an ounce of ugly."

"I may show you the bad me later," she whispered back.

"I like that. Take your mind off the case again."

"Yes, but not for long."

"Uh-oh. I don't like the sound of that," he said.

She sighed. "I have to go to Lexington in the morning. There's a horse trainer that we think might be able to help with the case."

"How long will you be gone?"

"I fly out tomorrow. I'll get my answers and try to get a flight back at night. If not, it'll be the following day. I'm sorry."

"You are good at what you do, Detective. I can't tell you not to go. It's your job. I can tell you that I don't want you to go and that I am going to sulk about it, but that is because I am selfish and want you here with us."

"I know, and I want to be here with you. It won't be long." She stood and put her arms around his neck, running her fingers through the waves in his hair. She grazed his lips with hers.

"Stop! Get a room," Megan said as she stepped out on the patio.

"Meg. We would, but you damn kids are always here," Brendan replied.

"Ouch and seriously yuck, Dad!"

"He's kidding," Holly said.

"No he's not."

"She's right. I'm not." He laughed.

Megan crossed her arms and stuck out a hip, typical teenager stance. "Did Dad show you what he was building you yet?" she asked.

Chloe and Maddie suddenly appeared. "Is the chicken ready?" Chloe asked.

"Yeah, Daddy. We're hungry," Maddie added.

"What are you building me?" Holly asked.

"Oh boy, I am really in trouble here. Thank God I'll have Petie when you move in. I'm going to be eaten alive by all you females," Brendan said.

"I warned you." Holly took his hand. "So. What are you building me?"

"Come on."

He led her around to the side yard. Brendan's place was situated on a double corner lot, giving him one of the larger backyards in Point Loma. He'd been able to do quite a bit with it, including building a swing set when the girls were younger, cultivating a flower garden and a vegetable garden, installing a Jacuzzi, and adding a lot of greenery. He had the green thumb that Holly didn't.

"I wanted to wait and hope you wouldn't discover it just yet, but we have big mouths in this family." He gave Megan the stink eye.

In front of them stood a rather large hole about eight feet wide, ten feet long and three feet deep. "What is it?" Holly asked.

"It will be your koi pond," Brendan replied. "Remember last year when we went to Sea World and you fell in love with the koi ponds and said you'd love to have one?"

"I do." She smiled.

"You're going to get one. It's my move-in gift to you. I figured it's getting close to the time when we put your place up for rent and you start packing. We only have a few months until we make this thing legal."

"We do. Yes. I love it. And I love you."

"Oh God, do not kiss again. Please," Megan groaned.

"No kissing. We want chicken," Chloe said.

Holly leaned her head on his strong shoulder. She was happy here, happy with him, and happy with their family. Happy in the moment and wishing she could stay, because she had no clue what the next few days would bring.

Somehow she doubted it would have anything to do with happiness.

CHAPTER
27

Early Monday morning, and Elena's nerves were rattled. Time to move Karma out to Sin City. She loaded the trailer with the necessities—grooming kits, liniments, medications, ice machines for the mare's legs, her blankets, all of the peripherals. Elena would normally have flown her in or had a professional hauler transport her. But there was something different about this time, other than it was the biggest event they had ever been to. Elena was filled with an unfamiliar urgency and felt the need to be the one in charge of her filly. Maybe it was because they had come so far together. Elena didn't know, but she was going to trust her gut.

She finished loading the tack room and headed to the barn to get Karma. Perez planned to drive out with the bug.

Reaching her horse's stall, she sensed someone come up behind her. She turned around. "O'Leary! You startled me."

"I'm sorry. You heading out?"

"Yeah. Just me and the girl."

"Wait a minute, you're hauling her? Alone?" he asked.

"Um, yeah. I've been hauling horses since I was seventeen. I think I got this."

"Oh, I know you're capable. But you got yourself an animal worth—what? If I had to guess, a cool few mil. She wins this race, and she's gonna be worth even more. And you plan to drive alone with her for the next seven hours?" He shook his head.

"You always did think like a thriller author. What? You think I'll get jacked and she'll be stolen. You really should write a book. I always thought so."

"Maybe I will. Maybe I am." He smiled. "But I'm serious, El. I don't like you doing this on your own."

She slipped the halter over Karma's ears and a chain up over her nose, attaching the lead rope. "What do you propose I do?"

"Take me with you."

"You're...wait a minute, you're serious?"

"As a heart attack. Yes, El. Do I think you'll get jacked out on the highway? No. But I really do think it's safer to have someone with you. I don't mean to push myself on you. I know I can be that way." He paused and met her gaze, real concern in his eyes. "But let me go with you."

She led the horse out of the stall and walked ahead of O'Leary. "You got your stuff with you?"

He held out a backpack. "I travel light. Pair of jeans, a couple of T-shirts, breeches, and my riding boots. I'm sure I can find a Laundromat out there if I need to."

"If I didn't know any better, I'd say you had this planned," she replied and kept walking. The clipping of the horse's metal shoes meeting solid ground echoed down the aisle.

He jogged next to her and the horse. "Nah. I was heading to the airport when I stopped by to see if you were around."

"What about your plane ticket?"

He shrugged. "I'm a nervous flier, you know that. The only real kind of flying I like to do involves four legs and dirt kicking up out the back. Besides, I can fly somewhere else some other time. Maybe I'll fly you to Cabo."

She shook her head, laughing. "You're lucky I'm taking you to Vegas."

"That I am. That I am."

CHAPTER

28

Where in this wide world can man
find nobility without pride,
friendship without envy, or beauty without vanity?
Here where grace is laced with muscle and
strength by gentleness confined.
He serves without servility; he has fought without enmity.
There is nothing so powerful, nothing less violent;
there is nothing so quick, nothing more patient.
— Ronald Duncan

Racehorses discover, when they are a year or two old, that they were born for a reason.

They learn to take a bit in their mouths—first something soft and gummy, then something metallic and cold.

They're doted on by veterinarians, prodded and poked and pampered.

They're shod, their legs are wrapped, they become familiar with the twitch.

They learn to bear a saddle, to stand in the cross-ties while a strap is tightened around their bellies, and then they learn to bear a rider.

CHAPTER

29

Monday morning came too quickly. Both Brendan and Chloe sulked as they drove Holly to the airport the next day. Brendan's good-sport attitude had lessened once the alarm went off. Megan thought it was cool that Holly was headed to Kentucky on official police work, and Maddie was thrilled to pieces that her best friend would be staying with them for a couple of days.

The drive to Lindbergh Field took only seven minutes. The early morning sky was already blue and clear—typical San Diego weather. They rode mostly in silence, with Chloe frowning and Brendan mirroring her. "Guys, it isn't like I'm going for a week," she said. "It's two days. Maybe three. I am flying in, going to go see this guy we want some answers from, and then heading home."

"I don't understand why Chad can't go," Brendan replied.

"For one thing, his wife is due to have a baby in the next couple of weeks."

"We're trying to plan a wedding in three months!" Brendan snapped.

"Oh, come on. New baby? Wedding?" She quickly realized how cold that seemed. "I'm sorry, Brendan." She did not want to argue in front of the girls. She took a deep breath. "This is my case. I am the lead investigator on this thing. I don't go out of town that often, guys. We'll make the plans when I get back. We agreed on small and quaint, Brendan. Right? It won't be that difficult. This will all come together."

"But you work all the time," Chloe interjected.

Now that hurt.

Holly sighed. "I promise everyone in this car that when I am finished with this case, we will go on some amazing vacation together and you won't even hear the words *crime, police, detective,* or *case.* Deal?"

Brendan eyed her. He finally cracked a smile. "I'm sorry, too. I miss you when you aren't around. And I need help keeping these three in line." He jerked his thumb over his shoulder and laughed.

"Oh sure, Dad. You let the girls do whatever they want. It's like party town at our house," Megan said.

Holly smiled. "Uh-huh, so the truth comes out."

"Megan. Isn't there a car you're hoping to get sometime in the future?" Brendan said.

"Oh. I mean, Dad is awesome with all of us when you're gone, Holly. I'm serious. When he says something, we all listen. Especially them." She pointed to the two younger girls.

"Uh-huh. You already dug yourself in," Brendan told her.

"I believe you." Holly turned around and winked at Megan. "I miss you guys, too, when I'm gone. But you all do need to keep in mind that this is my job, and trying to make me feel guilty is not good."

Brendan pulled up curbside in front of United's terminal. He got out and grabbed her bag from the trunk. She opened up the back door and gave each girl a hug and kiss. "I will bring gifts."

"Don't listen to them," Megan whispered. "They are *so* working you."

Holly smiled at the teen. "Ya think?"

Chloe hugged her mom but still didn't smile.

Brendan kissed her. "See you. Two days. Be careful."

"Always. You better hurry so you can get them to school on time."

She held back her own emotions and headed through the double doors with her carry-on and on up to the special security zone set apart for law enforcement.

Once she went through a complete security check and received approval to travel with her gun, she grabbed a Starbucks and sat down at the gate. She had about ten minutes before boarding.

As she settled into the seat, her cell rang. Chad again. "Hey, Inspector Clouseau, what's the story this morning?" she said.

"I may have something interesting, but I don't know if it means anything, so just hear me out."

"Always." She set her coffee down and watched as people walked by with their carry-ons rolling behind them.

"Okay. We know this guy likes to cat-and-mouse us some. We're theorizing, based on the notes he's left us, that he's working with someone else. But I dug deeper into the note, the clues there. The Carpenters' song 'We've Only Just Begun' is in John Carpenter's movie *In the Mouth of Madness*. Now get this, that movie is the third in a trilogy. An apocalyptic trilogy."

"How does that relate to a madman murdering influential people in the racehorse scene?" Holly asked.

"Not sure. But like you, I also have intuition. Only I call it a gut feeling. And if I were a betting man, which you know I am not, I would bet that this apocalyptic trilogy is significant to our killer. And I bet it is connected."

Holly closed her eyes and leaned back. This case was getting bigger by the second, and her head hurt. She hated to admit it, but something told her that Chad could be onto something. One killer. Two killers. Torture. Illegal substances. Now possibly an apocalyptic killer, which would cast an entirely new light on things. "You may be right. Share this with Amar and get his impressions. You heading out to Equine Health Systems for the employee interviews this morning?" They had agreed that, with Holly going out to Kentucky, Chad needed to be in charge of the process over at Equine Health Systems.

"Yes," he replied. "First I have to take Brooke to the doctor for a check. She hasn't been feeling well. After that, her mom is coming in to help so that will free up my day to spend at Scott Christiansen's place for those interviews."

"Good. I hope your wife feels better."

"Thanks. Me, too."

"What about Amar? I haven't spoken with him since we left Hodges's place. I figured it's a little early to call right now. I'll be in flight shortly. Can you give him a buzz, run this by him, and see where he's at with things?"

"No problem."

"Thanks. Hey, I have to go. They're starting to board."

"Be careful, partner," he said.

"Always." She clicked off her phone.

She boarded the plane, took her seat, and closed her eyes. She hated flying. It scared the shit out of her—and her experience from a couple years ago hadn't helped. She'd almost died when a madman she'd been tracking had crashed the small plane he was piloting. A shiver went through her as her memory took her back to that day. Gunter Drake had planned to kill her. She'd almost lost everything. Somehow she had survived. Thankfully.

Then another dark thought entered her mind. What did this killer, or killers, have in store for her? Did they know she was coming after them with a vengeance?

She would have to heed Chad's words and be as careful as possible.

CHAPTER
30

There is a reason why people call Kentucky the bluegrass state. As the puddle jumper descended into Lexington, the land spread out below with what Holly could tell was farm after farm—all with that green bluegrass growing abundantly.

There is also a reason that Lexington is called the horse capital of the world. No one walking through the small airport could miss the signs advertising the World Equestrian Games from 2010, Keeneland, race farms, and of course the university, which specialized in education in various equine fields.

Walking through the glass sliders, heading to the garage to locate her rental car, Holly saw life-size bronzes of what she assumed were famous racehorses off to the side of the curved walkway. They were gorgeous pieces of art. It was already after five by the time she got behind the wheel of the rental car, but she decided to take a chance and see if she could find Rafael Torres. She'd love to be able to get this little inquisition finished and add either another suspect, or at the very least some new information, to her notes.

The October day held on to some humidity as dark thunderclouds rolled in over the green pastures that spread out on either side of the road she drove after she exited the highway. The smells of must and earth filled the air. The place was beautiful. Plantation homes sat before the background of the pastures, some overlooking lakes dotted with ducks and geese. Horses grazed on the lush feed behind either black or white wooden fences. Cornstalks grew tall in some places, and grapevines climbed avidly the farther Holly drove out through Lexington-Fayette Urban County. She passed the world-famous horse park and, shortly after, found the street she needed, which wound into a few curves before she came up to the farm she was looking for—Donahue-Fields. A large wrought iron gate barred her entrance. Things could get tricky from here. She didn't want to involve local law enforcement—all she wanted to do was have a talk with Rafael Torres. No need to involve the locals. She just had to hope Torres was on the farm.

She buzzed the call button at the gate and waited. Nothing. She buzzed again. A couple of minutes later she spotted a golf cart headed in her direction. A security guard got out and came through the side door of the gate, stooping to talk through her car window. "How may I help you, ma'am?"

"Hi. I'm Holly Jennings. Detective Holly Jennings. I'm here to see Rafael Torres."

She showed the lanky, bald guard her shield. "What is this regarding, Detective Jennings?" he asked politely.

"It involves a murder investigation in Los Angeles, and it's possible that Mr. Torres may have some information."

The guard lifted a hand to his chin and scratched. "Oh, I don't think so. I think you'd better get on back to California."

Holly stepped out of the car. Her five-foot-five frame was no match for this guy. But her gun was, and she made sure he saw it as she moved her blazer just slightly off her hip. "Here's the thing… what did you say your name was?"

"I'm Harold."

"Okay, Harold. I am a nice cop. I do my job, and I do it well. My job has just sent me thousands of miles away from home. I have been traveling for about eight hours at this point and all I want to do is go to my hotel, have a drink and some food, and get some rest.

But first, I need to speak with Mr. Torres. Are you going to help me with that, or do I need to call local police to get involved? I'm sure you would like your day to end on time. But if we don't do this the nice-cop way, I can pretty much guarantee you that neither one of our days will end in a timely manner. That will suck for both of us."

He cleared his throat, looking away as if seeking the right answer from a pocket of air. He made up his mind quickly. "Follow me." He returned to the golf cart and opened the gate. Holly returned to her car and drove on through. She spotted Harold speaking into a walkie-talkie, surely giving a heads up to whoever needed one.

As she drove through the gates, an entire new world opened up. Straight ahead, along a circular drive, stood a replica of Tara from *Gone with the Wind*. She followed the golf cart, which veered off to the right of the driveway. On the right side of the drive, vines grew in intertwined succession, and to her left was a small lake with a floating gazebo, ducks, and a couple of swans. "Jesus," she found herself saying out loud. The road wound around and they came upon a racetrack on the left side, just after the lake. Straight ahead stood two massive barns that looked to be constructed out of cobblestone, their roofs a dark wood. Everything about it looked to Holly like old-world money.

In front of the barn on the right, handlers loaded horses into a semi horse trailer, one after the other.

Harold parked the golf cart. She pulled up next to it and got out. "Mr. Torres is over by the trailer. There." He pointed to a tall, dark, and—as stereotypical as she knew it sounded—handsome man standing next to the trailer. He was barking orders at the others.

She headed his way.

"Lorenzo, make sure all of the supplements for that mare are packed."

"I have, sir."

Dark and handsome nodded and then shifted his very direct look on her, as if studying prey. "Hello," he said.

"Good afternoon." Holly stretched out her hand. "I'm Detective Holly Jennings."

He looked surprised as he took it. "Rafael Torres. Detective? Not from around here, I'm guessing." He glanced over his shoulder at a horse being led up a ramp onto the semi. "Careful with that one." He looked back at Holly. "As you were saying."

"I'm not from here. I'm from San Diego, and I'm investigating a murder."

Torres cocked his head to the side. "Lyons's? Katarina's? Tieg's?"

"Yes. All of the above."

"Uh-huh. Not sure how I can help you, Detective. Scary, creepy, strange stuff, though." He leaned against the barn and crossed his arms.

"Very much so. But you know, you may be surprised. Sometimes I speak with people, and they say things that help connect the dots. I'm hoping, Mr. Torres, that you can help me connect even just a few dots. It's my understanding that you and Mr. Tieg had a history." She kept a trained eye on the man's body language.

He gave her that predatory look again, and she held his stare. Finally, Torres said to the guys loading horses, "I'll be a few in my office. When they're all loaded, let me know." He then started to walk off through the barn. Without looking back he said, "You can come with me, *Detective*."

She jogged through the barn, which looked cleaner than her home on most days, to catch up with him. The smell of straw permeated the air, and the whispers of live animals were obvious as the horses minded their own business.

He looked sideways at her. "I'd give you a tour of the place, but as you can see I'm busy and need to get packing."

"Oh. No problem. Where are you headed?" She figured a little small talk might soften him some.

"Vegas, for the Infinity."

"Oh. Nice. You have a horse running in the Infinity?"

"Yeah. He's on his way there now. I just have to be certain the two-year-olds are loaded and out of here without any problems, then I'm off to the airport. My assistant is traveling with a colt owned by the syndicate here. Donahue-Fields is a large operation, made up of several folks from the two families and then friends, business acquaintances. Keep an eye out for our colt. His name is Devilish."

"Cute."

"Yes. He's more than cute, and he is very fast."

"Sounds great for you," she replied.

He didn't respond. Small talk over.

At the end of the row, he opened a door to the right and entered. She followed him into a nice office. Dark woods, a caramel-colored suede sofa, a curio cabinet with trophies, and a good-size desk. Torres took a seat behind the desk in a leather chair, motioning for Holly to sit opposite him. She did.

"As I mentioned, I'm busy, and I'm not sure how I can help you." He kicked his feet up on the desk, crossing them.

"Let's start with the last time you saw Marvin Tieg." If he wanted the no-nonsense approach, she would give it to him.

"Last year when he fired me."

"Okay. I'd like to address that. I know there was some controversy around the colt you were training for him. Cayman's Cult?"

He nodded. "Yeah, and it was all bull. I don't give my horses illegal drugs. Ever."

Holly watched him as he rubbed the fingers of his right hand over a gold wedding band. He was clearly not comfortable with this discussion. "Why don't you tell me your side of the story."

He sighed and shook his head. "Fine. Maybe you will connect some of those dots. I've kept my mouth shut for some time because I'm a private man, and I didn't feel I had anything to prove. I don't rock the boat, and I believe karma wins in the end. I frankly don't care that Tieg is dead. What I do care about is that you catch the killer. From the stories running rampant throughout the racing world it would seem you, Detective, have a sadistic serial killer on your hands who is targeting industry people."

She tried to hide her surprise at his candor.

"And I knew both Tommy and Katarina. Katarina was set to be the first woman jock to ride a Donahue-Fields horse." He shook his head. "She was a good jock. Both kids were talented and good people."

"You believe they were killed by the same person who murdered Tieg?"

He shrugged. "It doesn't take a detective to put two and two together."

She leaned forward. "Do you think that if this is the same killer, it's someone who is involved with the industry?"

"I think you're the cop. I think that could be one theory."

"Any others? Theories, I mean?"

"Not really."

"Any ideas who could be capable of such crimes?"

"Lots of people work in racing. I don't know them all. I studied some psychology in my day and know enough that heinous acts like these are generally the work of sociopaths. And sociopaths are very good at fooling people."

"What are you saying, Mr. Torres?"

"Your killer could be anyone."

She already knew this, but hearing what this guy knew, or thought he knew, was a good way to gain new perspective. "Do you know a guy named Scott Christiansen? He owns a company out in Southern California? Equine Heath Systems?"

He shook his head. "I don't know him. Heard of the company, though. Seen the ads in some of the magazines. That's about it."

She observed his movements closely and from what she could tell, Torres was telling her the truth. "Why don't you expand a bit on the Cayman's Cult scandal?"

"Dermorphin. Racing commission is just getting on top of it, but there will be something else that comes along to take its place. Frog juice. Yeah. Know about it, did not use it, refused to use it."

"Were you asked to inject the colt with it?"

He took some time before he answered. "Yes."

"By whom?"

"Tieg."

"Tieg?"

He nodded.

"And you were investigated. Did you tell them—the racing commissioners—what you've just told me?"

"No."

"Why?"

"Because I knew at the time that it was unlikely the drug would be detected in the horse. There were suspicions but no hard evidence. I knew that if I started pointing fingers, Tieg was an ass who would do all he could to be sure I lost my career."

"But didn't your reputation take a hit?"

He laughed. "No. I've been in this business for thirty years. The people who know me know my ethics and practices. When it was all said and done, I just wanted to walk away."

Holly narrowed her eyes, deciding if he was being truthful. "If Tieg asked you to inject the horse with this frog juice, and you didn't, who do you think did?"

He uncrossed his feet and sat up. "I'm going to tell you some things that I don't want to get out there. I mean, I don't want others to know what I'm saying, you know?"

He certainly had no love for his former boss. "Okay. Discretion is something that comes with my job title."

"Good. As I said, I believe in karma, and Tieg got his. Jim Gershon, who now trains for Tieg, gave the horse the drug. He was my assistant trainer at the time."

Holly worked to process this information without signaling her surprise. "Jim Gershon. Okay."

"Gershon wanted my job. He's one who will do things that aren't always on the up and up. I refused. He complied."

"Where did they get the drug?"

"Perez is a punk. He always has been. He comes from some village in Guatemala. He's got some shady connections. He'd been riding some of Tieg's horses, including the colt. He told Tieg about a friend of his here in the States who was an out-of-work chemist and said that his friend could manufacture something that would go undetected and make the horses run faster. And be harmless. That stuff is not harmless."

"Were you privy to this conversation?"

"No. My brother was. My brother Frederico—he was my business partner, and he also worked with the horses, but he could sometimes be not as ethical as I am. He knew that if I caught wind of Perez's plan that heads would roll. He was right."

"Can I speak with your brother?"

"He's dead."

Holly sat speechless for a moment. "Dead?"

"Yes. Only two days after he told me about what Perez, Gershon, and Tieg were involved in, he died from a heart attack."

"You don't believe it could have been foul play, do you?"

"I don't know. My brother did have a heart condition, and that is what the autopsy report read. If those guys had a hand in it, I have to believe they'll get what is coming to them by something bigger than me. I went to Tieg and told him I knew about his deal. I knew that he set up shop someplace in Guatemala for this *chemist* to manufacture frog juice. He assured me that he'd had a change of heart, that what I'd heard was untrue. I was reeling from my brother's death. Cayman's big race was that weekend. I loved the colt. I wanted to see him win. Then the shit hit the fan the day before the race when blood draws came back inconclusive. There was skepticism all around and a lot of pressure on me. I advised withdrawing the colt because of the rumors. Tieg made sure he exposed that tidbit to my colleagues. But they knew the truth. The commission came back and said they were going to investigate. I was questioned up and down, but nothing came of it, except I was fired before I could quit working for Tieg."

Holly was rapidly running his story through her brain, attempting to make any connections that she could. "Did you not say anything to the commissioner because you worried about your brother's reputation? Did you wonder whether your brother was involved, and you feared tainting his name?"

He waited a few seconds. "You're good. My brother had two daughters, a son, and wife. They'd been through enough. That was part of the reason I stayed silent, and the other…maybe some fear. If these guys will go to extreme lengths to see horses in the winner's circle, what lengths will they go to in order to cover their asses? Do I think there may have been foul play in my brother Frederico's death? Yes. But, how do you prove it? You know my beliefs."

"Karma," she said.

He smiled. "I have to be going, Detective. Anything else?"

"Yeah. The colt? What happened to him?"

"The colt wound up suffering a career-ending injury a few months after Gershon took my place. A friend of mine has him.

She and her sister fronted the majority of the money to purchase him and then put a syndicate together for the rest of the shares."

"They needed a syndicate to purchase an injured horse?"

"The horse is still a stallion, and the hope is that he'll produce some real quick offspring. This is horse racing, Detective. Big business, lots of cash changing hands. Living, four-legged commodities. Many of these horses come with hefty price tags and require a handful or more of owners to make the initial purchase and support the upkeep. Injured or not, if they can breed, and they won on the track, they're still a commodity."

"If they can't breed, and they get hurt, or didn't win on the track, what happens then?"

"Each horse has an individual story. Some wind up living nice lives as a backyard horse for a kid. Some wind up healing and going on to work as jumpers, sport horses, other ventures. Some wind up in slaughterhouses."

Holly shook her head, remembering her discussion with Brendan about the cruelties of men. "And your friend who owns him, she lives here?"

"California. Her name is Elena. Elena Purdue. The horse is here, though. At her sister Leann's place. She has a few horses there for Elena for breeding, and she also runs a rescue facility. I volunteer there sometimes. You like horses?"

"I do," Holly said. "I'm an animal lover. My fiancé is a small-animal vet." Holly thought back to interviewing Elena Purdue after the jockeys' murders. Maybe this world wasn't as vast as it had seemed the other day back at the station going over everything with Chad and Amar.

"Oh. Great. You like fried chicken?"

"Yes." That was odd, but she was going with it.

"Then if you have some time before heading home, go see Leann. The rescue is open to the public, and she serves amazing fried chicken. Plus she knows Perez. He's actually riding the horse that Tommy Lyons won on the day he was killed."

"You know a lot about this case."

"I told you that I liked Katarina and Tommy. I don't like Perez. I warned Elena not to let him ride for her, told her that he's a bad egg, but sometimes people gotta find this stuff out on their own. Everyone in our world knows about these murders, and some folks are watching their backs."

Holly raised her eyebrows. "Know any details?"

"Nothing concrete. Rumors. That's it. Like I said, this is scary, creepy stuff. If I get something more certain, I will let you know."

"Thank you." She took one of her cards from her wallet and jotted down her cell number at the top, then handed it to him. "One more thing? Your friend's sister, the fried chicken connoisseur and horse rescuer." She smiled. "Leann. Right?" Torres nodded. "What does she think of Perez?"

"I think she feels the way I do, but she doesn't own the horse he's riding. Funny. The filly's name is Karma's Revenge. I find it ironic, anyway. Horse is one to keep an eye on. Perez doesn't deserve to be riding her, but he wins the races. And Elena is one of those people who believes in the good in all. She doesn't always see the truth in front of her. She's stubborn and one to try and prove people wrong."

"Anything else you want to add? Anyone else I should maybe speak with?"

"I think I gave all I know. I think you have some more dots to connect." He stood. "Have a safe trip home."

"Have a safe trip to Las Vegas."

Holly left the farm not knowing what to think of the man at all. He was sort of a mystery himself. One thing she did know, though. He was right when he'd said she had some more dots to connect.

CHAPTER

31

Holly had a lot to ponder as she sat down at the hotel bar. It was almost seven by the time she'd checked in and gotten settled. She'd called home, and Brendan and the girls had been warm toward her, missing her—and reminding her to bring gifts.

Brendan had brought up wedding plans. "I think I found us the perfect caterer. We could start with a sushi bar. We can go Mexican style and do a variety of ceviches, or we can go Japanese traditional with sashimi and some specialty rolls. I know you love sushi."

"Honey, that sounds terrific but expensive."

"Holly, I love you, and I am going to marry you. I want to have a celebration to remember when we are old and gray."

"You're an amazing man."

"That's why you love me."

"There are a few other reasons."

"I like that," he replied. "I can't wait for you to get home. I don't know much about flowers, so you have to help me on that, and music…we need to talk about a live band or a DJ. A lot to do."

"There is. I know, but remember we agreed to keep it small. No more than fifty people and between your family and mine we're already nearly there."

"I know. Small is good. It is good. Like you."

The way he said *like you* made her toes curl. His voice was always soothing—sexy. What was she thinking, traveling halfway across the country when she could be home by his side? Oh yeah... she was thinking that she was doing her job in hopes of catching a killer.

She'd said goodbye to Brendan and the girls, deciding dinner was in order. Processing the information she'd already gathered over a drink sounded good, too. She'd tried Chad again and still got the voice mail. She wondered if Brooke had gone into labor early. Dialed Amar to see if he and his team had any new information, but the call went straight to voice mail.

Halfway into her glass of red wine, she reviewed what she knew. She had a notepad and was waiting for a plate of spicy shrimp and cheesy grits that had come highly recommended. She began making connections as she had on the whiteboard back at the precinct.

She wrote down the name Rafael Torres. He knew both of the dead jockeys and was also connected to Tieg. She drew a line from Tieg to Torres to the jockeys. Then there was the frog juice scandal. He denied involvement but pointed fingers at Jim Gershon, the current trainer for Tieg, and Juan Perez, a jockey who had once ridden for Tieg and now rode for Elena Purdue. She drew lines from Elena's name to Tommy Lyons, who according to Torres rode her horse to the winner's circle the day he was murdered, then to Tieg, who had sold her Cayman's Cult. It would be interesting to see what Elena's sister had to say about all of this when she visited her farm tomorrow. She'd already looked the place up. It was called Golden Hearts.

Then there was Torres's brother Frederico and his death only two days after he'd told Rafael about the horse being drugged with the frog juice. Was that simply coincidence?

She rubbed her temples. She had to get this case under control, down to a manageable size. As the waiter approached with her dinner, Holly took a swig of wine. Something caught her eye as she set the glass back down, stopping her short. She heard herself suck in a deep breath. Felt her body heave and sink back into her chair as if she'd been sucker punched by some invisible force. She stared at the glass of wine, trying to focus. No. She hadn't had the entire glass, and God knew it took two full glasses for her to catch a buzz.

The waiter set down the plate. "Shrimp and grits. Enjoy."

She thought she muttered the words, "Thank you." Holly tried to move. Tried to stand. But her body betrayed her. The dark room spun a bit. Her mind reeled in an attempt to process what she was seeing.

Her husband.

Jack.

Dead.

Killed over ten years ago in an explosion.

Walking out of the restaurant with a dark-haired woman.

His arm wrapped around her waist.

CHAPTER

32

Quentin took in the myriad of orange hues as the sunset descended over the Pacific Ocean. A crescent moon already hung in the twilight sky. Something about that sky reminded him of Afghanistan.

What hell.

Funny how things change. One minute you're working for the country you love. You're doing covert shit and finding the deceivers and murderers hiding in their burrows.

Cowards.

Then, the next minute those same asses that you were fighting for, the country you strove to do everything in your power to keep safe, turn their backs.

There had been intel that Quentin felt should not have been overlooked. And to this day, Quentin was sure that the family he had gone to see with two other soldiers knew exactly the information he wanted. They knew the name of the connection who was taking the tax from their poppy seed field, helping them to manufacture heroin that in turn supported the Taliban and other terrorist organizations, and surely there was a money trail.

Quentin had been determined to locate that trail.

Sorry, but the wife deserved to be raped in front of her piece-of-shit terrorist husband and sons. And those sons deserved to be tortured and killed in front of their parents.

Didn't anyone understand anymore what was at stake? No one cared. After the shell shock of 9/11 had worn off, Americans had gone back to their mundane lives enjoying the independence and freedom that their military provided. They had no idea that the evil was already so deeply embedded, so steeped into society that the country—the *world*—at any moment could be taken down.

Quentin understood. And if the world was going to be taken down, he was going to be the one in charge. Not the bastards from the Middle East.

He was going to do it in a way that made sure the righteous survived and a new world would begin. A new world order would come to fruition.

Yes, Quentin was going to reign supreme.

He was going to control and rule the world.

He stepped off his balcony and headed into his office where he sat down in front of the graphic plans he had drawn up. It was all coming together.

He checked his watch. Yes. It was all coming together.

The countdown had begun.

And there was now an additional element. It was all so perfectly ironic. To think that the investigator—the CSI, of all people—trying to solve the murders he'd ordered...was none other than Holly Jennings. How insanely and beautifully ironic. Good stuff. Real good.

And he was going to string Detective Jennings along like the little mouse she was.

CHAPTER

33

Once Holly had gotten her bearings, she stood to follow the man and woman out of the restaurant. She had to see for herself. It couldn't be Jack. It just couldn't. Jack was dead. No one could have survived that explosion. Holly had been there. They had been on the case together. It couldn't be him.

But in the back of her mind a fact remained. No remains had been found. Three officers perished in the fire. Her husband had been one of them.

Her eyes were playing tricks on her. That's all. But she needed to be certain.

As she stood, a waitress rounded the corner, accidentally bumping her elbow. Holly spilled her red wine everywhere. By the time she recovered the couple was gone, and Holly had missed her chance.

She sat back down and rationalized. Everyone had a twin in the world. There was simply no way that man could have been Jack. If he had survived that explosion, he would have been found. He would have come home to her. He would have.

She ordered a second glass of wine and took it to her room. She drank about half of it down before trying to reach Chad again. Still shaken, but now convinced she had not seen her husband's ghost. Just someone who looked a lot like him.

Chad answered on the first ring.

"Everything okay?" Holly asked.

"Yeah. Why?"

"I couldn't reach you earlier and I was wondering if maybe Brooke had gone into labor."

"No. It's all good. She and the baby are doing fine. It could be any day though. I spent most of the day interviewing employees at Equine Health Systems. They give tours there," Chad said.

"What? I don't understand," Holly said.

"They give tours to groups, like different horse-riding groups. Vets, any professionals that want to come in here. They tour the plant, see how things are done, that kind of thing."

"I don't know what you're getting at, Chad. What do tours have to do with the murders?"

"I don't know exactly, but Christiansen needs neoprene to make his product. What if he was using the dive shop to purchase neoprene when it was in operation? Could he have mentioned that to one of these groups, or talked about it at all? Talked about the place being shut down and abandoned, about how he had to find a new source for his materials? He's the one who conducts each tour."

"Did you ask him?"

"I did, and he says that he didn't recall anything specific," Chad said. "I'm now asking everyone there if they recall mentioning the dive shop at any time to customers who walked in, or people who went on the tours. Also, Christiansen was mentioned in an article in the *Tribune* this morning. It's about the upcoming race, and he is quoted saying that he is against horse racing and that if trainers would use his products, horses could be saved."

"That doesn't mean a whole lot, though. He told us that himself. I know everyone looks guilty at the moment. Keep asking questions. Keep looking for answers. That's all we can do. What about Amar? Any word?"

"Spoke with him briefly and he's checking into this group called PAAC, which is People Against Animal Cruelty. I guess their big beef is with horse racing. There is word that they plan to stage some protest the morning of the Infinity."

Holly closed her eyes and leaned against the headboard of the bed. "Okay. Keep me posted on that. I'll probably give Amar a call, too."

"How about you? Get anything out there?"

She told him everything she had learned during her evening in Lexington.

"Quite a day, huh?"

"You could say that." She took the last swallow of wine. "I need you to go back and track down Gershon. Find out what you can about him possibly drugging that horse. Also, find out why he didn't tell us that Tommy Lyons had ridden a horse Tieg owned that had been put down. Run this stuff by him but keep Rafael Torres's name out of it. This could become a case of *he said/he said,* and I don't want that. What I want is the truth, and I want to know if Torres was telling me the truth. I think he was, and when we questioned Gershon, I thought there was something he wasn't being forthright about. Find him and dig. Dig deep."

"I will. Hey, you okay?" he asked.

"Um, yeah. Why?"

"I don't know. You sound a little off."

"Tired is all. Long day."

"You sure?" he asked.

"Yes. Stop worrying about me. I'm a big girl. I'm away from home and my people. It can make me edgy."

"I worry because you are the best damn partner anyone can have, and you're my friend."

"I know, Chad. The feeling is mutual. I'm fine. I swear."

"Okay. I'll take your word for it."

She hung up the phone. Chad knew her too well, but she could hardly tell him that she had seen Jack's ghost. He would have thought she was losing it.

For a while there, she thought that maybe she was.

CHAPTER

34

Joque had his eye on his victim. This was the hard part—learning patterns, especially when the victim was in a new locale. Fortunately, Joque had a head start.

He had been an insider in the industry, and he had known the victim he planned to take out very soon.

He sat up in the grandstand during the morning exercise—in the middle, out of sight. Baseball cap drawn low over his eyes. He knew how to blend right in.

His heart ached as he watched the young horses galloping down the track, pounding their large but delicate frames down onto tender tendons, immature bones, and suspensory branches that could tear easily. He shook his head and felt tears spring to his eyes. How had he not known this before? Or had he? Of course he had. He'd turned a blind eye because that is what his father had taught him to do.

And he'd needed the money. But money wasn't everything. He and Quentin agreed on that. Doing the right thing was everything. Seeking vengeance was everything.

Nothing like getting even.

Nothing like it at all. He wiped the tears away.

He was not his father. He'd let that go a long time ago. Joque was a man of ethics. A man of value, but he'd had everything he'd ever valued ripped from him.

He'd let that go, though, when the time was right. He was working on replacing the things that mattered.

He'd let his father's thoughts, affects, and beliefs go.

The day he'd killed him.

The son of a bitch should have never done what he'd done. He was not a good man. Not a good father. He was an equine vet who wasn't in it for the animals, but the money and the prestige of hanging around wealthy owners. His father would do anything owners asked him to. No ethics whatsoever.

His father's favorite pastime, other than big-wigging it with rich owners, was beating the crap out of him. His dad blamed him for his mother leaving them, but Joque knew his mom left because she had been his dad's punching bag first. They were both rotten—mother and father. Rotten.

The one decent thing that Dr. Ivy had done for Ted when he was about twelve was bring home a horse one of the wealthy owners' wives had given him.

"For you," Dr. Ivy said. "Nag can't be on the track any longer. Was going to put her down, but thought maybe you should have her."

Ted had been stupefied and thrilled. He'd named the horse Penny, because she was shiny red like a penny. She quickly became his life. Not one to have many friends in school, not one to succeed at school, not one to be paid much attention to, Ted found love and a friend in Penny. He'd race home every day to see her.

He had her for three years.

One day right after his fifteenth birthday, he'd come home and she was gone. "Where's my horse?" he'd asked his dad.

"Your horse? That was my horse." Dr. Ivy was drunk, which he'd been doing more and more often. He'd gotten into some trouble and his veterinary license had been suspended. The wealthy owners had faded into the background.

"I don't understand."

"Economics, son. That's all. Horses cost money and we don't have none. I made some money off of her."

"You sold my horse? *You sold Penny?!*" he screamed. "Where is she?"

"I suggest you stop screaming at me, son."

"Where's Penny?"

"Dead."

"What? No! What are you talking about?"

"Slaughterhouse. That was the only way I was going to get anything for her. She's meat headed to Europe by now, or into a can of dog food."

Ted had felt the rage, shock, and despair take over, but he knew attacking his father would have been no use. Dr. Ivy was a large man with a mean spirit and a hard punch. Instead, he planned. Like he was doing now. He waited. Like now.

Then, he killed.

His father was allergic to shellfish. One evening, a year after Penny had been taken from him, the time was right. Ted suggested he go and get some fish and chips for take-out. His dad thought that was a good idea. "Make sure it's just fish and chips, son."

"Of course." Ted had planned it all out. He'd skipped school that day and made the trek down south about three hours. He bought some crab in the shell. He drove back to Lexington. He ground up the shell nice and fine, and then he made his own tartar sauce in preparation for that night. He got the take-out. Brought it home and gave his father the doctored sauce. Dr. Ivy went into anaphylactic shock not long after he complained that the tartar sauce seemed to have sand in it. He died. The fish-and-chips place was at fault, they concluded, but not much was done.

Ted, being sixteen, began working from barn to barn as a hand. Finally happy to be rid of his father and around the horses.

He learned quickly, though, that horses were sometimes beaten by their owners or trainers just as he had been beaten by his father. Ted could empathize and knew he was among spirits like his own.

He was powerless to stop much of the abuse. At that time, he didn't have the money or the resources to rescue the horses. But a part of him that wondered...if he planned as methodically as he had his father's death, then could he, someday, bring restitution to the lives of some of the horses he felt so close to?

Years later, while spending time in prison for a crime he would have never committed, he prayed for a chance to get even.

Quentin was giving him that chance.

CHAPTER
35

Sheikh Farooq needed to see his trainer, Geremiah Laugherty. Whiskey was set to be flown to Las Vegas the day after tomorrow, the same day that the sheikh and Ayda would travel. However, he had gotten word that Mr. Laugherty would not be joining them until the following day, and he did not like that. They were already taking a risk flying the horse out so close to race day, but they had agreed that the colt was much happier at home. They'd learned that the more time at home, the better he seemed to perform on the track. And, the sheikh did not like to take chances with his horses. He had security beyond measure, and he had concerns about other places, although he had been told that the security at the Infinity was impenetrable.

Farooq found Laugherty in his office outside the main barn. He looked to be going over paperwork. As soon as the sheikh came through the door Laugherty glanced up and shuffled the papers, placing them back into a folder. He took his glasses off, stood, and shook Farooq's hand. "Your Highness."

"Mr. Laugherty." He nodded a curt greeting.

"Are you ready for the race?" Laugherty asked. As with the barn and all of the buildings on the estate, Laugherty's office was pristine, well lit and impeccably decorated in hues of gold and purple—the colors of Farooq Stables.

The sheikh sat down. "Of course I am ready. My question for you is, are *you* ready for the race?"

"Yes sir, I am."

Farooq leaned back in the chair. "There are whispers, my friend, that you have money problems."

"That's ridiculous," Laugherty replied.

Farooq folded his hands. He didn't speak for several seconds. "I trust you, Geremiah. You're a good trainer. My horses win under your hand. But this rumor of money issues…it is not the first time a rumor like this has swirled around you."

"I'm not sure what you're getting at." Laugherty shifted uncomfortably in his chair.

"Men with much on their minds make stupid decisions. They take shortcuts. They don't always pay attention. I want to be sure that you are paying attention to my horse. I want to be sure all precautions have been taken."

"Whiskey is the most important horse I have ever trained in my life. I am very careful with him."

"Good. I wanted to be reassured."

"In that case, I'm happy to be able to reassure you."

Farooq rose and started out of the office. "We will be leaving day after tomorrow at ten o'clock."

"Yes."

"And you will be traveling with us." It was a statement more than a request.

"I will."

"Good. I am going to see my horse. Keep your mind straight, Mr. Laugherty. There is no room for error."

CHAPTER

36

The rescue facility that Elena Purdue's sister Leann owned didn't open to the public until ten o'clock. Holly got up, took a long, hot shower and drank a lot of coffee. She had tossed and turned all night as strange dreams of Jack invaded her mind. One minute it was Jack in the dream...the next it was Brendan...and then images of dead bodies...and then of horses thundering down a track. Strange.

She went back over her notes, trying to connect more dots. She had a few more players to work with and decided it best to mull things over, let them lie for a while and then check in with Chad and Amar once back in California. Chad would likely get a hold of Jim Gershon before she returned home and put him through the ringer.

Her flight back to San Diego was scheduled for late that afternoon, so she had plenty of time to speak with Leann Purdue. After checking out, she put the carry-on in the trunk of the rental and merged onto the highway, passing more greenery, fat and happy brood mares, and large estates. About fifteen minutes along she spotted the sign to Golden Hearts.

She pulled in through the large wooden gates, which were flanked by vibrant pastures fenced in by the standard white-painted posts, just after nine o'clock in the morning. There were two horses in each paddock. A sizable wooden barn stood in the background, and on past that was a house. Signs along the way directed visitors to first stop in at the office, which was connected to the house. The place wasn't as impressive as Rafael Torres's farm—it offered less glitz and glamour and appeared to be more functional and down-to-earth—but it was nice.

Holly parked the car and took a pathway bordered by periwinkles and daisies. The home itself was painted butter yellow and had a stone roof. It looked as if it could have been transplanted straight out of Old England. The barn out front had a similar look, except it had been painted white.

A sign depicting a grazing horse with a rooster on his back read, *Welcome to Golden Hearts. Come on in for carrots,* and was hooked to the handle of the door.

Holly entered and was engulfed by the smell of good comfort food in a fryer. Her stomach rumbled, reminding her that she'd only had coffee for breakfast. "Hello?" she called out.

A minute later a petite, blonde woman came around the corner, wiping her hands on an apron. "Oh, hi. I'm sorry. I'm trying to do too many things at once. My fiancé usually mans the desk, but he's on a haul to Colorado picking up a couple of rescues. I'm Leann Purdue."

A German shepherd came charging around the corner, barking at her. "Rascal, stop it! Sit!" Rascal listened. Holly reached out and let the dog sniff her hand, which he did, and he followed that with a vigorous licking. "He likes you," Leann said. "Sorry. He looks ferocious, but he's a good boy. We got him about four months ago from a rescue place."

"I love dogs. No problem. He's a sweetheart." Rascal lay down at her feet.

"He is."

"Sorry. I'm Holly Jennings." Holly stretched out her arm and shook Leann's hand. She held off announcing her detective status. That could wait.

"Good morning. Officially." Leann smiled brightly. "Our first tour doesn't begin until eleven fifteen, and then I serve up some lunch."

"I know. I have a flight back home today, so I wanted to stop by as soon as I could. Rafael Torres suggested I come here for a visit."

"Great. Rafael is a good guy. Friend of my sister's and mine. Trained one of the stallions we have here. Cayman's Cult. A big deal on the track." She smiled. "Here, give me a sec and I can show you around and maybe send you on your way with some lunch. Where's home?"

"San Diego," Holly replied.

"Lovely place. Hang on."

Leann came back a moment later, apron off, and a pair of paddock boots on her feet, carrying a bucket of sliced carrots and apples. "Shall we?"

"Certainly." Holly followed her out the door.

Rascal followed along as well.

"I'll take you over to the main barn first." They walked through the aisle opening. There were six stalls on either side. "This is where we keep Cay. That's what we call Cayman's Cult. And there are a few older stallions housed here, too. I have to juggle horses in and out, since we're in the process of building a new barn. We keep taking in more strays. Takes a lot to fund this place."

They stopped in front of one of the stalls. A large, reddish horse with a star marking on his face peered out at them between the bars of the stall. "How much do you know about horses, Holly?"

"Not much, I have to admit."

"This pretty chestnut here…that's his coloring…is Cay. You may have heard of him. There was a bit of a scandal surrounding him last year, and then he had an injury that kept him from going back to racing, so my sister and I, along with a handful of others, put together the funds to purchase him, and now he's ours." She smiled.

"He's gorgeous."

"Yes he is."

Leann opened the stall and slid through, handing the horse a carrot. "I'll let you give some of our older guys some treats." She slid past the stall doors. "Shall we see a few more?"

"I'd love to," Holly replied.

They walked on through the barn with four-legged onlookers nickering at them. The barn opened out into the paddock area. Upon spotting Leann, horses trotted over and stopped at the fence. Leann handed Holly a carrot. "Hold it in the palm of your hand. This is Sprite. We pulled him off the back of a slaughter truck headed to Kansas. This horse gave all that he could on the track, won over a half a million dollars. Then, when he couldn't run any more, he was sold off from owner to owner, lost an eye, and given up on. When we got him here, he needed to gain three hundred pounds. He's been here now for ten years and just had his twenty-fifth birthday."

Holly held the carrot out to the old guy, who greedily sucked it down, his whiskers and soft lips grazing the palm of her hand. She then rubbed a hand down his face. He was almost black except for the graying whiskers and a strip down his nose. "Hey old guy, had a tough time of it?"

Leann nodded. "He did. I have story after story like that. This place runs on volunteers and donations. My fiancé, sister, and I put in our own funds to keep things moving, but it's not easy when you're looking at a hundred head. And we get calls every day about more of these guys needing homes. I've got two semis constantly on the road. They're both out now bringing back six horses from different places. We're hoping to expand and open a facility up in Arlington as well. We'll see."

"It's amazing that you do what you do," Holly said.

"Wish we could do more, though. It's just not enough." She frowned and handed the horse next to Sprite a carrot. "This is Ridge. He had a tendon injury and was sold off to a family who then wound up not being able to afford him. The kids wanted to keep him, but in their efforts to give him some shelter they nearly starved the poor guy to death. There are a lot of people, Holly, that just are not meant to have these animals. And there are not enough facilities like ours to take them in. It's a sad state we're in. And, now all of the tracks have been closed down in Canada. That's going to pose a huge problem. Lots of people are out of work, and they're euthanizing the foals. It's not good."

"What? Why?"

"Because racing has been getting a bad rap for some time. Eight Belles, Barbaro—horses the people were rooting for—had catastrophic, fatal injuries out there. You couple that with the scandals that crop up and the seedy side of gambling, and people begin to pay attention. Throw in animal activists and things are bound to get heated. Change becomes a requirement, or at least a demand. Right now, there is a bill in Congress to federally regulate the sport here in the States. There are some tracks where certain drugs are legal, some where they aren't. It's a state-by-state thing."

"What's your position?" Holly asked.

Leann sighed. "It's tough. I agree that changes need to be made. I think since we haven't seen a Triple Crown winner since Affirmed in 1978 that we as breeders need to look at the problem from that standpoint. Have we bred them too lean? They break down faster these days. They aren't the sturdy animals we once had out there on the tracks. These guys are far more fragile, and when fragility is on the track at three years old, you get one problem compounded with another. The real issue, though, isn't with your high-stakes races and higher-profile tracks. It's the racinos—racing casinos—cropping up all over the country. Purses are worth more money than the horses. They are racing casinos. Young, poorly bred, not-well-trained horses with inexperienced jockeys and greedy owners and trainers give the sport a bad name."

"Sounds awful," Holly said.

"It is. We can't turn a blind eye to that kind of damage out there. We need to raise awareness, and if the federal government getting involved does that, then so be it. I am creating a breeding program here that I hope will help build a stronger Thoroughbred again."

"You think these horses should be raced when they're older?"

"I think that's a start. What I don't think is that racing needs to be shut down. Yes, there are some real jerks in this world. There are people in this game who are in it only for the money, the greed. But there is a flip side. There are a lot of us who love these animals. We love the tradition and the sport. We are devastated when we lose a horse. Every single one of these animals, whether they are rescues or our breeding stock, is loved. I have a relationship with each one. When I hear it said that all people in racing are shady, I shake my head, because the fact of the matter is that these animals are bred to do exactly what they do—run. And giving their all for the jockey on their back is what they do best. They love it. They really do."

Holly could appreciate the woman's passion, and it was nice to see someone who felt so much for these animals.

"I'm sorry. I don't mean to ramble, I just have some opinions."

"Opinions are good," Holly replied.

Leann smiled. "How do you know Rafael?"

It was time to be truthful. "Actually I'm a detective, Ms. Purdue. I'm investigating the murders of Tommy Lyons, Katarina Erickson, and Marvin Tieg."

"Oh." She looked stunned. "Horrible situation, and it has a lot of people talking."

"I'm sure it does."

"I suppose you came here to ask me some questions then, rather than visit the horses."

"Both, actually. Getting your take on the industry is good, and the horses are beautiful, but yes, I do have some questions. Can you tell me about the victims? Anything at all? Mr. Torres believed that you could help me out."

"Why don't we go back to the house? Maybe I can help."

CHAPTER

37

Holly followed Leann to the house, where they walked into a quaint family room painted in a light beige. White wicker furniture with a floral print on the cushions sat atop an oak hardwood floor, and artwork featuring famous racehorses adorned the walls. Leann sat down in an oversized chair and motioned for Holly to take a seat on the sofa.

Leann reached over to a small jeweled bowl, removed a large diamond ring, and placed it on her finger. She smiled. "Just got engaged recently. I take the ring off when I'm out with the horses." She flashed the marquise-cut diamond at her.

"That's beautiful," Holly said. A twinge of guilt wove through her, bringing to mind the wedding plans Brendan was so excited to make. Leann glowed when simply sliding the ring onto her finger. It wasn't that Holly didn't feel excited about her upcoming nuptials, but as with everything in her life, she had compartmentalized her emotions. A little stick in her heart made her wonder if she was so different from other women. "When are you getting married?"

"In about six months. Danny, my fiancé, is a great guy. Wish you could meet him. He should be in sometime tomorrow with the load from Colorado. We have the same love and respect for the animals, and it's just worked out for us."

"That's great. I'm engaged, too."

"Wonderful."

Holly smiled. "Thank you. I don't want to take up too much of your time, Leann. I know you have a business to run, but Rafael Torres suggested you might be able to help me. Very interesting guy."

Leann laughed. "You can say that again."

Holly grew serious. "Can you give me any insight into these cases? Do you know anything? Why did Rafael send me to see you?"

Leann leaned back. "As you said, Rafael is interesting, and he's also discreet. He's a big deal in our world. He may have sent you to see me because he knows I'm not shy with my opinions."

"Okay. I'm all ears."

Rascal came in and lay down at Holly's feet.

"Rafael sometimes helps me with the stallions when Danny is out of town. He was over here two days ago, after Tieg had been killed and the news started spreading. He was working with the older stallions we keep here, and I invited him in for some dinner. It got late, and we had some drinks with our dinner and started talking about Tommy, Katarina, and now Marvin. And I couldn't help thinking of Geremiah Laugherty."

"Geremiah Laugherty?"

She nodded. "Laugherty trains for Sheikh Mahfuz Farooq. The sheikh is a wonderful man. He's given a lot to the sport and, like us, he loves his animals. Laugherty is one of these trainers who, I think, isn't quite the man he pretends to be. I think Rafael agrees with me but won't say anything because that's how he is."

"I met Laugherty in San Diego after the murders of Katarina and Tommy. Katarina was riding one of the horses he trains."

"I know. Good horse, too. Owned by Farooq. I was surprised to see Katarina on one of the sheikh's horses. It was a bold move, considering his culture. I think he did it because of Laugherty."

"Why is that?"

"I don't want to speak ill of anyone, especially the dead, and I didn't know Katarina, but there were rumors that she was sleeping with Laugherty to work her way up the ladder."

"It's our impression that Katarina and Tommy were an item," Holly said.

"I don't know about that." Leann shrugged.

"Why do you think Laugherty might have something to do with the murders?"

"He's a weird man. We dated briefly. I haven't shared it with anyone, not even my fiancé, but Laugherty knocked me around some and was controlling. He also has a thing for gambling, and I think he runs into money trouble here and there. There was something that he said to me one night about how if I didn't mind him, he knew people who would make sure that I did. He'd been drinking. It was after he'd had a horse win a major stakes. He was celebrating. But Geremiah is one of those guys who turns mean after a few drinks. He told me there were things he'd done in the past, things he'd been in charge of, that would make me mind him if I knew."

"I sensed there was something wrong with that guy when I interviewed him. All charming and manipulative."

"That's him. There's a story from ten years ago that Laugherty and Tieg were tied into—it was shut up real quick and people moved on, but some of us home-growns wonder if there was something more to it than what came out."

"What's the story?"

"Tieg owned a farm here before he became famous. Laugherty trained his horses. Tieg had some very nice horses. His place and the horses were insured for a lot of money. One night the barn burned down and killed all nineteen animals. A farmhand who was trying to get the horses out also perished. It was a tragic loss. One horse in particular, named Dirty Games, was a real up-and-comer.

I think he was insured for several million by Lloyd's. Anyway, turned out a groom who had an issue with both men set the barn on fire. The groom was convicted and I think got fifteen to twenty years in the state pen."

"But you think there's a part of the story that never came out?" Holly asked.

"I think Laugherty is a bad man. I know he is. I think maybe the groom agreed to start the fire because they were going to pay him. But that didn't happen. I don't know. I was living in Europe at the time, helping exercise horses in the UK. I moved back about a year after that, but the word was still around that maybe Laugherty and Tieg had been more involved than they let on."

"Why would you even consider dating Laugherty then?"

"Years passed, and I stopped believing the rumors. So did most people. The groom—I think his last name was Ivy—had admitted to the crime. I met Laugherty at a party. He was good looking, charming, polite…at first. Things changed after we started sleeping together, and then after that night, the things he said to me, I had to wonder about what had really happened with that barn fire. Had Tieg and Geremiah been in financial straits and needed the insurance money? It's happened before in the horse world. It will happen again."

Holly nodded. "And this Ivy? The groom, he's in the Kentucky State Penitentiary?"

"As far as I know. It's a few hours from here. Up in Eddyville."

"And Laugherty? He's back in Lexington at the sheikh's farm? Or is he still in California?"

"I assume he's here. I heard that once Whiskey was invited to the Infinity, they brought him home. However, they're probably on their way to Vegas by now. My sister already has her horse there. I can get a hold of her if you'd like and ask."

"That would be great."

"Hang on." Leann took the cell phone off the table next to her. Holly glanced around the room. Warm and cozy. She saw a photo on the stand next to where Leann had been sitting and picked it up. Leann stood next to a nice-looking man, his arm around her, both of them smiling and looking ecstatic. Her stomach sank as that same guilt of not being with Brendan and her family washed over her, because she knew she would not be making the afternoon flight back to San Diego.

Rafael Torres had been right. Leann Purdue was a wealth of information, or at least had some insight that no one else had given her.

"My sister just texted back and said that Farooq and his horse aren't expected until late tomorrow. That means Geremiah is still in town."

Holly nodded. "Know where I might find him?"

"When he's in town, you can pretty much find him having a late breakfast at the track café at Keeneland. But I steer clear of it because of him."

Holly stood. "Thank you for everything." She patted Rascal on his head and left Golden Hearts. She needed to ask Geremiah Laugherty a few questions, as well as drive up to the state pen. If there had been some kind of cover-up and this groom Ivy had been framed or coerced, could he be one in a duo of killers? She was feeling a bit like Clarice Starling in *Silence of the Lambs*, but it was a possibility. Killers got ideas from books, movies. What if this groom was a regular Hannibal Lecter?

Holly needed to find out. And if he was, who was his Buffalo Bill?

CHAPTER

38

The recurring nightmare had awakened Joque again in the wee hours of the morning and he had not been able to go back to sleep. It was now nearly noon. Though tired, he had a job to do.

And the nightmare fueled his desire to seek revenge, to get the job done. His adrenaline surged.

He touched the side of his face. The scars were barely visible, and the lies he had told as to why they were there had been convincing enough. But the truth of it had been nothing short of excruciating. From the moment he had been framed for a crime he could never have committed, to the scars on his heart, body, and face, to the moment he had been attacked behind the prison walls and left for dead. Seven years of hell, and now he was getting even.

With Quentin's help. With Quentin's help, Joque had become unrecognizable in a world that had ostracized him, and with a new identity he had been able to start fresh.

CHAPTER

39

March 3, 2011

"There's no need, man. We're good," Quentin said, his hand on the door of his Porsche. Ivy had followed him out of the bar and to his car. As planned.

"No. No. I'm in. I am. What do I do?"

Quentin smiled. "Get in."

"Okay."

Quentin waited for the guy to question him again. He didn't. He got in the car like a good boy.

They drove a mile or two before Quentin spoke again. "As far as the world is concerned, you, Ted Ivy, are dead. I arranged it so that you got out on good behavior. I also arranged it so that you are a dead guy."

Ivy looked confused, which was exactly what Quentin wanted.

Quentin nodded. "Yeah, you poor son of a bitch, you got some kind of nasty illness in prison and try as they might, you didn't make it very long after your release."

Ivy shook his head. "How?"

"Oh Christ, man! Again, how did you think you got sent up in the first place? Did you do those things they accused you of? Huh?

Did you? Did you start that fire? Kill those horses? Cause the death of the worker? Did you?"

"No! Of course not!" he snapped.

"Right. I know that. I know what slimeballs these pricks are. They killed my family." Quentin pressed down on the accelerator. The Porsche moved at nearly 100 mph. "They killed my family and got away with it!" He slammed his hands on the steering wheel.

Ivy jumped in his seat.

"And I want them dead, Ivy. You should, too, for what they did to you, and I can make that happen. You know, my wife…my sweet wife was like you. She loved horses. She'd grown up with them. Those bastards destroyed nineteen beautiful horses, and you took the fall. Then they destroyed my wife and daughter."

Once again, Quentin had told a partial truth—he had gotten Ivy out early. Money had talked. The part about him being dead on paper was not so true, and Quentin was banking on it that the guy wouldn't go looking for answers, other than the answers that Quentin provided him.

No. Quentin needed Ted Ivy alive.

"I want them dead, too," Ivy said quietly.

"Good."

They pulled into a private landing strip. A chartered jet sat on the tarmac.

"What's this? What are we doing?"

"New life, Ivy. New life. Let's fly. What do you have to lose? You're dead. You don't have a dime to your name. I know. I've been following you since you got out two days ago. The money you spent on the beer is probably the last dollars you had, unless one of the dipshits who picked you up while you were hitchhiking gave you some cash."

"You've been following me?"

Quentin nodded.

"Why didn't you stop and pick me up on the road then?"

"Not how I do things, Ivy. Not even close. Get on the plane. Start your life all over."

Ted Ivy followed Quentin onto the plane.

CHAPTER

40

Holly left Golden Hearts and headed to Keeneland hoping to find Geremiah Laugherty, as Leann suggested she might.

She called Chad on her drive over to see if he could gather any information on Laugherty regarding the fire at Tieg's place ten years before, and also anything on the groom who had gone to jail. The call went straight to voice mail.

She hadn't spoken to Amar since Sunday. Maybe she shouldn't have taken his remarks about turning over every stone so personally. The guy had obviously been through a painful loss. Maybe it had been his way of warning her to be careful rather than trying to tell her how to run the investigation. She gave him a call. No matter what he thought about the case, she needed some help in gathering intel, and she certainly couldn't do it while driving. The trip to the state pen would take almost four hours. She knew that if she found Laugherty and had a discussion with him, she wouldn't get up to Eddyville until it was too late to speak with Ivy. She figured she would make the drive anyway, find a place to stay and visit the jail early the next morning.

Amar answered the call on the first ring. "How are you?" he asked.

"I'm okay. I'm knee-deep in this, and I've gotten a lot of information, but I need your help."

"Of course."

"Can you gather as much information as possible about a fire that happened here ten years ago, and everyone involved?" Holly went on to explain everything Leann had told him.

"I can do that. I'll call you with what I find."

"Thank you. Anything on your end?"

"Chad tell you about the protestors going to the Infinity?"

"Yes."

"I've learned that Scott Christiansen and his wife are involved."

"No kidding?"

"No. In fact, Mrs. Christiansen is very involved in the PAAC group," he replied.

"Have you passed that on to Chad? That is really interesting. How much do we know about Mrs. Christiansen?"

"She works side by side with Scott. She manages the finances at Equine Health Systems and seems pretty solid. She volunteers at a youth center on the weekends, as well as being involved with PAAC. I have to tell you that I would find it difficult believing that either husband or wife might be even remotely sociopathic—much less serial killers. We know their alibis have checked. Chad is still running interviews with the employees at EHS. I did leave him a message. He isn't answering his phone at the moment."

"I know. I hope his wife is okay. If he calls you first, have him give me a ring, please."

"I will. Stay safe, Detective."

She pulled into the famous racetrack shortly after noon. She had not called home yet to let them know that she would not be home again tonight—she dreaded that call. No one was going to be thrilled, but if the rest of her day went well, then she would be heading back tomorrow afternoon.

Keeneland's grounds were pristine. The main colors of the track and outbuildings were green, white, and gold. A large sign in gold stood at the front entrance. She wound around the drive, spotting the building where the yearling sales were held annually. Leann had told her which way to go. She saw a green sign displaying the words *Track Kitchen*. She parked and got out. The barns were close by.

She walked into the kitchen. Numerous racing photos hung on the walls. The place was emptying out. The smells of bacon and other food floated all around. A hostess offered to seat her.

"I'm looking for Geremiah Laugherty."

The young woman smiled. "Mr. Laugherty is at his regular table." She pointed to a corner table, where Holly spotted the man.

She thanked the hostess and headed over to the table. Laugherty looked intent on some papers spread out in front of him and didn't glance up until she sat down. When he did, he seemed quite surprised. "Detective?"

"Hello, Mr. Laugherty. How are you?"

"Pardon me if I don't recall your last name."

"Jennings. Detective Jennings." She did not offer her hand. This guy was slime, and she had pegged him from their initial interview back in San Diego. He had been a tad too charming, too congenial. Now she knew the truth. He had a foul temper. Liked to knock women around and had a lack of self-restraint when it came to money, according to Leann.

"That's right." He smiled his smarmy smile and snapped his fingers. "What brings you all the way out here to bluegrass country?" He took a sip of coffee. "Did you find Tommy and Katarina's killer?"

She shook her head. "Afraid not."

"Oh."

"I'm sure that you're also aware of Marvin Tieg's murder."

"I am. It's awful. I don't know what's going on." He shook his head. "Just horrendous. Do you have any leads?"

"That's why I'm here, Mr. Laugherty. I've spoken with some folks regarding these cases and your name came up. A couple of times, actually."

A waitress walked over and asked if she wanted any coffee. Although the place smelled great, she decided she ought to focus on why she was here. She turned down the coffee and offer for a menu.

"Oh? My name came up? Why is that?" He shook his head and put his papers in a pile, turning them over.

"It's my understanding that you and Mr. Tieg used to do business together."

"We did. But I haven't had any dealings with Marvin in nearly ten years."

"I see. Is that because you two agreed after the barn fire at his place that it was probably a good idea to part ways?"

Laugherty's face drained of color. "No, Detective. I moved on. I've been working for Sheikh Farooq for some time now. Before going to work for the sheikh I trained horses for various owners."

"So why did you move on from Tieg? Did you get any of the payoff from the insurance company?" She was going in for the kill with this asshole.

His face turned red. "That's ludicrous! Who would say something like that? I don't have time for this nonsense." He stood.

"I think you should sit down. You may very well be in danger," she said calmly. Laugherty stared at her, his eyes wide and somewhat empty. Now Holly could buy that this guy might actually be a killer. She had seen eyes like Laugherty's before, and they were usually on the face of a psychopath. "I'm very serious, Mr. Laugherty. You could be a target for this killer."

He sat back down. "Why do you say that?"

"Tell me about the groom in prison for that fire. Think maybe he could have anything to do with the murders?"

"Ted Ivy? No way. That guy is sitting in a jail cell for the next ten years. He was sentenced to twenty." He shook his head. "And for the record, no one was set up. That idiot even admitted he'd committed the crime. So why you would come in here and say something so ridiculous to me is mind-boggling."

She ignored his comment. "Do you think that maybe this Ted Ivy has a vendetta, even though he *admitted* he was the one who started that fire and caused the deaths of that man and those horses? Think that maybe the guy has some anger toward you, toward Tieg?"

"I don't know. He's a sick bastard, just like the one who killed the jockeys and now Marvin."

"Exactly." Holly smiled. "This killer is a sicko. And sickos create all sorts of scenarios in their heads. They tend to believe their own lies. They manipulate people. They can even *charm* the pants off people." She stared hard at him, even though she doubted he understood her meaning.

"What are you getting at?" he asked.

"Ted Ivy…he have any good friends you know of?"

"How would I know? I barely knew the guy ten years ago. Where are you going with this, Detective, and why would you tell me that I might be in danger?"

"Have you seen the movie *Silence of the Lambs*? Or maybe a better analogy is the book *Red Dragon*, same author. Not quite as popular as *Silence of the Lambs*, but the story is just as creepy. Although *Red Dragon* was a better book. I thought so, anyway. Critics even say so. Not sure about the movie. I do think *Silence of the Lambs* was a better flick than either adaptation of *Red Dragon*—"

"What the fuck are you getting at?" Laugherty yelled.

She smiled and let out a chuckle. The real Laugherty exposing himself. "Basically, I am suggesting that one killer may be leading another. I'm a detective. I see a lot of shit. But I have to say that both of those movies scared the crap out of me. You know, guys in jail meet all sorts of other inmates. They bond. They make agreements. They lie. Imagine that. One might tell another who is getting out before he is that he has a lot of money socked away. Maybe he promises it to him in exchange for a favor."

"Ivy didn't have a pot to piss in, and no, I never saw either movie. And I don't read fiction. If you think Ivy has someone on the outside doing his evil bidding, I think you'd better look at other possibilities. Ivy wasn't that bright." Laugherty gathered up his pile of papers. "I've got to go now. I have a horse to prep for travel."

"I bet you need that horse to win. Big purse like that would help, wouldn't it, Mr. Laugherty?"

He stood up again.

Holly continued to press. "You have a bad habit, I understand, of not managing your finances all that well. Bet you'd do almost anything to stay afloat."

He placed both hands on the table and shot back at her. "I don't know why you came to see me. I don't know what your game is. And I don't like being fucked with, Detective."

"I bet you don't." She lowered her voice to a near whisper. "Especially by a woman."

"I think you should go back to California. You won't find a killer here."

She stood up and eyed him. "And I think you should watch your back. You never know where a killer lurks, really. Now do you?" She turned and walked out ahead of him. Pleased she'd gotten under his skin.

CHAPTER
41

The fabulous Infinity grandstand and grounds blew Elena away. Never before had racehorses been given double stalls where they could move in a twenty-four-foot-square space. There were plush accommodations on the grounds for owners, trainers, and jockeys as well. She couldn't get enough of the place and, surprisingly, she could not get enough of O'Leary. He was all she had been thinking about—besides her horse and the race. Their long drive had been pleasant. They'd flirted and they'd talked seriously, finally falling into the familiar rhythm of comfort that they'd had and then lost so many years before.

But since they'd arrived, she hadn't seen much of O'Leary. She'd been busy with Karma and he'd actually been hired by Rafael Torres to exercise the colt he had running, after his regular exercise rider wound up injuring himself the day they'd arrived. It was a lucky break for O'Leary. What he didn't know was that Elena had been watching him during morning workouts just as much as she'd watched Natalie on Karma. O'Leary looked good on the colt out there. She hoped he would find himself a horse again that would take him to the top. No matter the controversy in his past, Elena knew he was a good man who deserved another break.

And he wanted another chance with her. He hadn't had to spell that one out, but she knew, and she was scared. He had broken her heart. He'd lied. He'd been paid off by her dad and she didn't know if allowing him back into her life was a smart thing to do. She'd known, or should have known, that once she even slightly opened that door, she could easily be sucked in. Dammit.

Karma stood in the cross ties. Elena swiped a brush along her back. She then found the pressure points along the horse's top line. She spent the next thirty minutes applying pressure to various spots. The filly stood quietly in the cross ties, relaxing under Elena's touch. Elena spoke softly to her as she worked. Every once in a while she would slip a baby carrot from her pocket and feed it to the horse. Spoiling her girl was as much fun as it was important in order to keep the horse happy and healthy. Karma had the best of everything—food, health care, exercise, bedding. Whatever this horse (or most any horse racing at her level) needed, she would definitely have the best of.

As she carefully scanned her legs for any cuts, scrapes, bites, or swelling, she heard a voice behind her. "Hey, El."

She stood and turned around. "O'Leary."

He smiled. He held a basket in his hand. "She is looking gorgeous."

"Yes, she is."

O'Leary walked over to Karma and stroked her neck. "Like you."

Elena rolled her eyes. "What's in the basket, Pete?"

"Dinner."

"Oh."

O'Leary set the basket on a bench along the side of the barn. "We all have to eat, and you did say we'd have dinner together. I was hoping that tonight might work. Haven't seen much of you since we got here."

She shook her head. "You always did have that way about you."

"What way is that?"

"Kind of charming."

"Oh, I'm charming, huh? You flirting with me, Purdue?"

She laughed. "Let's have that dinner."

"Got an empty stall on this row?"

"As a matter of fact, there is one." She pointed three stalls down.

"You put your girl away, and I'll set up," he said.

"Okay then."

"Okay then."

She watched as O'Leary walked into the stall, basket in hand. She undid the cross-ties and led the mare back into her stall, where dinner already awaited her. Things were quieting down around the barns for the evening.

She closed the door and headed to the stall where O'Leary had set up dinner. Opening the door, she was taken aback. In a few short minutes O'Leary had turned the empty stall into something magical, and damn if her stupid heart didn't skip a beat. He'd laid out a thick blanket, along with two folding chairs and a pop-up table with a tablecloth. A vase holding two red roses sat atop the table. He had an iPod set up with a small speaker playing Sade. Music from when they had been together.

He motioned for her to sit down. "When did you sneak this past me?" she asked.

"I have my ways. When you were out with Karma on the grass. Lucky for me, you bring her in on the other end and didn't pass by this stall and spoil it."

"I'd say, lucky for me. If I didn't know better, Pete, I'd say you're trying to get into my pants."

Ha laughed and practically choked. "You know me too well. But no. I mean, that would be great. Don't get me wrong. That would be wonderful. I know it would..."

She knew it would, too. "The roses. Nice touch."

"I thought so. One for you. One for the filly. Won't be long before you see that blanket of roses draped across her neck."

"I sure hope so."

"She's got it. That mare has the speed, the determination to do it. I've watched her. I've been out there clocking her."

"She's special."

"Like you," he said. "And as far as us sleeping together tonight: as much as that sounds perfect and I am totally all in, I believe that would make me a bit of a jerk, don't you think?"

Elena caught that sparkle in his eyes. She wasn't so sure that would make him such a jerk. Making love with O'Leary had given her some of the best moments of her life, but for now she decided to agree with him. "I suppose it would."

"Right. Just making sure you agree with me. I think for tonight, we just hang out. Have some dinner and visit."

"You are still a charmer after all these years."

"And you are still the most beautiful woman I have ever known."

She swallowed hard. "Wine?"

"I did bring some, but not for me. Only for you."

"Really?"

"Really. I stopped drinking, El."

"You did? When?"

"The day we had breakfast. So, what, three days ago? Look, El, I've done some stupid shit in my life. Made mistakes I'm not proud of. But the biggest mistake I ever made was trading you in. I should have told your dad to forget it. But I was stupid. I don't want to make that mistake again. Now I have no idea if you are even interested in me at all. I wouldn't blame you if you told me to go screw myself and get out of your life. I wouldn't blame you. I'm hoping…I'm *praying* you won't do that. And if there's the slightest chance with you, I know it's time to get my shit back together. I gotta get straight. I just do. I've been watching you all these years. I know we run in the same crowd, and I've been biting my tongue.

When you were with that jackass Carter, I wanted to tear that guy's head off. Then, when he broke your heart, I could see how bad you were hurting. And I wanted to tear my own head off because if I hadn't hurt you in the first place, you would have never wound up with that guy. So..."

"So what?"

"So, should I go screw myself? Or..."

"Or what?" Yes, she wanted to make him squirm a little bit.

"You interested?"

She reached for his hand across the table. "Yeah, Pete. I'm interested."

CHAPTER

42

What delight
To back the flying steed, that challenges
The wind for speed!—seems native more of air
Than earth!—whose burden only lends him fire!
Whose soul, in his task, turns labor into sport!
Who makes your pastime his! I sit him now!
He takes away my breath! He makes me reel!
I touch not earth—I see not, hear not. All
Is ecstasy of motion!
— James Sheridan Knowles

The starting gate can scare some horses.

It can take days for them to become accustomed to the noise.

They're led to the gate, over and over. They sometimes jig side to side, nervous about the strange, confining space.

Trainers can work for months with a horse, to soothe a filly or colt into the gate, to teach her to not startle at the bell, to urge him to run when the gates open.

CHAPTER

43

Farooq checked on Whiskey. His colt had settled in fine. The flight had gone well and Laugherty had heeded Farooq's subtle warning to get himself together. He had shown up for the flight on time, which took off at 1:30 EST and landed in Las Vegas at 3:30 PST. By the time Whiskey was unloaded from the sheikh's personal 767 cargo compartment—refitted specially for his horses so that they would not have to ever fly public—and transported to the facility, it was dinnertime.

The colt appeared happy and relaxed. The larger stalls helped. Farooq was impressed.

However, his heart was heavy. No matter that the event of his best horse's life was to take place in a few short days.

He performed his regular ritual, rubbing his hands down Whiskey's legs. On the back leg, the one with the white stocking, there was a small wind puff—an inflammation to the fetlock. "What in the world? Geremiah!" he called. The trainer was right outside the stall.

"Yes, sir?"

"What is this?"

Geremiah came into the stall and ran his hand down the leg. "I don't think we need to be concerned, sir. He's had some inflammation on and off, but this is nothing."

"Nothing? Nothing!"

"It's so slight. I think this could even be an insect bite."

The sheikh stood and crossed his arms. "Get him on ice and call the vet."

"Sir, I don't think we want to alarm anyone. There will be a jog out daily here. This horse is sound. I promise you, Your Highness. The colt is completely sound."

The sheikh studied Laugherty for a moment. "I want him iced anyway. You'd better be right."

"You've see him move. You know as well as I do there's no lameness."

The sheikh nodded. His phone rang. He looked at the number and his stomach sank. "Watch him. Report any change to me immediately."

"Of course."

Farooq walked away. "Yes?"

Waqqas said, "We need another transfer of funds."

"No. I am busy."

"Sheikh, I suggest you think again. We need fifteen million dollars."

"That is ludicrous!" he hissed into the phone. "Money like that gets noticed. I can't do it."

"Find a way. We have a cause to move forward." The phone line went dead.

Farooq looked back at Whiskey's stall. He felt tears come to his eyes and quickly blinked them away.

He was stuck. An image of Wallid came to mind. God, how he hated Naqeeb Waqqas!

Farooq sighed and wiped perspiration from his brow. He knew what he had to do.

CHAPTER
44

"This case is a hard one," Holly said into the phone. "I miss you guys."

"We miss you, too," Brendan said. "It's not the same here without you. Our girls run all over me."

"You're the dad. Make them mind."

"I will. I have a surprise."

"Another surprise? Brendan, the koi pond is plenty."

"This is a little different."

"Um…okay."

"Remember the kitten I told you about? The one in the tailpipe?"

"Yes."

"The girls named him Piper."

"Brendan!"

"I know. I couldn't help it. The people who found the poor baby in the pipe didn't want him, and he can't go to the shelter, and the girls will take such good care of him. He's a mess, but he's going to live. I think he'll see out of one eye."

She couldn't help but smile. He knew how to take the edge out of her. "I can't wait to meet him."

"Get home. Love you."

"I love you, too." She hung up the phone.

The motel room in Eddyville was not exactly a five star. She turned on the TV for some noise, thoughts of home and family warming her heart. She hoped the dreams about Jack would stop before she got back. Ever since she'd seen the man who looked so much like him the other night in the hotel, her subconscious mind had been bringing him to her nightly, in her dreams. She still had the plumeria charm with her. She'd moved it from her sweater into a pocket of her purse. Why hadn't she just socked it away? If she was honest, having the charm with her made her feel like Jack was around, made her feel like his spirit was close by guiding her through the case. That was stupid, but that's how she felt. She wished that she'd been able to say goodbye to him—a wish she'd repeated nearly every day for ten years.

She decided to check in with Chad and Amar. She finally reached her partner.

"Any news?" she asked.

"Big news. My baby is on the way!"

"Oh my God. Is that why your phone was off earlier?"

"Yeah. Brooke was having an ultrasound. I meant to call you back, but things moved quickly. I'm sorry. I don't have anything more to add on the interviews at Equine Health Systems. I was already at the hospital by the time I heard Amar's message about the Christiansens being heavily involved in PAAC. Brooke is seven centimeters, so I should be able to get back over there tomorrow at some point and continue questioning people. As far as Gershon goes, I can't locate the guy. He's not answering his phone. I think we should have Amar see if he's still around."

"He might be in Vegas. Seems that's where all of these people are going. Makes me wonder if one of us should be there, too. Our guy could be setting up to strike before the big race."

"He could. I think you'd better see what you can find in Kentucky, and then we can regroup."

"Agreed," she replied. "And don't worry about getting back to Christiansen's company. Stay with your wife and baby. Get someone else over there. If they find anything, let me know."

"Okay. Thanks…Uh-oh. My girl is in pain. Contraction coming on."

"Do whatever she tells you to do!"

"I am."

"Smart man. And, Chad, congrats. You're going to be a great
dad. My love to Brooke."

"Thanks, partner."

Holly hung up the phone not feeling as low. New babies could
do that for people, it seemed. A renewed sense of urgency rose up
in her chest—she really wanted to find the answers to this case, get
home and meet the new addition to Chad's family, and then spend
time with her own.

Amar hadn't called her back. He said that he would. It was
already past six in California. Holly ate the Subway sandwich she'd
picked up on the drive to Eddyville and settled into a comfortable
position on the bed.

In the middle of the turkey and cheddar, her text notification
chimed. Amar had written, *Check your e-mail.*

She turned on her laptop and navigated to the email from
Amar—a forward. He wrote his own message at the top. *I think we
need to look into this. One of my guys found this IM exchange between
Tieg and an unknown contact inside the Kentucky State Penitentiary.
The exchange was from four months ago. The IP address originates
from within the pen, but it will take some time to establish the identity
of the direct contact.*

She read further and was stunned by the e-mail exchange
between Tieg and someone he referred to simply as *Contact.*

It started with Tieg: *How's our boy been?*

Contact: *He's out.*

Tieg: *What? When?*

Contact: *A year ago.*

Tieg: *And you didn't think to fucking let me know?*

Contact: *I am quite busy. I didn't think he was a threat.*
Tieg: *You didn't?*
Contact: *No. The man was completely beaten when he left here. You know how he was burned on his face and hands, and then the number your guys did on him. I arranged that, and I don't feel so good about it. I don't owe you.*
Tieg: *The hell you don't.*
Contact: *Trust me. That guy is not coming back for you. He worked with shrinks. He did his time. He just wanted to start a new life. That's all. Told me he was moving to the Caribbean.*
Tieg: *You believed him?*
Contact: *Yeah. I did, and you need to cut the shit. If the guy wanted your blood, don't you think he would have come after you by now? All he wanted was to get out and start over. I don't think he would risk going back to prison. It was more of a hell for him than most people. Face it. The man was innocent. You know that, and if you want me to continue to keep your dirty secret, I suggest another payday. I guess you shouldn't have contacted me. I was happy until you did.*
Tieg: *Fuck you!*
Contact: *Same to you. You know how to wire funds. You know my expectations. I suggest you get on it.*

That was the end of the correspondence. Holly blew out a deep breath. She picked up the phone and called Amar.

He answered on the first ring. "You read the exchange."

"Yeah. How did your man get this?"

"He's one of the best. It wasn't easy, but cyberspace isn't as protected as most of us like to think."

"There is so much here, Amar. This case keeps revealing more twists and turns. This exchange has to be referring to the groom from the fire. Ted Ivy."

"I think you're right. You were not able to get to the prison in time today?"

"No. But I'm headed there first thing in the morning. If we're right, and if Ivy has been let out, I think he's our guy. He's the one killing these people."

"Why the jockeys? He had a motive to kill Tieg, and he may be going after the other guys involved in the fire frame-up. Do you have background on that?"

"Laugherty would be on that list, and maybe Jim Gershon. I talked with Chad. His wife is in labor, so he's unavailable for us. He wasn't able to locate Gershon. Santa Anita closed yesterday and Gershon mentioned that he didn't have a horse running in the Infinity."

"Maybe he went to Vegas to watch."

"Maybe. Amar, we need to find him. I'll call after I see what I can find out from the prison. Do you have a photo of Ted Ivy?"

"Yeah. There's one from the newspaper stories back then. Kind of grainy. You should be able to google it."

"I will. Let's touch base tomorrow."

"Holly?"

"Yeah?"

"Watch your back. I got a bad feeling."

"Listen to you, Amar. I think we're friends."

He laughed. "I think so, too."

CHAPTER
45

Holly got up early the next morning and went for a quick run around Lake Barkley, near the motel. The prison was also close by and she'd learned at the sandwich shop the night before that locals called it the Castle on the Cumberland. She knew she wouldn't be able to get into the prison gates until ten and her nervous energy fueled the run.

Maybe it was the proximity of the prison. Maybe it was being a lone woman jogging along the lake. Or more than likely she was edgy as all hell and had the feeling of being watched. She didn't like that feeling at all and pushed herself harder and faster.

She got back to the motel and showered, leaving the TV on to keep her company. She opened up the small closet to retrieve her bag and grab the same pair of jeans and blouse she'd worn yesterday. If she was here any longer, she'd need to pick up some clothes. Bra and underwear on, she bent down to get the rest of the clothing when hands grabbed her from behind.

She struggled, squirmed, kicked, and tried every tactic she knew from her cop training. But this guy was strong. How had she not even heard him? She had no time to ponder the question as a handkerchief was placed over her face, and she soon passed out.

CHAPTER

46

Holly struggled to open her eyes. As consciousness slowly crept into her brain, reality did as well. Her hands and feet were bound, and she was gagged.

She was in deep shit.

Her vision began to clear and as it did, she was shocked by her surroundings. *What the hell...* She would have to take in every detail that she possibly could quickly. She had no idea if she would be knocked out cold again, or worse, but if she had any kind of guardian angel watching over her—and she'd always thought that angel was Jack—then maybe she would get out of this alive.

She was locked inside a bedroom, a large one that spoke of a lot of money. The bed she was lying on, a four-poster, was made of some kind of dark wood. The linens were all white; black velvet curtains on the windows were closed and hung down to the floor. She wondered what was on the other side of them.

Red roses filled a vase on one of the nightstands, next to a lamp that was on. A black-and-white sketch of a nude woman hung on one wall, on the other a sketch of—what else? A horse. But this horse wasn't racing and did not look to be a Thoroughbred. She'd learned a few things about horses since she'd been on these cases, and the breed looked to be an Arabian.

Where the hell was she?

She went to logic. What was the last thing she remembered before getting knocked out cold? She went jogging. Planned to go to the prison. She was in that tiny hole-in-the-wall motel room. How had someone gotten in without her hearing? How had they taken her without being noticed? She recalled the strength in the arms that had been wrapped around her.

Where was she? What in hell had happened?

She closed her eyes and heard the lock on the door.

When she heard her name and opened her eyes, everything in the room began to swirl. She grew dizzy; her stomach sank. She blinked several times. She spotted her plumeria charm on the nightstand next to the bed.

Was she dreaming?

No.

Her heart raced. Sickness rose in her stomach and confusion swirled around in her brain. How could this be? Could this really be?

As if he'd read her mind, something he used to be quite good at, her husband, Jack, who she thought had been dead for ten years, said, "I'm real. It's me."

CHAPTER

47

Holly didn't pass out, but every nerve stood on edge. Her body shook, and as he came closer to her and she could see that it really was Jack, the burn of tears stung her eyes.

He came to the edge of the bed and sat. She tried to push herself back and as far away from him as she could. This had to be some kind of nightmare. There was no way this could be real.

"I know what you're thinking. I know you. And this is real. I am real. It's me. Jack."

The tears began to stream down her face. He reached out and wiped them. She shrank from his touch as memories flooded her, and questions ached to escape her. So many questions.

"I know you have a lot of questions, and I'm sure my answers will never be good enough."

Her brain kept replaying the thought: *ten years, ten years of questions. Ten years of—YOU WERE DEAD.*

"Listen, I am not a bad guy. I know about the case you're working. I need to talk to you about what you're investigating. I promise that I'm not bad. If I take off the gag, do you promise not to go insane and scream?"

She nodded.

"Okay." He untied the kerchief stuck in her mouth and she spat it out. For seconds no words were spoken, until she finally whispered, "A good man doesn't leave his pregnant wife, allowing her to believe for *ten years* that he's dead, only to suddenly pop back into her life by kidnapping her. You may be Jack Jennings, but you are not the man I married. Where are we?"

He lowered his hazel eyes, his long lashes shrouding them. He looked almost the same as he had a decade ago, except for some silver scattered through his hair. "We're back in Lexington. I knew I needed to get you here, and I doubted you would come if I just asked."

She could not believe what she was hearing. "What? Why? *Why*, Jack?"

"I had to do what I had to do, Holly. If my death hadn't been faked, then it's more than likely neither you nor I, nor *Chloe*, would be here today."

"Don't you say her name." Holly's words were laced with disgust.

"Holly, you have to trust me. I would never in a million years have hurt you, but I had no choice."

"What do you mean, you had no choice?"

"The case we were on back then, ten years ago...what you didn't know was that I had been working with the CIA."

Her mouth dropped open. "What?" Had her entire marriage been nothing but lies and deceit?

"I couldn't tell you. I was investigating the cartels, and there was a price on my head—and yours."

"No. I don't believe you. You could have found a way." She shook her head, not completely grasping his words. "Who else knew?" she asked, raising her voice. "Someone else had to have known!"

"No one knew. No one on the force, that is."

"How in the hell do you expect me to believe that you were on a task force for the CIA, and no one in the department knew?!"

"From my years in the military," he replied. "I still had contacts there. There was so much about that case, Holly, that even our department didn't know about. I was approached by a former acquaintance from my Marine days. They needed my help."

"They needed your help? They needed your help! And you agreed? You faked your own death, Jack. You left! What about me? I was your goddamned wife! Don't you think that I needed your help?" Tears streamed down her face as she grew angrier by the second, disbelief giving way to hurt and rage.

He shook his head and sighed. "Honey, I had no idea it would go so far. If I had known, I would have turned down the assignment. If I had known that I would be ordered to leave you to keep you and our baby safe, then I would have told them forget it. I thought I was doing the right thing. I thought wrong." He brushed his own face with the back of his hand.

"You could have come home. You could have told them no!"

"No. I couldn't have." He walked over to a desk in one corner, where he picked up an eight-by-ten envelope. He pulled out a stack of photos and set them down on the bed. "I knew you wouldn't believe me. I mean, why would you? The whole situation is insane. But it's true."

The photos sickened her—a woman with her throat slashed, her child next to her. There was another photo with an older couple slain in the same fashion. Jack pointed to the mother and child. "DEA agent Pedro Suarez. Remember him?"

She did. The slayings of his wife and daughter had been all over the news. The cartel had been suspected. Suarez was later found hanging in his garage, presumed to have killed himself because of the pain of losing his family.

Jack pointed to the photos of the older couple. "CIA agent Bill Benington. These are his parents. Again the cartel was suspected. I was next. *You* were next. There was no way in hell I was willing to risk your life, or that of our daughter. No way. The CIA got me out of there. I've been working undercover for several years in the Middle East, and my current assignment brought me back here—and it now involves you."

Holly was so confused. She didn't know what to think, or how to feel. "The cartel, though. The guys we were after are gone now, or in prisons around the world."

"But they weren't that long ago."

"You could have come back. You would have been out of danger. *We* would have been out of danger."

"Not likely, Holly. The cartel has far-reaching branches and long memories. The risk will always be there, and besides, even if I felt it might be safe, I had to question whether it was fair to you and to Chloe. You had a new life, a new love."

Brendan.

"It would not have been right or fair," he continued.

"Then why do you think it is now?" she screamed at him, her voice filled with rage, her body shaking.

He touched her shoulder and then reached out to wipe her tears again. She continued to shrink back. He untied her hands and feet.

"I'm getting the hell out of here!" She stood.

Jack grabbed her wrist. "Please don't run, Holly. Please hear me out."

CHAPTER

48

It had been four years since Quentin was relieved of his duties for the United States government.

He had been working with an informant named Zahoor, who was in tight with the Taliban. Money talked with some of these guys, just as it did with a lot of people. Money remained the universal language.

Quentin was also in deep, working side by side with a guy he thought was his man—someone who had his back.

Jack Jennings.

Quentin had gotten Jack out of that mess in San Diego ten years ago. If he hadn't, the guy surely would have been dead at the hands of the cartel, and not an easy death at that. Jack's wife and unborn child would have been murdered, too. The government had gone in to pull off a fake death and stage a rescue—Quentin had gone in and rescued the guy—seeing that Jack had been an asset.

Jack turned on him, though.

If Quentin didn't have a master plan to manage, he would be taking some time to harass Jack's wife, Holly, in her pursuit to catch her man. He'd like to do that out of spite, but had no time, and, anyway it was all going to work out rather nicely. Detective Holly Jennings would get her man. Joque. Ted Ivy.

Afghanistan had been hell.

Is hell.

Quentin thought Jack wanted the best for the world. That was not the case.

He'd learned that when Jack had turned on him.

Zahoor had told him about a family that lived in one of the villages. They were working for the Taliban. They grew poppies that were turned over to another group who manufactured heroin, which was then shipped stateside to be sold on the streets. The funds all came back to the Taliban and fueled terrorism all over the world.

Jack and two other agents had been with him when they'd surprised the family, bursting into the shack without warning. Jack had stood guard with one of the other guys outside. Even then, Quentin wondered if Jack had the stomach to do what needed to get done.

He hadn't.

Quentin had used the necessary tactics to get the information needed. He got a name and he aimed to use it.

Afterward, they set the house on fire.

Jack grabbed Quentin by the shoulders and shoved him.

Quentin regained his balance. "What the fuck was that for?"

"You didn't have to do that!" Sweat streamed down his face.

"The hell I didn't! They weren't talking!"

"That was savage, Bradley. Brutal savagery!"

"What the fuck? You don't think they were savages? What the fuck do you think we're dealing with out here? This is a goddamned war and you work for the United States government. We are here to better the world!"

"You think that torturing and terrorizing and brutally killing people who were already victimized by their own countrymen is making the world a better place?!" Jack wiped his forehead with the back of his hand.

"I think you're a fucking pussy, Jennings. That's what I think. Now get in the jeep. We're out of here."

"No. I'm not going with you."

"Oh, Christ. You are an old woman. Get the fuck in the Humvee!"

"Fuck you!"

"Stay out here and die then, asshole!"

Quentin and the other two soldiers took off. Jennings stayed behind. He was obviously rescued by some other asshole who worked for the United States government.

Quentin had found the group manufacturing heroin, and he and the two other men went in and blew those fuckers to the next town.

But not before Quentin got a name.

Naqeeb Waqqas.

There was another name that was told to him before he shoved the face of a man into an outhouse toilet and drowned him in his own shit.

Muhammad Farooq.

The son of Sheikh Mahfuz Farooq.

CHAPTER

49

"Wait a minute, you've been able to hack into my e-mails within the department and see what I'm sending Chad and the other detective I'm working with?" Holly asked. "Who the hell are you?"

Jack frowned. "Listen to me. I thought that maybe I could help you out somehow from afar."

Holly crossed her arms. "That's rich. Real rich. I think you should explain." She'd calmed down some, and Jack had been trying to explain his interest in her case. She'd decided to stay but still wasn't buying his incredible story.

"As soon as I spotted you, I knew you were here as a cop. Obviously Chloe isn't with you. Or...Brendan."

Holly swallowed hard. "What do you know about Brendan?"

Jack shook his head. "Anyway, it didn't take long for me to make some calls and find out what case you're on. I was ahead of you at the pen. There was a payoff made to the former warden there, Kyle Junket. I've already gone to visit the man. Junket talked to me."

"Excuse me. Where is this guy and how did you get him to talk?"

"It doesn't matter, but he talked and yes, he was paid off—more than once—and that's why I had to take you." He sat down across from her. "Someone was willing to pay a lot of money to get Ted

Ivy out of jail. Whoever it was has a far reach, and Junket claims he doesn't have the name of the guy. I think you're in trouble."

"What? I'm a cop. I would have gotten these answers on my own. I certainly didn't need you riding in on your white horse to rescue me. Couldn't you have left it alone?" She felt the tears wanting to come again. Her throat tightened as she said the words, "Do you have any idea how long it took me to get over you?"

"I'm sorry," he whispered. He looked at her with those soulful eyes of his—eyes that used to easily seduce her. Eyes that used to make her smile. Eyes that showed how much he adored her, loved her.

"Why are you even here? You know I am capable enough to have worked this on my own. So, why, Jack? Why now? *Why* now?"

He didn't reply.

"You owe me that much. You have me captive, for God's sakes. Why are you even in Lexington?"

He sighed. "I'm on assignment. There is a possibility that Sheikh Farooq—I am sure you know of him—"

"Yes. He has a horse racing in the Infinity and he's obviously a key player in keeping things diplomatic between the US and the Middle East."

"Right. There is a chance that his son is dealing in laundering money for the Taliban. The night I spotted you, I was at the hotel restaurant after getting word that Muhammad Farooq—the sheikh's son—had a meeting scheduled there. Then I saw you and knew I had to leave before you recognized me. I went to work trying to find out what you were out here for. It didn't take me long."

She crossed her arms. "Shouldn't you then be working on your own assignment? I am a big girl, remember. The woman you left as a widow." She started to pace across the hardwood floor.

He cringed. "I deserved that. Yes. I know." He paused and looked away. When he spoke again, he said, "I know you can manage your cases. I know that you're a good cop. I can't deny that the real reason I took you is…when I saw you, so close, I had to talk to you. I knew I needed to hear your voice again. To try to explain everything. I wanted to be near you."

She didn't respond for a minute, trying to keep old emotions deep at bay. "I need to call home. They'll be wondering why I haven't checked in yet today," she said, her voice cool and level.

He nodded and went to retrieve her cell phone.

She stared at him. "Can I have some privacy?"

Jack walked into the other half of the suite.

Holly called the house phone. She knew that Brendan would be at work and the only one home at the moment would be Megan. Holly wasn't sure if she could keep her nerves out of her voice if she spoke to Brendan. She probably should have called him directly, but she was afraid. She had to sort through her emotions first. Megan answered the phone, and Holly told her that she would not be home for at least another day, and she would be checking in later.

She hung up and fought back her tears again. She walked out into the suite to find Jack staring out a window. "I need you to tell me everything that happened. *Everything.* Don't leave any of it out. You say you needed to see me, be with me again. What I need from you is the entire story. All of it."

He turned to her and nodded. "Okay."

They sat down on a couch and he began to talk. He talked about how he'd been recruited to the cause by a former connection from his Marine days. He told her about the secrecy, the vital mission he'd been helping with. He took her back to that day ten years earlier and told her how he'd been taken from the warehouse as planned. Two operatives got him out of the building just before the explosion and into a boat on the harbor. He'd flown out of San Diego that night and landed in Washington. "I was briefed and told what would happen next."

"So you knew going into that operation that you wouldn't be coming home?"

"Yes."

"You knew that you might never see me again?"

He nodded.

She stood up. "It's late. I need to think, and I need some sleep."

He stood, too. "For what it's worth, I never wanted to leave you. I really didn't. As I said, if I had known what was coming, what was going to be asked of me, I would have turned the assignment down. I never would have left you."

She walked toward the other room and without turning around, not wanting him to see her tears, she replied, "But you did."

CHAPTER

50

Jim Gershon had flown to Saratoga a few days after being questioned by the detectives regarding Tieg's murder. That woman—Detective Jennings—man, she had made him jumpy. But he had already been a ball of nerves. He thought he had done a decent job keeping his nerves hidden. He hoped so, anyway.

He hadn't been totally forthright with her. He never mentioned that Tommy had ridden a horse for him once—Tieg's horse. But it was inconsequential. He had wanted to get rid of those damn cops. He needed to be sure that none of them went digging into the past.

He didn't want to go to Saratoga but he had horses running that Hodges owned, and when that guy told him what to do, he obeyed. He was disappointed, and he knew Hodges was, too, that they didn't have an Infinity contender, especially since Hodges had been the main investor in the track and casino. But those were the breaks. Gershon hoped he didn't lose his job over it, but there was nothing he could do. There wasn't a three-year-old running real strong in their barn.

He thought maybe he'd found some good horses in Saratoga and he left Hodges a message. Not losing his job was on his mind and so were the murders of Tommy Lyons, Katarina Erickson, and Marvin Tieg. The sight of Tieg's dead body still haunted him. With the jockeys, Gershon didn't think much of it, didn't get alarmed.

But with Tieg, he started to wonder. He started to look over his shoulder.

But why?

He was pragmatic. Logical. Paranoia wasn't going to help him any.

But still…the day before he found Tieg covered in needle holes and burns, staring at him with dead eyes, Tieg had told them they needed to talk. Talk about Ivy.

A name Gershon hadn't heard in a long time and wanted to forget.

He had a secret. Tieg had a secret. Laugherty had a secret. Gershon wondered if Laugherty was thinking about all of this. Wondered if he was scared.

Probably not. There probably was no reason to be afraid. It was his paranoia and his conscience bugging him, nothing more. Gershon knew that what they had done ten years ago had been wrong. But Tieg and Laugherty had given him no choice.

He'd had no choice but to do what he did.

It had been wrong, and Gershon had tried to go to confession, but he couldn't get the words out.

He could not even tell the priest in the confessional that he'd been a part of framing a man for arson and murder. And that man had been badly burned in the fire—adding insult to injury. There was so much at stake—it had to go down the way it did. A lot of money had been involved, and although Gershon didn't get the payout the others did, he was too scared to ever talk. Plus, who knew if Ted Ivy was even alive? If he was, he had to still be in jail. If he was out and seeking revenge, then why kill Tommy and Katarina? That didn't make sense. That made no sense at all. Those kids wouldn't have even been teenagers ten years ago. Nah.

Paranoid.

He passed by a group of grooms. It was the end of the day and they were all shooting the shit.

He took a walk through the barn and checked the horses. The security guards were all coming on as the day shifted to evening. He was tired. It had been a long flight from California.

Gershon needed a shower and a drink.

He headed back to his hotel. He stopped at the hotel restaurant, where he sat at the bar and ordered a whiskey and steak. He took a couple sips of the drink. It warmed him and began to ease his mind. His dinner soon came, and he dug in, his cares slowly slipping away.

"How's the steak?" A guy in a suit and tie sat down on the barstool next to him. "I'm hungry and have an early morning."

"It's okay," Gershon said.

"I'll have a steak and a Corona."

Gershon felt his shoulders tighten. Goddamned paranoia. Ted Ivy used to drink Coronas. That was all he ever drank.

"Nothing like a good steak. I'm Frank Halorin." He turned to Gershon, who didn't feel like making small talk.

"Jim Gershon."

"Here on business?"

"Yep. Horse racing."

"No kidding? I love watching the races. I don't know a thing about horses but man, they are cool to watch."

The bartender set a Corona on the bar, and the talkative guy said, "Oh hey, can I get a couple of limes?"

Gershon took a large gulp of the whiskey. Perspiration beaded the top of his receding hairline. This was ridiculous. Just because Ted Ivy used to put two limes in his Coronas meant nothing. *And, for God's sake, Ted's face was scarred badly. Severely burned. This guy has no scars. None. Stop it.* But caught up in his paranoia, he set the drink down and asked, "Do I know you from somewhere?"

"I don't think so. I'm from Minneapolis. I do insurance."

"Ah."

"And you do horses."

Gershon nodded. There was a creep factor oozing from the straightlaced coat and tie dude.

"You ever need some insurance, I can get you some amazing deals."

"I think I'm good," Gershon replied.

"Never have enough insurance," he said.

"Yeah, well. My wife would probably agree."

"Wives." He laughed. "That Infinity race, huh? That's a big deal. All over the media. You going?"

"I don't have a horse running. No."

"Bummer. Big deal, though. How about those murders? Kind of a damper?"

"I thought you didn't know much about horse racing." This guy was getting on pretty much every one of Gershon's last nerves.

"Horses no, but man, that stuff has been all over the media."

"I don't watch the news."

"Yeah, but the people you work with must be talking." The guy downed the rest of the beer.

"A little, I guess. That's the problem with the media. They blow these things up."

"Blow things up? That dude killed three people. Not a nice guy, you know." He snorted.

"No."

"Did you know those people he killed?"

"You know what, I have a long day tomorrow, and I'm beat." Gershon set forty on the bar and left. He didn't give a shit about the change. He just wanted to grab a shower and go to bed.

Once in his room, he leaned against the door and started laughing. How stupid had he been? Stupid.

He turned on the TV and headed for the shower.

Fifteen minutes later he was clean and relaxing in his bed, watching an old episode of *Two and a Half Men*. The guy in the bar was not on his mind.

He grew tired and turned off the TV and the light.

He slept like a log for about four hours.

He woke and tried to turn to his side. What the hell? There was a pain in his arm. It stung. He'd been stung by something. Oh hell. He had a bee allergy. He needed to get up and get to his EpiPen. Who would have thought a bee could get into his hotel room?

But he couldn't move.

At all.

Panic set in.

And then a dim light turned on.

A man stood there with a flashlight under his chin.

What the hell?

Gershon blinked and tried to focus on the guy standing over him. This had to be a nightmare.

"Don't bother, Jim. I shot you full of Ketamine. You know Ketamine, don't you? Of course you do. Nice paralytic we use on horses."

Gershon's vision swam, then came briefly into focus. Oh God, the guy from the bar.

"You know, you have good instincts. You always did. You knew good horses. You knew my boy, my horse; he was a good horse. Dirty Games. Loved that horse like O'Leary supposedly did. O'Leary, was he in on this, too? He didn't seem to help me much, didn't stick up for me when you shitheads started pointing fingers. No problem, though. I'm going to find him, too."

Gershon knew who the man was, but how…how had he been able to change his face? He wanted to say to him that the horse had not even been his horse. He had been a piece-of-shit lowly ass groom.

"But neither you nor Tieg nor any of those other assholes cared at all about what you did that night. All for the money. All for the money. Bastards," he whispered. "And you, Jim, you are probably the worst bastard of them all. You and me, man. It was you and me. We groomed those animals. We loved them. Or at least I did.

"Those horses that you helped kill, they were far more decent than the animals that you and your buddies are." Ivy sighed, big and dramatic, and a spike of fear lodged in Gershon's throat. "Well, you won't be around for long."

Gershon tried to squirm, but it was no use. He had been completely paralyzed by the Ketamine. He knew he wasn't getting out of this. He couldn't even cry. Jim Gershon began praying and confessing. He wanted to scream at Ted Ivy that he would see him in hell.

"Why did you do it, Jimmy? How much did they pay you?" Ivy stood. "You know what, it don't matter." He held up a twitch. "You always liked these. Put them on countless horses. Oh yes, it releases endorphins." He twisted the twitch in his hands. "So the horses have told us fucking humans that when we put the loop of chain or rope around their lip that it relieves stress. That it feels good. Sure!" He paused. "How about when you take the wooden handle of the twitch, which I saw you do, man, and smack the horse over the head? Like this!" He hit Gershon on top of the head with the twitch.

He then forced Gershon's mouth open and shoved the chain past his teeth. "Can't take a chance on being heard. Oh wait. You know where a twitch probably really releases endorphins? In your balls, huh?"

Ivy pulled back the covers, yanked down Gershon's pajama bottoms, attached the twitch to his testicles and squeezed.

Pain flared out from Gershon's testicles, rippling over his whole body.

"Yeah, feels good, huh? This is gonna feel better." Ivy held up a blowtorch and all Gershon could do was stare ahead in dire pain and pray for the end to come quickly.

Ivy started the torch.

"Remember that night? The screams of the horses? Their fear? Remember? I sure do, motherfucker. I got to spend eight years in a cell remembering every horrifying second I went in to try to save them. I tried to save my boy. Where the fuck were you?"

He shook his head and brought the torch first down on Gershon's hands. He singed the hair and burned the skin as he continued the tirade. "You should have looked at my hands. Not my face. You thought you knew me, and you did. At the bar. But you kept looking at my face. If you had looked at my hands, you would have seen the burns. They're still there. Makeup helps, but if you'd looked close, you would have seen them. But you didn't look close enough, asshole."

Ivy lit the torch again and moved to Gershon's legs. Gershon began to fade. "Know where you were that night? In a bar, because that is where *they* told you to go. Then you did everything else *they* told you. You framed me."

Gershon had a vision of that night. Everything Ivy was saying was true.

"Now you have to pay, as I have paid."

Ivy brought the torch up to Gershon's face, burning his skin to complete black.

He stuck a carrot in the charred skull's mouth and headed to the airport to catch his flight to Las Vegas.

CHAPTER
51

"And Allah took a handful of southerly wind, blew His breath over it, and created the horse... Thou shall fly without wings, and conquer without any sword. Oh, horse."
— *Bedouin Legend*

Horses don't run alone on the track.

Their bodies jostle against one another and dirt kicks up from the hooves of the horse that's ahead. The noise of the track, the flashbulbs and frenzy and flowers—the world of the track is entirely man-made.

CHAPTER

52

After Quentin had learned that Naqeeb Waqqas and the sheikh's son were in cahoots, smuggling drugs into the US and then laundering money that went back to the Taliban, Quentin set his sights on bringing them down.

But his own government and military had set their sights on him.

And they did.

But not for long.

"You are officially relieved from your duties." Those words echoed daily in Quentin's mind.

The group he had worked for within the CIA was so covert, so deep, that it didn't even have a name. Only a few knew about its existence.

And yet, they still took him down. They fired him, cut him off.

And now...he was sure they regretted not *really* taking him down.

Taking him out.

He was sure that a few of his former colleagues were looking over their shoulders on a regular basis. Including Jack Jennings.

The irony was that he was in plain sight. Right out there in front of everyone. Bradley Security Systems was now the largest private security firm in the country. No one had put two and two together. Bradley was such a common name.

The name Bradley—the one part of his former life that he'd kept the same.

It was amazing what good plastic surgery could do for a person. Colored contacts. Hair color and style—from buzz cut to longish dark brown. When one had money to blend in, put a business together, plant oneself in the middle of the movers and the shakers, changing an identity wasn't hard.

He lived very nicely on the money that he had taken from the Taliban drug lords. Millions of dollars.

After a stint in Brazil, where he'd had his extreme makeover, Quentin, with his new look and his new identity in place, left South America for his new life.

He had a condo in Cardiff-by-the-Sea near San Diego, and a lake house out in Colorado. He maintained an apartment in Manhattan as well. His offices were in Colorado so he spent a good share of his time there.

It was at the lake house built from cedar, oak, and walnut that Quentin had gone to work to find the perfect patsy after he had decided what he needed to do.

Finding Ted Ivy wasn't easy. Quentin knew the kind of guy he needed for this job, and it was a narrow role to fill, a specific kind of guy.

He got real lucky with the man who, like himself, had a thing about names. His guy Ivy preferred to be called Joque.

He fit the profile perfectly.

Quentin had started his search for the perfect guy with scandals. Kentucky was filled with them. The racing world was filled with them.

He found murder, abduction, money laundering—the Mafia even had their hands in Lexington at times.

Then he found Ted Ivy.

Quentin's training and experience told him the guy's conviction smelled funny. He read the newspaper articles from the case. He knew who the players were to an extent.

He sat behind his desk inside his office, rubbing his hands together—thinking and pondering. Supposing Ivy wasn't guilty of setting the barn ablaze and killing nineteen horses that were insured up the wazoo. Supposing he wasn't guilty of manslaughter. Supposing he'd want to get even...

Or maybe the guy was totally guilty. Maybe the guy had a real beef with Tieg and his compatriots.

Either way...Ted Ivy was looking like a man who could use some help, and certainly after eight years of claiming innocence, and eight years spent inside the Kentucky State Pen, this guy would want to get some revenge.

Quentin planned to help him, because if Ivy was who he thought he might be—a man with a need to see justice truly served—then he was his man.

His patsy.

CHAPTER

53

O'Leary had finished with the horses. Riding Karma during her morning workout had been amazing. What a fast and lovely animal. And spending time again with Elena felt even more amazing. The love he'd had for her ten years ago hadn't faded at all. And he kicked himself for ever letting her go. What an ass he'd been.

Elena was busy filling out necessary forms for the race and spending time with her mare. He admired and respected her for what she had done with the filly. He hated that Perez had the privilege of riding Karma for the race, and Perez knew it. Perez was also aware that O'Leary and Elena were hanging out again. They hadn't made it a secret. Perez and O'Leary had been cordial to each other for Elena's sake, but O'Leary knew he stuck in the guy's craw, and he didn't care one iota. If anything, O'Leary enjoyed watching the asshole squirm a little.

The Infinity grounds were top-notch, and he now sat in the Jockey Stop, an excellent eatery next to the barns that served home cooking.

Waiting on a plate of meatloaf, he jotted down more memories on his legal pad. Once back at his room, he'd get on the computer and transcribe everything.

The night of the fire.

O'Leary had left Tieg's farm around three o'clock that day. He and Ivy had downed a few more beers together, and then Ivy said he needed to get back to work.

This was all stuff that O'Leary had said in court.

He'd told the judge everything the way he recalled it.

The prosecutor asked, "Did Mr. Ivy say that he'd had an argument with Mr. Tieg and with Mr. Laugherty the day before the incident?"

"Yes," O'Leary replied. "But, I don't think—"

The prosecutor held up his hand.

The judge said, "Just answer the question with a yes or no, sir."

"Yes." O'Leary glanced at Ted Ivy slumped over in his chair next to his state-appointed defender. The burns on Ivy's hands were purple and grotesque. The burns on the side of his face didn't look as bad, but must have been painful all the same. O'Leary had wanted to say that he didn't think Ted Ivy started the fire. The prosecutor never gave him a chance.

O'Leary had always questioned Ivy's conviction. If the man had wanted to destroy Tieg's place out of spite, why would he have risked his own life trying to save the horses? Why wouldn't he have taken them out of the barn before setting the fire? The prosecutor claimed it was an arson job gone bad. They claimed he confessed and then recanted. To O'Leary, none of it added up. Not then and not now.

O'Leary had his doubts for sure.

Ivy cared for the horses in that barn, and when O'Leary had left him that day, he wasn't drunk. Maybe he was tipsy, but he wasn't drunk. He especially cared for Sucio—Dirty Games—and so did O'Leary. Just thinking about the sweet, handsome gray colt brought emotions up in O'Leary that he had not ever really dealt with. That horse had been a real good boy. Special—and he was special beyond the speed he had, the speed O'Leary was developing with him. He was one of those horses that had a real soulful way about him. Karma reminded O'Leary a lot of Sucio.

Good horses.

Back in court, evidence proved that Ivy was way beyond the legal limit with a blood alcohol level of .18. Supposedly he had gone on to have some drinks with Gershon after O'Leary left, which O'Leary found odd because when he'd chatted it up with Ivy that day, Ivy didn't seem to care much for Jim Gershon.

"That guy is a jerk, too," Ivy had said. "He's trying so hard to get in tight with Tieg and Laugherty. Tells me the other day that I'm a peon. That he's going to be moving up, and moving up in big ways."

O'Leary had told all of this to Ivy's attorney. O'Leary recalled the slimy-looking attorney who represented Ivy. Slicked-back hair, cheap suit, bloodshot eyes—O'Leary now wondered if the attorney hadn't been paid off by Tieg to do a piss-poor job for Ivy. He wouldn't doubt it. And now Tieg was dead.

Katarina and Tommy were dead, too.

O'Leary still thought Gershon was a creep.

O'Leary set his iced tea down as the waitress brought his meatloaf plate. He dug in. Excellent!

He ate his food and continued thinking. He knew that Ivy had gotten fifteen to twenty years in prison for the "crime." If he were out of lockup, O'Leary would have to wonder if Ted Ivy had murdered Tieg. But the guy could only be halfway through his sentence by now.

Somehow Tieg and the kids were all tied together. He shook his head. It was useless trying to figure out the murders. Way above his head. But maybe he could figure out what had happened the night that Tieg's barn burned and those nineteen horses and one farmhand died. Maybe somehow O'Leary could help Ted Ivy prove his innocence.

O'Leary knew that after the Infinity, he needed to go see Ivy up in prison.

He wrote a few more notes, then heard a voice he recognized at a table nearby. He cringed. Juan Perez.

"You got no idea, man. She's a wildcat in bed. I tell you what, I am going to do whatever I need to do to win her over."

O'Leary saw that Perez was talking to his agent—Warren Walker. Another slimy bastard.

"Be careful, hombre. You have a good thing with this. Don't mess it up," Walker said.

"You know, she's got a tattoo with a four-leaf clover on the left side of her ass. It's cute," Perez said.

O'Leary swallowed hard.

"I don't care if she has a tattoo on her clit," the agent replied. "Ride the horse, not the broad."

O'Leary closed his eyes. The clover was their thing. He looked at the tattoo he'd gotten the night they'd decided they were lucky together. His was on the inside of his arm. Elena had slept with Perez. Dammit. O'Leary felt sick. He got up and paid his check at the counter. He didn't look at Perez. He wondered if the ass knew he'd been sitting there at the booth only feet away.

It didn't matter.

O'Leary wasn't the jealous type. And he knew it had only been days since he had started seeing her again, but he had never stopped loving Elena. Never. He hated thinking of another man being with her, especially one like Perez. But he wasn't so naïve as to think that Elena didn't have sex. He'd certainly been no angel over the years.

Still…

Overhearing Perez only cemented in O'Leary the fact that he wanted to be with Elena that much more. He never again wanted another man to have her.

CHAPTER
54

March 4, 2011

Ted Ivy woke up slowly and in pain. He tried to say something. A pretty Brazilian nurse stood over him. She rubbed his arm. "It is okay. We will give you something for the pain." He watched, his vision blurring as she put something into his IV. He could feel the bandages on his face.

He drifted in and out of a drug-induced sleep. Memories of the past twenty-four hours swam in and out of his mind.

Meeting Quentin in the bar.

The plane ride.

The palatial estate.

Dr. Arroyo.

"You will recover nicely here," Quentin had said, showing him first around the estate set against a hillside in Diamantina in the state of Minas Gerais. "Every desire will be catered to. You will have nothing that you do not want or need. When Dr. Arroyo is finished, you'll be amazed at what you look like."

The idea that the scars on his face would be gone was almost unbelievable. But everything Quentin had promised so far, he had done. He had saved Ted from a life of poverty and depravity.

Quentin was his guardian angel.

When Ivy came to again, the pain was somewhat less severe. The nurse offered him some dinner. "That would be good."

Twenty minutes later an incredible filet mignon, a seafood risotto, some greens, and what had to be quite expensive red wine arrived in his room.

He couldn't eat much because of the pain, surgery, and meds, but what he did get down was delicious. After living eight years in a prison cell, he would take the current pain and all the luxuries that accompanied it over the hellhole of prison any day.

When he finished his meal, the nurse took his tray away and moments later came back with a state-of-the-art laptop computer. Taped to it was an envelope. "For you," she said. "I will be back. Press the buzzer if you need anything before I return."

Ivy thanked her.

He opened the envelope. The first thing he spotted was a huge wad of cash. He counted it. Twenty thousand dollars.

Twenty thousand dollars!

There was a letter as well.

This is the first installment of many to come. Get online. I have set up an encrypted e-mail account for you. It is a private account, meant only for our communication. If someone else gets into the account, I will know, and there will be immediate consequences. Your first lesson is in the first e-mail. You have a lot of studying to do. I have faith you will do a wonderful job. Q

The e-mail account and password were in the letter.

Ted opened the laptop and went online. He did as he had been directed. Went to the e-mail site and logged on.

That is when he learned his new name, his new residence, and the first step of many on the way to the final act.

CHAPTER

55

The next morning Holly was up before the sun. Not that she had slept much anyway. She had lain awake all night wondering about her life with Jack, trying hard to decipher what had been real and what had not.

The thing was, as angry and hurt as she felt, she believed him. The man she had married had been honorable, and when he'd joined the CIA he probably really felt it was for the good of the people. And it was for the good of the people—all the people except for her.

She also couldn't deny that feelings for Jack were still there. They had come rushing back with each passing second as she began to accept that he was still alive.

But...

She was in love with another man. She had a new life, a new partner in Brendan. She could not deny that.

And although what Jack had done—leaving her and faking his death—was likely necessary given the lengths the cartel would go to in order to destroy people, she couldn't get past the fact that he had never told her. He never told her that he was working for the CIA. He never told her that he was involved with a special task force.

They were married, for God's sake. They were supposed to be a team, supposed to face challenges together. They could have figured it out. Couldn't the CIA have gotten her out as well? Couldn't they have disappeared together? Been together? Raised their daughter together? She couldn't stop herself from wondering why he'd never included her. Had he been looking for a way out? How much of her life, her love, and her marriage with Jack had been a lie?

She finished showering and put on the robe hanging on the bathroom door. She walked out and found a shopping bag on the bed. There was a card inside. *Thought you might like a new set of clothes. XOMLJ.* She forced away the smile. He was getting to her. The sight of the signature he'd always used when giving her gifts, starting with the plumeria charm...

When he'd handed her the jewelry box in Hawaii and she read the card, she looked up at him. "XOMLJ?"

"Kiss, hug, much love, Jack."

She'd smiled, leaned across the small table between them on the balcony overlooking the ocean in their hotel suite, and kissed him. She opened the box and took out the charm. He stood and guided her arms around his neck. He picked her up and carried her into their hotel room, where they'd made love for hours. Lying in bed afterwards, she whispered in his ear, "XOMLH." From then on, they'd adopted those signatures.

How dare he use it now. After everything.

She did gratefully remove the clothes from the bag—new panties, new bra—a little lace on them, nothing extravagant. Ivory. She felt her face flush. He remembered her size and what she liked. She then took out a V-neck cashmere sweater in a dark gray and a pair of jeans—again right size and her style. She slipped into the new clothes and as she finished buttoning the top button on the jeans, there was a knock at the bedroom door.

She opened it and there stood Jack, coffees in hand. "Thought you might want this." He handed her a cup.

Like the clothes, he remembered how she took her coffee. After all these years, she still knew how he preferred his, too. She walked out into the family room of the suite to find a breakfast spread set out.

"And I thought you might be hungry as well." He pulled a chair out from the table and motioned for her to take a seat.

She did, and he sat down across from her. They didn't speak for several long moments. As she ate breakfast with Jack, she realized suddenly how comfortable it was. How easy. She closed her eyes for a second and sighed, thinking about Brendan. What did all of this mean with Jack here now? He obviously still worked for some task force within the CIA. He obviously was undercover. How would this affect her marriage to Brendan? Oh my God, could she even marry Brendan? Would it be legal? This was all crazy. She had to know. She set her fork down.

Jack looked up from his plate. "Yes?" he asked. Always so confident. Always knowing what she needed.

"I'm getting married."

He nodded and wiped the corners of his mouth with his napkin. "I know."

"I love him. I love Brendan."

"I know that, too." He took a long sip from his coffee.

"What does this all mean then, Jack? You're alive. I know you're alive. Can I even legally remarry?"

He set the cup down. "For all intents and purposes, Jack Jennings is no longer alive. There are only a handful of people who know who I really am. That list now includes you. But your knowledge doesn't change anything. If you want to marry Brendan, then that's what you should do."

"What do you mean *if* I want to marry him?" She could hear the upset in her voice escalating and tried very hard to remain cool. "Of course I want to marry him! Just because you come back all, all, all..." She shook her head, exasperated. "Riding in on your white horse announcing, 'I'm alive!' what am I supposed to do?

Call home and say to a man who would never, ever leave me, never betray me, 'Sorry, Prince Fucking Charming is back! Wedding is off, babe.'"

Jack wore an amused look on his face. "Prince Fucking Charming? That's a new one."

"Yeah, well, that's you." She stood, threw her napkin at him, and walked back into the bedroom wanting to scream. He had gotten under her skin. He'd always known how to do that. She hated him for it. And she knew him so well. Their old song and dance came rushing from her memory bank to the forefront of her mind. She closed her eyes and counted down from ten. When she got to one, she heard the click on the door. He stepped in and walked up behind her, placing his hands on her shoulders. "No," she said. "Don't go there. I have a call to make. It's after seven in California and I have people to check on." She walked out from under his touch and picked up her phone off the nightstand. Once Jack had returned it to her, he hadn't asked her to give it back. She could have at any moment throughout the night called home, called Chad, called someone and told them about Jack.

But she hadn't.

She called Chad now, questioning why she was still in the hotel suite with Jack.

"Hey partner, it's about time. I was getting concerned since I hadn't heard from you in a day!"

"I was giving you some time to be with your new family. How is Brooke? The baby?"

"Everyone is fine. I'm worried about you, though. It isn't like you to leave us all hanging, and Brendan said you talked with Megan but not him. Is everything okay? You have us all a little freaked out. Amar was, too. He said the last you guys spoke you were going to the prison to talk to Ted Ivy. That was yesterday. What the hell happened?"

Holly knew she should have called Brendan. Dammit. But could she have kept the angst out of her voice? He knew her so well. "I promise you that I'm fine. Been looking for Ted Ivy is all."

"Amar told me that he'd been let out. Or at least that's what you guys thought. Did you confirm it?"

"Yes. I did. Dirty former warden. Long story, but Ted Ivy is out, and we suspect he changed his identity."

"We?"

"I mean me. I do. I planned to talk with you and Amar and was sure you'd agree with me on this. I'm tired." She tried to brush it off.

Chad didn't respond right away. She glanced at Jack.

"No kidding?" Chad said. "Changed his looks?"

"No kidding."

"You think he's our man?" Chad asked.

"I think there's a very strong chance."

"So what about our theory? Do you still think there's another killer involved? I suppose Ted Ivy, without changing his appearance, would have to keep a low profile."

"He would. Honestly, Chad, I'm not sure what to think." She knew that she couldn't make her partner privy to everything Jack had told her. There was likely another man behind Ivy—someone had paid off the warden. Who he was at this point was an unknown.

"You don't know where he might be?"

"No. And I don't know who he is working with, if he's working with anyone."

Chad sighed. "I have something that may be interesting. I don't know. I've been chewing on it until I could get you. Now I'll let you gnaw on it."

"Give it to me."

"Equine Health Systems. Scott Christiansen's company…"

"Yeah?"

"The tours they do and all that. Well, they also give a lot of product to facilities in need. Places where handicapped people go to ride, war veterans, and horse rescue places. That place you went to and spoke with that woman—Leann."

"Purdue. Yes."

"Her facility has taken some donations from them. And after going through their sign-in sheet for tours from last spring I saw the name Golden Hearts from Lexington, Kentucky. I asked Christiansen if he remembered the folks. He said that it was just one guy, a Dan Creswell. And get this, this guy was talking about his wedding and where they were going on their honeymoon. Fiji. To scuba dive. Receptionist told him that the dive place was closing in a matter of two days and that he could probably get a good deal on dive equipment."

"Oh my God! Chad, I've gotta check something. I'll call you back."

"You better, and you better call your fiancé."

"I will." She clicked off the phone and stood up. "We have to go, Jack. I think I know Ted Ivy's new identity."

CHAPTER
56

"Elena, I have to talk with you," Perez said.

Elena stood in the filly's stall, rubbing liniment down each of the horse's legs. "Yes." She stood up. "What's going on?"

Perez shifted uneasily. Natalie the bug was with him. Uh-oh. Had he knocked up the nineteen-year-old kid? Hell, say it wasn't so.

Natalie was a pretty young thing who had been making eyes at Perez since she'd walked into Elena's barn. She was a good kid, from what Elena could tell. Same height as her, dark brown eyes, long dark-red hair. She wanted to be a jockey. Elena wanted to give her that chance, but she had a lot to learn. She knew the kid was from a broken home—a real broken one—so giving her an opportunity to exercise her horses was the least Elena could do, and she had noticed Perez had taken the kid under his wing. She had warned him not to take her into his bed, though. "What is it, guys?"

"It's O'Leary," Perez replied.

Elena came out of Karma's stall and closed the door behind her. "O'Leary? What about him?"

Perez looked at Natalie. "Tell her what you heard."

Natalie swallowed and looked down at her feet. "I, uh, I heard O'Leary talking to some of the grooms and stuff."

"Okay." Elena had a sinking feeling in her gut.

"They were doing some shots."

"They were?"

"Yeah, tequila."

Oh no. O'Leary had told her he'd stopped drinking. It had only been a few days, but she thought he'd been sincere about making an effort.

"And he was saying how he was going to get the ride on Karma. He said that he was going to get the ride because you still wanted to be with him."

"What?" Elena said. She was incredulous. "Are you sure that's what you heard?"

Natalie bit her lower lip. She nodded. "I was right there. That's what I heard. I was inside Karma's stall. I swear. I'm sorry."

Elena shook her head. "No. It's okay. Thank you for telling me." She felt emotion grab the back of her throat and tighten her chest. Her fear that O'Leary had come back into her life with guns blazing, only to hurt her again, was true. He didn't really want to be with her. He never really did. Even back in the day when her father bribed him with good mounts, he'd chosen the horses over her.

And, it looked as if he had done it again.

CHAPTER

57

O'Leary spotted Elena heading toward the accommodations. She was supposed to have gotten in touch with him already. They were going to have dinner together again. He called out her name. She didn't turn around.

He jogged up alongside her. "Hey, El. Forget something? Or someone?" He nudged her.

"No." She kept walking and didn't look at him.

"Um, yes, I think you did. Me." He tried to put an arm around her, but she shoved it away. "Hey. What's that all about? Are you upset with me?"

She stopped walking, crossed her arms, and stared at him.

Oh no. He recognized that look. That was look on her face the day she'd told him to go to hell after her dad had put him on one of his best horses. But this time he had no idea what he'd done.

"I should have known better, Pete."

This was bad. She called him Pete. There were two times she ever used his name: if she was in the throes of passion or really pissed off at him. They certainly weren't making love at the moment. "I'm sorry, El, but I have no idea what you're talking about."

"Really? How about your little drunken soiree with some of the grooms? Where you told them all you were working me so you could ride Karma in the Infinity?"

"What?! That's ridiculous. I told you I stopped drinking, and as far as running my mouth off with stupid shit like that, that's something I would never do. I'm not working you. Do I think Perez is the right jock for your horse? No way. But I'm not trying to take his ride. I'm not like that. I'm in this for you."

She laughed, but with some cynicism. "Right. Like you were when my dad gave you a fat check. Money talks, doesn't it, Pete? People don't change." She tossed up her hands. "I can't blame you. Look at you. Big fall from grace from who you once were out here on the track."

She was fighting back tears. He could see it. He tried to say something, but she cut him off. "Then you see my filly, me, and think, 'Oh, bet I can sweet-talk Elena. Get in good. Get her in bed.' Nice idea. Bet tonight was supposed to be the big culmination of your plan." She clapped her hands. "Bravo. But, you didn't plan on the fact that you would be talking smack and drinking with the grooms and then, lo and behold, my bug hears you say that shit about me and the horse!"

"Excuse me? Your bug? That kid? The girl? The one diddling Perez?"

"She's a good kid. She isn't a liar like you are, and now I know why you keep throwing Juan Perez under the bus."

O'Leary shook his head. He could not believe this. He couldn't even speak for a few seconds. In a calm voice, he finally said, "You know what, El, if you want to believe the bug and Perez about me, go ahead. That's on you. I know what I was in this for. And it wasn't to ride the filly. It was for you."

She didn't say anything.

She didn't have to. O'Leary could see the doubt in her eyes.

He turned and walked away, fighting his own tears.

CHAPTER

58

June 23, 2011

Ivy's wife had died on 9/11. Quentin could not have designed it more perfectly himself.

Quentin loved three things in life: He loved his capacity for control. He loved Tarantino movies, thus the name change. And he loved the idea of the apocalypse.

Which he would cause.

And survive.

And the world would be a much better place.

His world.

The detailed e-mails he had been sending his patsy contained everything from falsified police reports from when "Tieg had killed his family," photos of his "deceased wife and daughter," addresses on Tieg and every detail about his life, Gershon, Laugherty, and of course how Ivy was to pursue his new life with his new identity—the people he would need to meet and align himself with.

Then, the e-mail that would push things to the next level.

This was one of those make-them-or-break-them moments.

By this time, Ivy had a new face and looked like a nice-guy-from-next-door type. The only thing that Dr. Arroyo could not fix completely was the man's hands. They had been severely burned. That bothered Quentin, who considered Arroyo a master.

"There is only so much I can do with his hands," he'd said.

"What do you mean?" Quentin asked. "Give him new hands."

"When we spoke of this man…" Quentin never told Arroyo or anyone Ivy's real name. No one asked. It seemed that everyone had the understanding that Quentin was a dangerous man, so not asking questions was prudent on their part. "I did not know how severe the burns were. They cannot be made new. They can be made better, though."

Quentin cracked his neck. A regular guy under these circumstances would have thrown his fucking gin and tonic against the floor-to-ceiling glass doors that led to the atrium inside the estate.

Quentin was not a regular guy. He drank the gin. Watched the doctor.

The man wasn't lying.

It was a risk.

A calculated risk.

He would take it.

He had come this far.

"Do what you can."

He'd gotten back on the plane, and Dr. Arroyo had gotten to work.

Quentin composed the first e-mail and gave Ted Ivy information about his new identity.

Now he was about to send e-mail number 203. The big one.

It was an e-mail about Katarina Erickson and Tommy Lyons.

He had a feeling he was going to have to fly down to visit his patsy after he sent this e-mail. Ted Ivy was a murderer. Quentin knew that. But he had to turn him into a *killer*.

He chartered the flight.

When Quentin arrived he was faced with the question he knew Ted Ivy would ask. "But these guys didn't do any harm to me. To us. Why do I need to kill them first?"

"Here is the thing, my friend: have you ever heard the term 'casualties of war'?"

"Of course."

They were seated outside by the pool; a waterfall bled into the water, splashing droplets at their feet. The air was hot and humid; hummingbirds buzzed overhead. Who would have thought such ugly plans for destruction would be created in such a peaceful, beautiful place as this, situated on a hillside in Brazil?

"The jockeys are casualties of war. It's a way to confuse the police."

Quentin needed the police to not get too close too fast to Ted Ivy. He also needed to test Ivy's loyalty. He'd tested people before— like Jack Jennings—and they'd failed. If Ted murdered the jockeys in cold blood, Quentin would rest assured knowing that he would carry out all of his requests.

"I'm confused," Ivy said.

Quentin had used many tactics over the years to guide people into doing what was necessary, and Ivy was no exception. He would use subtle suggestion to help create the kind of killer he needed. "You love the horses. You loved that horse more than anything. The one that died in the fire, Dirty Games. Sucio."

"Of course."

"These jockeys...they don't love the horses. Why should they make all the money they do and have access to these horses? Why?"

Ivy nodded slowly.

"They shouldn't! You should have been a jockey. You would have been kind and decent. You never would have allowed one to get hurt, would you?"

"No."

"What if you had been a jockey? What if you had been called Jock? Those jockeys you will kill are as guilty as the rest of them."

Quentin could see that the rhetoric and technique was working on Ivy. By the end of the day, Ted Ivy had chosen the nom de guerre Joque. Quentin had laughed with him over that. By the end of the day, Ivy believed that he and Quentin were buddies and partners. And by the end of the day, Quentin knew he would do as he'd been told. He would kill both Tommy Lyons and Katarina Erickson. And he wouldn't stop there.

CHAPTER

59

They drove to Leann Purdue's place. Holly had filled Jack in on everything she knew about Leann and the rescue facility, and most everything else that had been uncovered in the case.

"It makes sense that Ivy would take cover with this woman," Jack said. "She's a decent human being and accepted in the community but not considered a player. It's her sister who is big into racing. Ivy could have been using Leann, who through Elena may have information about where certain people are located, or what races they are attending. He's likely learned how to listen, how to pay attention. I am sure his time in prison taught him other skills as well."

Holly's cell phone rang as they made the run into Golden Hearts. It was just past two o'clock and the sky was darkening rapidly. She saw who it was. Her stomach tightened.

"It's Brendan, isn't it?" Jack asked.

"Yes."

"You need to take it. You're a cop. You're investigating. Play it cool."

She nodded, but God, this felt like an awful lie she knew she was about to tell. "Hi," she said, answering the phone.

"Honey! I was getting worried."

"B. I'm fine. I've been working this thing hard so that I can get back home," she said.

"I know. But you're out there on your own without your partner, and I got concerned when Chad hadn't heard from you."

"I called and talked to Megan."

"I realize that, but I thought you might have called and talked to me."

"I…figured you would be busy at work. I needed to go interview someone. I've got a gun. I'm fine. I've had a break in this case, I think."

"That's good news," Brendan replied. "You sure you're okay?" he asked.

"I am. I will do what needs to get done here and come on home."

"Good. I love you," he said.

"I love you, too."

She ended the call. Jack didn't say anything. She stayed quiet, too. This was a messed up situation. That's all there was to it. Really, really messed up.

The gate at Golden Hearts was closed. Jack pressed the buzzer. No one answered. He buzzed again. Holly pulled out Leann's card and called the numbers. Both times she got voice mail. She shook her head. "Dammit! I know this is our guy, Jack. I know it. We have to find him, and Leann is our best source."

He nodded. "I agree. Call back again. If she doesn't answer, leave a message, let her know it's important."

Holly did and left the message Jack suggested.

"She'll call back," he said.

"What do we do now?" Holly asked.

"I say we go back to the room and wait for her to call."

CHAPTER
60

O'Leary had paced in his room for some time. He'd been hurt and now he was getting angry. He couldn't focus on his writing. For a minute he thought about having a drink but knew that was stupid. No matter what, he wanted to stay clean.

Why in the hell would the bug tell Elena such a lie?

O'Leary changed his shirt and headed out the door. He was going to find the bug himself and ask her.

He searched the grounds and finally found her in the restaurant eating with a few of the other bugs. O'Leary pulled up a chair. He looked at the three other riders and said, "Get lost." They scrambled to get up, and O'Leary focused his stare on the girl. "Natalie…it's Natalie, right?" She nodded. "We need to talk."

Natalie's face paled, and the other kids took off. O'Leary knew that even as a small man he had a certain air of intimidation about him. Back in the day, a few people teased him about his Napoleon complex.

"What do you want?" Natalie asked, pushing strands of red hair back behind her ears.

"The truth. Why would you tell Elena Purdue that I was trying to take the ride away from Perez and that I was using her?"

She shook her head. "I don't know what you're talking about."

O'Leary slammed his fist on the table, hard. Natalie jumped. A few people turned and looked. "Bullshit. Perez that good in bed, bug? Is he? Or did he pay you to say those things?"

Natalie stared at him.

"You know, everyone thinks Juan Perez is the man. But he's a slimeball and a snake and eventually, dear girl, he will turn on you, too."

"He's going to win the race," she said.

"I don't care what he's going to do. What I want *you* to do is tell the truth. Take it from me, if you don't, no matter how much that guy promised you, your conscience will eat away at you. You seem like a good girl. Do the right thing. Tell the truth. Eventually Perez is going to drop you. Maybe you'll have a few extra bucks, but not for long. And if I am right, and Perez goes down, you'll go with him. The truth always comes out. You can shed light on it today. Or, you can wait for it to come back and bite you in the ass."

Natalie looked scared to death. O'Leary got up and left her alone, hoping the bug did the right thing.

CHAPTER

61

"Tell me about her," Jack said. He picked up the bottle of red wine he'd ordered from room service. They had spent nearly twenty-four hours together at this point, and Holly had not brought up their daughter. She had been waiting for him to do so. She had tried calling Leann again but still got no answer. The day had worn on, and they mostly talked about the case. They tiptoed around the elephant in the room—their relationship.

Holly held up her hand. "I'm on duty." Jack still poured the wine.

He'd ordered up crab cakes, obviously remembering that the dish was a favorite of hers. He'd also had salads and the specialty for the evening—filet mignon—brought up. She never remembered them eating this well on their two-cop salaries. She thought about his question and then took a sip of wine. Her nerves were on edge. "Chloe?"

He nodded.

"She's smart, funny, sweet, precocious."

He laughed. "She gets that from you. I know she's beautiful like you, too." He held up his glass.

Holly shook her head. "She has your eyes. She likes to play the piano and read. She's a little shy, but comes out of her shell when she's around people she knows. Her best friend is Maddie." Holly took another sip.

"Brendan's little one."

She sat back in the chair and stared at him for several seconds, her heart pounding hard against her chest. "How much do you know about us?" she asked.

"Enough," he replied. "I needed to know he was a good guy."

"He is. Very much so. The best." Again that clenching, tight feeling settled in her throat, making her feel as if she was suffocating.

"Are you happy?" he asked.

She set down the glass. "Yes. I am happy. We have a good life together. He is very good to me. To us. He understands me. He loves me. Brendan is a sweet, honest, funny, hardworking man." She looked away.

Jack didn't say anything. He took a sip from his wine.

"Are you happy?" she asked.

"Wow. Uh…" He gazed at her, setting the wineglass down. "No. I'm not. I haven't been happy since I had to leave you."

Holly didn't know what to say. "What about love? What about the woman you were with the other night?"

"She works with me."

"She's beautiful."

"She is. Competent. Dedicated."

Holly nodded. "There must have been women, or a woman?"

"I'm a man. I am human. I have needs. Yes. I have been with other women. But no one I love. I haven't loved anyone since you."

"I don't know if I should believe you," she said.

"I never thought I'd see you again, Holly. Not up close. As far as you were concerned, I was dead."

"You still are," she replied, hating the hurt she saw in his eyes. "I have someone else now. I have someone who loves me, who would never choose his career over me." She felt on the verge of tears.

He stood, pulled her up from the chair and nudged her into the wall, holding her arms above her. "I chose your *life*, Holly. I chose yours and Chloe's lives! You! I did choose you!" A small cry escaped his lips.

"What are you doing?" she felt the heat rise from her gut into her face, but it wasn't just angry heat.

"I've missed you," he whispered in her ear. He kissed her neck. "I love you, Holly. I've never stopped loving you." He held her gaze for a loaded moment then kissed her hard on her lips. She started to resist. His kiss grew heated. She let herself fall into it.

His hands began to wander over her body. He pulled away and looked at her, his eyes telegraphing his intense arousal. She felt it, too.

His hands grazed her face. He ran a finger over her lips. Her mind screamed, *No! This is wrong!* Her body told her different.

This was her husband. How could it be wrong? Jack was her husband.

Then her conscience kicked in to remind her that he *had been* her husband. To her and to the world, Jack was dead.

But he wasn't dead. He was right here, running his hands over her skin, brushing his lips against hers, setting her on fire with his touch…his words of love that had never died echoing in her ears. Her heart raced as her body warmed.

His fingers moved down to her blouse as he continued to kiss her with years of pent-up urgency. She let her ache for him drown out all of the voices in her head that were telling her that this would be too complicated and allowed every carnal feeling in her body to take over. She kissed him, unrestrained, holding nothing back. All the years she'd mourned him, all the emotions, everything escaped her as Holly found herself somewhere between hell and nirvana.

God he smelled good, the way he always had. Musk, spice, clean. Jack. "Jack, Jack," she breathed.

He lifted her up and carried her to the bed, laying her down and quickly unbuttoning her pants. He turned her over and kissed her down her entire body. She heard the echoes of pleasure escape from her lips, but they sounded distant as if they belonged to someone else. Maybe they did. They belonged to who she was ten years earlier—the woman married to this man.

Jack's hands all over her were strong but gentle, and again memories flooded her. Memories of what it had been like to be with him—all of the intense, heated passion they had shared.

He caressed, stroked, and kissed her everywhere. In that moment, Holly forgot every other being, thought, feeling she'd ever had. There was only Jack and her and the life they had once known together. As they made love, neither had to tell the other what they felt. Easily moving into a familiar rhythm, it was obvious after ten years of being separated, of lies keeping them apart, of different lives created, that the love they'd once shared had not been lost.

CHAPTER

62

"Are you okay?" Jack asked.

"I don't know," Holly replied. They had been quiet for several long intense moments after they'd brought one another to sheer ecstasy. The tears she had held back flowed freely now. Guilt crept in and consumed her. *Brendan.*

"Holly, what just happened proves our love is still there. Here."

She nodded. "But, it isn't just about you or me...us...any longer." She stood and started to dress. He reached for her hand and she pulled it away. "I can't. I can't hurt him. I can't do this to Chloe, who only knows Brendan as a father. I can't do this to Megan and Maddie. There is so much you don't understand. So much at risk now. I can't do it."

"What about you? Can you live a lie?"

"My love for Brendan isn't a lie. It is not. What this was..." She motioned to the bed and then pointed at him. "What this was for me was closure. That's all."

"That didn't feel like closure, Holly."

She didn't know what to say. Before she could form her next thought, she was interrupted by the ringing of her cell phone. Her stomach plummeted. She grabbed her phone off the table. "Hello."

"Detective Jennings?"

"Yes."

"It's Leann Purdue. I'm sorry. I just got your messages. I just got in. My cell phone needed to be charged. I'm glad you called. I think I need to speak with you. I think you should come to my place."

Holly clicked off the phone, looked at Jack and said, "Leann Purdue is home. Let's go. We are done here." She finished dressing and grabbed her purse without another word. Jack followed her, not speaking either.

CHAPTER

63

They were both silent on the drive to Leann's, until Jack spoke her name.

"No. Don't talk. Not now. Please," she said.

He didn't.

It was nearing ten o'clock, and she was tired and disgusted with herself. A mixture of confusion swept through her brain, her heart, her soul. What had she just done? She hated herself. She had not thought at all. How selfish and stupid. Then she glanced over at Jack, and some of the emotion from only an hour earlier rushed back. He was still her husband, and every moment they had shared in that hotel suite had been passionate, loving, and unencumbered. But now, rationality and reality set in, and yes...she hated herself. Unequivocally.

She had to admit that she was happy to see the lights on in Leann's house. Leann opened the front door as soon as they walked up, looking surprised to see Holly there with a man. Holly wasn't sure what to say at first. They hadn't talked about how they would handle the investigation together.

Jack took over. "Good evening, Ms. Purdue. My name is Mack Twinnings."

He lied with ease. He didn't even blink. Holly flinched ever so slightly. He eyed her.

"I'm with the FBI, ma'am, and we are helping Detective Jennings with this case."

"The FBI?" Leann took a step back, her face paled. "Goodness."

He smiled and Holly could see Leann warm up a bit. Jack had always had that way with women. "Please come in. Can I get you some tea, coffee?"

They both shook their heads. "You said that you wanted to tell me something," Holly said. She wanted to see what Leann might have for them before she started the questioning.

She nodded and tears sprang to her eyes. "It's Dan. My fiancé."

Holly glanced at Jack. "What about him?"

"I don't know. I think he's in some kind of trouble. He's been lying to me. He said he'd gone down to Colorado to pick up some horses the other day. But he came home with an empty trailer. He said that the people were gone and that there were no horses there. I got a call this morning from a guy out there who asked why he hadn't come and gotten those animals. I tried getting ahold of Dan, but he isn't answering. I went to get those horses myself. I just got back, got them all unloaded, and I was in his office looking for some bute, which is an anti-inflammatory, for one of the horses who is badly arthritic. I didn't mean to pry. I don't usually go in there. I keep meds in the house but I am out of bute. Dan is…he's private about his things and his space. He had an abusive mother, and she was always getting into his things. So, when he moved in here with me, I gave him his own office and told him that was his space and I wouldn't ever bother it."

"What did you find?" Holly asked.

Leann went to the kitchen counter and brought back a pile of newspaper articles. They were stories about the murders. "I think maybe I can't get ahold of him because he is seeking justice for these deaths. He was really upset when the jockeys were murdered, and although we knew Marvin Tieg and thought he was a jerk, Dan has a real good side to him. Maybe this is what he's up to."

Jack crossed his arms. "Has your fiancé acted strangely before? Is it odd that he would have those clippings?"

Leann's hand trembled, and the newspaper articles fluttered. "No. He's a good man."

"How long have you known Dan?" Holly asked.

"About nine months."

"Where did you meet?"

She smiled weakly. "He actually came here saying he wanted to volunteer. He wanted to help with the horses. He had some background in working with horses out in Texas, where he's from, and so I agreed. I need all the help I can get. Especially volunteer."

"Well, how did he make a living?" Jack asked.

"Danny is a simple guy. Probably why we get along so well. Neither of us needs much. He had some money from his father who passed away a couple of years ago."

Holly nodded. "Why do you think Dan isn't answering his phone?"

Leann gave a halfhearted shrug. "As I said. He might be off trying to be a vigilante. Play superhero. He is a just man. But I think he could be in over his head."

"Is that what you really believe, Ms. Purdue?" Jack asked.

She looked confused and a little frightened. "I don't understand."

"Did you call us here because you think your fiancé is on a manhunt for a killer? Or did you call us here because you think that maybe he *is* a killer?"

Holly shot him a dirty look. Leann was a simple woman but she was kind, and she deserved a little more gentleness.

"What are you saying?" Leann asked.

"I think we'd better sit down," Holly said. "You need to hear what we have to say."

CHAPTER

64

Leann Purdue insisted that Holly and Jack were wrong about Dan, but she began to come around when Holly mentioned Equine Health Systems.

"They donate a lot of product to Golden Hearts. Mr. Christiansen is a wonderful man. He loves the horses. He came out here last year and brought product to us, brought his family. Told us if we were ever in San Diego to stop by and see his place. So when Dan went out there to pick up a couple of former racehorses, I told him he had to go by there. They toured the place and Scott gave him a bunch of product to bring home. He also brought me a dive suit. For our honeymoon. We're planning to go scuba diving in Fiji. He said there was a shop right next to Equine Health Systems and that he'd gotten a good deal."

Holly didn't know how to break this to her. She reached out and touched the woman's knee. Leann looked at her with a bit of confusion masked on her face. "What's going on?" Leann asked.

"Listen, this isn't, uh, easy. But, Leann, you know I've been investigating the murders of Tommy Lyons and Katarina Erickson, and now Marvin Tieg."

Lean nodded. "Yes. I know, but just tell me what is going on here, exactly."

"We have some information that has come to light about the murders." Holly shook her head, not wanting to spell it out for

Leann. "And I'm afraid that it's very possible that your fiancé is involved."

"No. No! That's not true." Leann jumped up. She went to the window and pulled back the drapes. She stood still, her back to Holly, gazing outside.

"Leann, the jockeys Katarina Erickson and Tommy Lyons were found murdered in the back of that dive shop," Jack said. "I'm sorry, but we think that your fiancé could be connected to those murders."

"What?"

Holly nodded. "We think that there is a possibility that Dan is lying about who he is."

"What? This makes no sense! You're wrong!"

Holly stood and went to the window. "Can you tell me if Dan has any scars? Anything indicating he may have had surgery, or even been burned at one time?"

Tears welled in Leann's eyes. She crossed her arms and frowned, nodding her head and sucking back a sob. "His hands. He burned them in boiling water as a child, and he has a scar on his face…" She tried to muster a smile as if recalling the story he had told her. "From a barroom fight when he was, you know, only twenty-something."

Holly placed a hand on Leann's shoulder. "I'm afraid he has been lying to you. We think he fabricated all of that. A history, stories…lies…he told you whatever he had to so you could provide his cover."

"I really don't understand."

"We believe that your fiancé is really Ted Ivy," Jack said.

"No. No! The groom? From the fire? Tieg, Laugherty…that fire? That can't be. Ted Ivy is still in prison. See! That's not possible." Leann was visibly shaken. "It just could not be him. I think you need to go now."

"We've checked. Ted Ivy has been out of prison for two years. We believe he had extensive plastic surgery and is getting his revenge on the people who sent him to jail."

Leann brought her hands to her face, visibly shaken. "Why? Why would he do this, and why would he get engaged to me?"

"To blend in. To get back into this culture," Jack said. "You are a good alibi, but we think there is something even bigger going on with him. We need to see his office, and I need a current photo of him."

She nodded. Holly felt for her. The poor woman. She went back into the family room and took the photo that Holly had seen of the two of them the other day. "This is the most recent picture. We took it the day we got engaged. Follow me."

They followed her out to the barn. The office she led them to appeared to have been broken into. Leann looked ashamed. "I had to break in. I jimmied the lock. Dan has the keys. But I couldn't let that horse suffer and it was too late to call the vet."

Holly doubted her story, as Jack already had. A facility like this would have medicines readily available, and not in the one office that was kept locked up tighter than a drum. "Leann, did you break in because you needed meds for the horse, or because you had your own questions about your fiancé?"

Leann didn't reply. She just sobbed and looked down.

Holly's cell rang. Amar. "Holly, Jim Gershon was found murdered. In Saratoga. Looks like he was killed last night by our guy. Carrot, blowtorch. The whole deal."

"Oh my God," Holly replied.

"I got word that the feds are on this now," Amar said.

"Hold tight, Detective. I have some information, too. I'll be in touch soon. I'm looking into something right now."

Holly hung up the phone. "He struck again. He killed Jim Gershon in Saratoga last night."

CHAPTER
65

O'Leary spotted Perez before he had a chance to think. Edwin Hodges, the host of this shindig, had invited anyone and everyone to his pre-race party—including O'Leary.

People were dressed to the nines, and champagne flowed.

Perez stood over by one of the bars laughing it up with none other than Geremiah Laugherty. Now *that* was interesting.

Perez's eyes widened as he spotted O'Leary. O'Leary shoved him as hard as he could. Laugherty stepped back, shocked.

"What the fuck?" Perez yelled.

"What the fuck? What the fuck! I'll tell you what the fuck, Perez! You fucker! Why would you tell Elena that the only reason I'm with her is to get the ride on the filly?"

Music played on with people out on the dance floor, but a few had noticed the brewing situation and stopped to watch and listen.

Perez started laughing. He blew his chest out. "Cuz it's true, bro. Everyone knows your digging that because you want my horse. No way, man. Not gonna happen! Not taking my ride!"

O'Leary had had enough. He pulled his right arm back and clocked Perez in the face. Perez grabbed his nose as blood spurted everywhere.

"Hey, man!" Laugherty grabbed onto O'Leary.

O'Leary pulled out of the man's hold. The group of onlookers stood stunned by the explosion between the jockeys.

"Pete!" It was Elena running toward them.

"The nose is for her." He pointed at Elena. "Don't ever disrespect her again, you fucker!"

Perez spat at him. "I will get even," he growled.

"Go ahead. Just try it. I'd love to have another chance at you. And this time it'll be for me. I'm not an underhanded piece of shit like you are." O'Leary looked at Laugherty. "And for that matter, like you!" he yelled. "You're both crooked as hell, and everyone knows it. You just got lucky that Elena has a good heart and doesn't believe gossip. But I know. I know for a fact that the two of you are crooked motherfuckers who will do anything and everything to win a race, and one day...*one day*...it's all going to come out. It will all come undone for you. So enjoy the limelight while you have it." O'Leary turned and took two steps away.

"Hey, Pete. Watch your back," Laugherty said.

"With guys like you around, I am always watching my back, *Geremiah*. Maybe you should do the same."

Pete O'Leary left the party with a smile on his face. He might not have been riding in the Infinity, he might have lost his girl, but he wasn't going down without a fight, or without exposing a couple of snakes in the grass.

CHAPTER

66

"Pete! Pete!" Elena called from behind him. O'Leary was headed in the direction of his room. "Please stop! Please!"

O'Leary finally stopped. His head down, he turned to her. He looked as if he needed to cool off.

"Look at me," Elena said.

"I'm sorry, El, but I had to do that. Perez is a liar, and if you want him on Karma that's up to you. I told you that there is no way in hell I was trying to take the ride from Perez. I told you that he was full of shit. But you chose not to believe me."

"I'm sorry, Pete. I was wrong. Natalie just came to see me. She told me the truth. Perez promised her a big chunk of money if she lied to me about overhearing you. He also threatened her, told her he would fix it so she wouldn't ride on the track again if she didn't do as he asked."

"You believe me now." He shook his head.

She didn't respond.

"Funny, your first impulse was to believe Perez and the bug over me. Perez is the guy who wants to screw you over. Wait, he doesn't just want to screw you over, he wants to keep screwing you!"

She took a step back.

"Yeah, that's right. Mr. Ego-Slash-Testosterone back there only wants in your pants. He don't care about your horse. He don't even care so much about the money. He cares about what you have between your legs! And that you could be a real nice meal ticket for him. You don't think jocks talk shit? They talk, and I know you slept with him."

Elena felt the tears sting her eyes. "That was before us."

"I don't care. One thing I would not do is lie to you."

She straightened herself up to her full five feet. "Really? Because you lied to me before. And I'm supposed to believe you've changed just because you wine me and dine me, and say a couple of pretty things?"

O'Leary shook his head. "Believe what you want, El. I'm a different guy now. I suggest you go nurse your jock."

O'Leary spun around and headed to his room, leaving Elena shocked, hurt, and knowing that he had told her the truth. He hadn't lied to her about a damn thing.

She walked inside to where Perez now sat at a table, an ice pack on his nose. Laugherty handed him a towel. "Hey, man, I'll see about getting a medic over here, make sure that thing isn't broken."

Perez nodded. He spotted Elena. "I am so sorry, Elena. I am terribly sorry you saw all of that."

"Shut up, Juan. You're fired."

"What? You can't fire me! We have a race! We have *the race* to run tomorrow! Calm down! You can't fire me!"

She turned on her heels and yelled back, "I can. And I just did."

CHAPTER

67

It was nearing seven in the morning. They hadn't slept at all and were running on the coffee and the food that Leann had supplied the night before. Holly had interviewed Leann, asking her every minute detail about her relationship with the man she knew as Dan Creswell, the guy that both Holly and Jack were convinced was Ted Ivy. She had also gone through the files in Ivy's office, the couple's bedroom, anything that might possibly give them insights into Ivy and where he might be at the moment. Leann tried calling him a couple of times and leaving messages. He didn't answer.

Jack spent his time going through the man's computer and working on cracking passwords. "Is this Dan's only computer?" he asked Leann.

"No. He also has a laptop. It isn't here."

Jack frowned. "What I might be looking for, and I am not even sure what that is exactly, could be on that laptop only. But I might find something here." He had been able to get through to the banking information. Holly didn't know how he did it, and she didn't ask. They could see that several deposits had been made into a private account in the Cayman Islands under the name of Dan Creswell. "At least there's a money trail here. That's something," Jack said.

An hour later, just as Holly was feeling as if this was a wild goose chase, Jack exclaimed, "Oh bingo! Damn!"

"What?" She looked over his shoulder.

"I'm into his private e-mails. The correspondence is with someone going by the initials of BQ. I'm guessing he wasn't real smart about this. He's been using both the laptop and the desktop to access e-mails. I doubt this guy—this BQ who, from what I'm reading here, orchestrated everything—would be thrilled that he did this." Jack shook his head and let out a sarcastic chuckle. "Guess you should be real careful who you hire to do your dirty work." Jack's expression changed abruptly. "Hang on. These e-mails from BQ detail a lot of stuff…" Jack grew quiet. "Oh no."

"What is it?"

"I think I've got it. BQ is planning on having Ivy assassinate the sheikh at Infinity."

"He's giving orders like that over e-mail?" she asked.

"Not explicitly, no. But there are directions here telling Ivy that a plane would be waiting in New York to take him to Vegas. This is from a night ago, the night Gershon was murdered. From these other details, I'm positive that this guy has set Ivy up to take out the sheikh. BQ is a bigwig and a master manipulator. I have a feeling about him, Holly. I have a feeling I know exactly who he is. And if I'm right, he made one big mistake here." He took a deep breath and met Holly's gaze. "And if this guy is who I think he is, he's trying to set up the beginning of the end. Listen, I'll explain in flight. We have to get out to Las Vegas."

CHAPTER

68

Twenty calls. Twenty calls, and O'Leary hadn't answered Elena. It was close to midnight. She finally sent a text: *I am only going to try one last time. Please answer. I am sorry.*

He sighed.

His phone rang.

On the third ring, he picked up. "Yes, El."

"Listen, Pete, I'm sorry. I am. I should have trusted you, I know that. I know that now, and if you were here…" She was crying. "If you were here, I'd throw my goddamned arms around you and show you how sorry I am. I love you, O'Leary. I never stopped loving you, and I should have listened to you."

O'Leary didn't say anything for a few seconds. Then finally he said, "I love you, too, El."

She gasped and sucked back a sob. "Will you do it then?"

"What?"

"You know what."

"I know. But I want to hear you ask me. I want to hear you say the words. Don't you think you owe me that much?"

"Yes. I think I do." She sighed. "Will you ride my girl tomorrow?"

"I think you know the answer," he replied.

"But I want to hear you say it." She laughed.

He laughed with her. "Yes. Yes, El, I will ride Karma to the finish line."

"One more thing."

"Okay," he said. "What's that?"

"Will you come over? Come to my room?"

"I'll be there in five."

CHAPTER
69

Holly and Jack had boarded a chartered jet at ten-thirty that morning. They would be landing in Vegas at eleven Pacific time. They had photos of Ivy. They still did not have an ID on BQ, though Jack had his suspicions. Jack had people on his end trying to break the IP address that the e-mails had been sent from. So far they'd had no luck.

Jack was on the phone with another agent. "Listen to me, Paul. This is him. This is Darren Bradley. I know it. It reeks of him. Get me what you can." He hung up the phone.

"Who is Darren Bradley, and why do you think he's BQ?" Holly asked.

"Darren Bradley worked for the government, the same agency that I work for. He's the one who was in charge of getting me out of the warehouse ten years ago. He brought me into this. Technically he saved my life and yours. But Bradley is a loose cannon. He holds extremist views of what the world should look like. As I worked closer with him, I learned that he didn't have limits. He's one of those guys who think that the end justifies the means. He did some horrendous stuff while we were in Afghanistan. Ultimately he was let go from the agency, and I helped send him on his way. I knew we could have a problem with him out in the world on his own.

"I told the people I work for that he needed to be watched. They didn't pay attention, and he wasn't watched closely enough.

He fell off the radar. My radar, too. This is a guy with some means. He took a lot of money from the Taliban. Money that he stole from them, which I guess I can't really fault him for. But the point is that this guy has connections and vast sums of cash. Plus he is a genius and he knows how to utilize his brains. He used to spout apocalyptic shit to me all the time—part of the reason I know he's dangerous. But he made a mistake."

Holly's mind began ticking at the apocalypse reference. "What?"

Jack shook his head. "Proves none of us are infallible. I did not find one e-mail instructing Ivy to delete all the other e-mails. They used encrypted addresses, but nothing is foolproof. Maybe Ivy was instructed to delete by a direct communication, but he decided not to. He was likely given the laptop by Bradley and told to e-mail only from that machine. Ivy isn't all that sophisticated, from what we know. Maybe the fall guy isn't as vulnerable as his boss is hoping for, or maybe he's dumber than his boss assumed."

"Why? I mean, what is this all about?" Holly asked. "Why does this Darren Bradley want to take out the sheikh?"

"Bradley is the one who brought us the original intel that the sheikh's son, Muhammad Farooq, was working to supply money to the Taliban. He implied that the sheikh was somehow involved, but he had no real evidence. We couldn't accept Bradley's gut feelings as actionable intel. Sheikh Farooq helps maintain peace. We couldn't just go in with guns blazing on a man who has helped create policy and who has done some very good things for the world. Bradley being who he was, he felt like we blew him off. I think he's taken it into his own hands."

"You really think he plans to kill the sheikh?"

"Probably. Yes."

"How does Ted Ivy fit with Bradley? How do they know one another?"

"I'm not sure. I'd bet that Bradley got Ivy out of jail. He's a patient man. I've gone over the Ted Ivy story. This guy was framed. Plus he got burned in that fire, and I learned that an inmate tried to take him out while he was in prison. Cut his face."

"We found an IM exchange between Tieg and someone in the prison about that. It mentioned that he'd been brutalized in prison. Tieg tried to have him killed," Holly said.

"Yeah. I think Bradley bought Ted Ivy, an innocent man, who I believe was coerced into a confession on the arson because Tieg and his associates had the cash to make that happen. Bradley purchased Ivy a new face and a new identity, and I think he's using him to kill. And his endgame may be for Ivy to kill the sheikh. Bradley was an expert target sniper. I mean, this guy could have taken out a fly from a hundred yards away. My guess is,—since he and Ivy have been planning this thing *together* for some time—Bradley schooled Ivy in sniper techniques."

Holly shook her head. She felt as if there was something more. Something they were missing. "Why have Ivy murder others, then? Why the jockeys, especially?"

"Tommy and Katarina were exactly what the note said—sacrificial lambs," Jack said. "They were meant to throw off the police just enough to buy Bradley time. He's framing this guy to take the fall. The notes that led your partner, Chad, to the Carpenters' song and then the movie trilogy about the end of the world, that was for real for Bradley. It wasn't as subtle as it appeared. Bradley knew that he needed to make Ivy look Unabomber crazy. If a peacemaker from the Middle East who spends a good share of his time in the United States is assassinated, imagine what that would create around the world."

"It'd cause chaos."

"Bradley likely believes that it will cause more than chaos. He's hoping it heats up tensions, and he's also hoping to further the war and have the country get behind it."

"What does he get out of this?" Holly asked.

Jack shrugged. "Ego, power, who knows? A sociopath like Bradley may think he's going to run the world. He actually said that to me one day. A few days before…"

"Before what?"

"I can't talk about it. It's too hard. All I can tell you is that he claimed the world would be a better place under one world leader and that he aimed to make it happen. That he planned to be that leader. I thought he was joking. Now I'm not so sure, Holly. I think he meant it, and I think he believes it. If he causes destruction, or causes harm to anyone, I'll never live this down. I should have been more emphatic with my people about what I thought this guy could become." He shook his head and looked out the window.

"Do you think Bradley has Ivy set up so that can we find him *after* he assassinates the sheikh?"

"I think that yes, he wants us to get Ivy quickly. He'll want Ivy to tell his story. Ivy is the perfect patsy to commit these crimes, from Bradley's perspective. If I were Bradley, my thought process would have been like this: Ivy loses his wife on September eleventh, so he's looking to blame someone. He's also going after the guys who sent him to prison. Bradley is banking on the fact that Ivy looks like a guy who's gone rogue, whose rage is just escalation, and who is going to further piss off the Middle East by his action. Maybe start a larger war. Being that the sheikh is a big deal in both parts of the world, it's not a leap to expect people to believe that Ivy would take him in a misguided revenge plot."

Holly shook her head. "When I thought that Ivy was still in jail, I had this strange idea of him being like Hannibal Lecter, and I wondered who his Buffalo Bill was. Ironic. It was the other way around. Ivy is Bradley's Buffalo Bill. How do you think they planned to get past all of the security?" Then it hit her. "Oh my God."

"What?" Jack asked.

"Bradley Systems. Edwin Hodges mentioned the security system in his home was the best. I noticed the name on the alarm panel
in his house. The logo was shaped like a Q. And there's something
else. Oh my God. I missed it. Can I get cell reception up here?"

"You may be able to get through, but you'll probably have better luck with a text."

She looked at her watch. It would be nine at home. She took
the chance at sending the text, hoping Amar would get it. She
recalled a name with Bradley in it when she scanned the investor
list Hodges had handed her, which she'd then given to Amar to
follow up. She knew that was probably a low priority for Amar, as
the case had escalated since then, and he'd been looking into PAAC
and Gershon. Who would have thought that anyone who invested
in the track would be orchestrating these killings? She furiously
typed out a text: *Is there anyone on the investor list with the name
Bradley in it?*

About ten minutes later, Amar responded. *Yes. A Bradley
Quentin.*

"BQ!" She looked at Jack. "Bradley Quentin builds security
systems and he invested in the Infinity."

Jack shook his head. "He used his last name for his first name,
invested in the Infinity. What a brilliant son of a bitch. Think of
it—he's out in the open, playing the role of financier and security
planner. How would anyone in the world ever suspect that this guy
would be gunning to kill Farooq?"

"We have to stop him," Holly said.

"We will." Jack dialed a number on his cell.

Holly held up crossed fingers.

A few seconds later, Jack gave her the thumbs up, indicating
he had reached his contact. "Paul, can you hear me okay? Good. I
think we have an ID on our man. He goes under the name Bradley

Quentin now. Wealthy investor who...get this...owns a security systems company. I'm sure of it. Look him up. Get all you can. I have a feeling, Paul. I do." He hung up the phone. "There will be a ground team meeting us at the airport, and I'm certain that agents are working on this already. We will find Bradley and Ivy. We'll do it together." He stood and went to the back of the plane, where he opened up a closet and took out a carry-on bag. He came back, unzipped it. He pulled out a Glock 22. "I know you're comfortable with the nine, but if you need to take someone out...this will get the job done."

She nodded. "Okay."

"We're a good team, Holly. We always were."

The plane touched down at McCarran International and was directed into a private hangar. Jack's words of partnership echoed in Holly's mind and hung between them.

CHAPTER
70

Three other agents met them when they landed at the airport. Jack had informed her they had come in from Los Angeles. One was the woman Holly had seen Jack with at the restaurant in Lexington. Young, long dark hair, bright brown eyes, porcelain complexion. Her name was Samantha, but Jack called her Sam. The other two were introduced to Holly by their first names only—Paul and Alex.

Paul was the older of the two men. As they sat in the back of the car on their way to the track, he opened a file and handed them each photos of Bradley Quentin, formerly known as Darren Bradley. "We went to work on this as soon as we got your call, Jack. This guy is a big deal, so I sure in hell hope you're right about this."

"I'm positive it's him. I know damn well and so do you that Bradley always had a major hard-on about taking down the Middle East at all costs. On top of that, he's crazy. He is truly fucking crazy. I knew this guy. I worked side by side with him, and his Armageddon rhetoric in those last days he worked for us was almost all he could talk about."

Holly looked at Jack, knowing exactly what he was feeling, and if this had been ten years earlier, she would have taken his hand and reassured him that he was right.

Paul did the reassuring now. "That's why we're here, Jack. You're good at what you do. Samantha, Alex, and Holly will need to start searching the grounds immediately and see if they can find

Ted Ivy. He won't be in the open. He's going to be high up some-where. You believe that Bradley trained Ivy in sniper techniques?"

Jack shrugged. "He was the best. That would be his MO."

"We have a map here of the most likely places that would offer a direct shot at Farooq once he's in his seat. We already have other agents sweeping the area," Alex said. "There's a chance that Ivy could be on low ground and that's why we thought the three of us should be on ground level searching for him."

Holly couldn't help but notice how young the man was. Strong, attractive, but he couldn't have been over twenty-five. Who were these guys? What agency did they work for within the government?

They pulled up to the rear of the grandstand. It was a little after eleven and the race was set to go off at one. "Listen, we have had to be real careful with this," Paul said. "If Bradley guesses that we're here, we'll never get him. He'll run. Our guys have kept a low profile this morning."

"How?" Holly asked. "How do you keep a low profile in a situation like this?"

Jack looked at her. "It's what we do best."

Point taken.

"Everyone have their weapons?" Paul asked.

Holly nodded. The Glock was tucked in her holster. Everyone else said they were prepared.

"If you spot Ivy, call for backup," Jack said. He showed Ivy's photo to the others.

Two men in suits waited as they parked. "We good?" Jack asked as they got out.

The men nodded, and one of them handed out badges that passed for security. "We have you cleared as extra security under the cover story that there may have been a breach in the barns. We've been able to build a story that one of the horses may have been targeted by someone looking to cause the animal harm. We can take you through the back gates. There are men stationed at high points four, seven, eleven, and fourteen." These were the locations that provided a direct line of fire to the sheikh.

Everyone started heading toward the gates to the back entrance. "Holly..." Jack grabbed her arm. "Wait. Just a minute."

She stopped. "We have a job to do."

"Listen to me, please. I meant what I said. Can't we try this? Try to be a family?"

What she wouldn't have given only a couple of years ago to have this chance. "I can't, Jack. I meant what I said, too. I love someone else now."

"But you love me, too. What happened between us, that was not just sex. It was not even closure, Holly. I love you, and you love me."

"Of course I do!" She shook her head. "But I have a family with Brendan. I love him. I love his girls. They are my girls now, too, and Chloe...they are the only family besides me that she has ever known. I can't change their lives because you decided that it's time to *live* again, and because we are...we are..." She sighed. "I just can't."

She turned and walked through the gates of the grandstand, knowing that what she had wanted to say was that they were perfect together. They always had been.

CHAPTER

71

The day of the race had arrived. The last day that Farooq would know life as it was. But he had a plan, and it had to be done. His conscience could no longer allow him to live this way. But before, he would allow himself one last joy. He would see his colt to the winner's circle.

As he always did, the sheikh went to have "a talk" with Whiskey. Laugherty was there, but his jockey was not. Farooq recognized the jockey standing there and shot Laugherty a look. "What is this? Where is Mike?" he asked, referring to Whiskey's jock—one of the best in the world, if not the best.

"Sick. Real sick," Laugherty replied.

Farooq frowned. "I don't like this."

Juan Perez walked up to him. "Sir, you know my record. I like your colt, we've been talking. I think he likes me, too." He laughed.

"You don't ride my colt!" Farooq shot back. "Pull him from the race," he said to Laugherty.

"What?"

"I said pull Whiskey from the race. None of this feels right to me."

Laugherty shook his head. "Your Highness, this colt is meant to run this race. He is meant to win. He will win. Mr. Perez here is a very adept jockey. This horse is easily adaptable. I respect what you are asking me to do, and I'll follow your orders, but I sincerely feel that Whiskey is going to win this race, that he wants to run this race, and that your colt will go down in history."

Farooq looked at the men, weighing his options. He nodded. "Fine. Now leave me. Leave us."

Laugherty and Perez left as Farooq had asked.

The sheikh closed the stall door, his elegant, long robes hanging loosely around him. He placed a hand on the majestic animal's neck and rubbed him. He walked around to the rear of the horse, where he rubbed his hands over the lucky white stocking. The inflammation was not evident. He came around to the front and slipped a treat from his pocket into Whiskey's mouth. The colt's soft nose twitched over the sheikh's palm, making certain he got every last morsel of the treat.

The sheikh leaned his head against the horse's face, tears in his eyes, and said, "I am so sorry, so very sorry. Win this for us today. For you. Win because you can. Because you are the greatest of all horses." He backed away, breathed into the horse's nostrils and then took a deep breath in, as was their custom. He drank in the animal's soul and then stood back, looking into his warrior's eyes. This would be the last time he would ever again be this close to the horse. The deal had been made. When this was over, Whiskey would be going with Elena Purdue. It had to be this way, he reminded himself again. The world needed to know that his son was evil, and so was Naqeeb Waqqas. They needed to know what had happened to Wallid Waqqas, a man whom Farooq had loved desperately.

Everyone needed to know that Naqeeb had been using Farooq as a cover to wash dirty money from heroin. It was money used to grow poppies in Afghanistan. The poppies were turned into heroin to be sold on American streets, the profits of which were used to fund terrorist activity. Farooq had unwillingly played a major role in terrorism. He could no longer take part in such evil, and his life as he had known it would now be over.

He had just placed a call to the one man he thought could help him. He only knew this man by his first name—Jack—and knew that he worked for an American intelligence agency. He had spoken with Jack on a few occasions. The man had questioned him once about his son and about Naqeeb, but Farooq had covered for them. He was finished lying.

He sought comfort in the colt's eyes. But something seemed wrong. He rubbed his hand over the horse's face. "What is it, my boy?" Was he sad, anxious? There seemed to be something different in the eyes.

"Your Highness?" Laugherty stood outside the stall door. "We need to be getting ready."

Farooq sighed and looked again into Whiskey's eyes. Maybe it was nothing. It was his paranoia and angst about what would happen when the day was done. "I will miss you, my friend," he whispered as he left the colt's stall.

He looked back one last time as Laugherty slid a bit into the horse's mouth. He fought his emotions and headed to the grandstand.

CHAPTER

72

Holly was in awe as she entered through the gates. She also felt numb. Jack had gotten under her skin and was remaining there. She needed to focus on the job before her.

The grandstand grounds exuded a magical quality only present in places like Paris or, for a child, Disneyland. The gardens were pristine. The landscaping and architecture boasted roses in all shades of red, pink, yellow, and the greenery was lush; she could almost imagine being on a tropical island. Shrubbery was shaped into the forms of horses and jockeys. A large three-tiered waterfall gushed in the center of the paddock, where Holly knew that the horses would soon be paraded prior to the big race.

Large crowds milled about with their drinks in hand; laughter, energy, and a lot of chatter filled the air. High fashion was apparently the order of the day as many of the women were dressed to the nines in hats that would make the Queen of England proud, and the men wore jackets and ties.

Holly pulled herself together, knowing the clock was ticking. Making her way through a throng of people, she headed down a corridor and into the first section she was assigned to sweep. Even the more common area was plush. The leather seats reclined and were quite wide. Holly noticed control panels on their sides, and small tables in between them. From what she could tell, the control panel was used to buzz for food and drink service. Obviously no expense had been spared.

She looked out onto the beautiful red clay track, which contrasted with the green grass around the outside and inside. The infield boasted a crystal blue lake with swans floating on its surface. If this were any other day—a day when she could have been here in the seats, champagne in hand, her love at her side…But no, this wasn't like any other day. Somewhere out there, an assassin planned to take out one of the world's most influential peacemakers at the orders of a madman.

Holly continued searching. "Give me something. Dammit, anything," she said under her breath.

She continued on through the next several sections as people began taking their seats. This seemed impossible. She had not heard anything over the two-way radio. Doubt was setting in when her cell phone rang. She recognized a Lexington area code. "Detective Jennings, it's Leann Purdue."

"Yes, Leann?"

"I found a receipt in a pair of *his* pants pockets. It was from a costume store in town. He rented an EMT outfit."

"A paramedic. Thank you!" Holly hung up and called her team to tell them what she had learned.

Alex told her to wait while he checked something, then came back on. "Okay, Holly, there are four tunnels that lead onto the track. Two of them have a vet team with horse trailers ready to go in case there are injuries with the horses. The others have ambulances ready for jockeys. There are also three other ambulances stationed behind the barns."

"Oh shit. We don't have time to check them all out," she replied.

"Start with the tunnels." He gave her the locations. "I'm closest to the north side. You go the other way, then I'll head out to the barn area."

"If we find something, what do we do?"

"Call for backup. Do not try and take Ivy alone. If you do, Detective, you may wind up dead."

CHAPTER
73

As the horses had been led out to the starting gate, O'Leary dipped his fingers into his breeches pocket. The precious trinket was there. It was good luck. He rubbed the top of the great filly's mane and leaned in slightly over her neck, cooing to her. "It's all right, big girl. It's all right. We've got this, baby. Easy. Easy." She was emanating urgency and anxiety, and it was his job to bring her down and channel it in a way she understood—in a way that would encourage her to run her heart out.

Perez and the sheikh's colt reached the gate first. They had the position right next to O'Leary and Karma. "Oh yeah, you got this, huh, motherfucker?" Perez said.

"How did you get the ride away from the other jock, Perez? You got something on Laugherty?"

"Regular jock got real sick this morning."

"Huh. I bet he did."

Perez continued to heckle.

O'Leary ignored him. He wasn't about to let the jock's negativity take him down and transfer onto the filly.

"Sure, you got this, you old drunken asshole."

He was only trying to get under O'Leary's skin. O'Leary had stopped drinking. He had reasons to live again. Reasons other than booze. He wasn't going to let any of this get to him. He was going to run a good and honest race with Karma's Revenge.

CHAPTER
74

Quentin smiled at the senator from Nevada and held up his glass of champagne. "Great day for a race, eh, Senator."

"Indeed, Mr. Quentin. Indeed," the man replied.

And it truly was a glorious day for the big race. Not a cloud in the sky. No one in the Prestige Box seemed to have a care in the world. Before long, they truly wouldn't.

Quentin looked at his watch. In a little less than five minutes he would be down the elevators and headed to the limousine parked at the south gate. The car would be waiting to take him and his true partner to the airport.

He took a quick glance at her—his gorgeous partner. It was all so brilliant. Who would have ever thought?

She was the one who had helped him plan it all.

Ayda Farooq.

He sipped the champagne. Made niceties with the rich and famous and kept an eye on the clock as the countdown had begun. Their plans had only just begun—his and Ayda's.

Quentin almost couldn't believe that Ayda Farooq had become the love of his life. But she had. She had originally been a small part of his plan—a way to possibly discover her father's patterns, his contacts, anything he possibly could learn about Farooq.

Quentin had learned enough about Ayda before meeting her at an art gallery where an event for a close friend of hers was being held. He'd approached her as she studied a piece of art. "I know it's cheesy sounding, but this piece is not nearly as beautiful as you are," he'd said and pointed to the painting.

She didn't look at him at first, but he had noticed her glancing at him earlier in the evening as champagne was being passed around. "You are right. It is cheesy." She turned to him, her dark eyes flashing with a fire that Quentin recognized. It was a fire that motivated people to achieve. He knew he had it in his own eyes.

Three hours later they were in bed. A weekend together and Quentin had learned there was no love lost between father and daughter. Ayda felt her father had always chosen his horses over her and through his techniques, Quentin had fueled that belief. Funny—and fortunate for Quentin—that that kind of resentment born in childhood, along with the lack of attention from her *great* father, would in part cause the man's demise.

But it had. Ayda had been a willing participant. They had agreed that together they would build a new world. Leave the old one behind. Joque would take the fall. Empires would be destroyed, and Quentin, with his new queen at his side, would make the next moves in ruling a world gone awry.

"So who did you put your money on, Bradley?" It was the hideously egotistical Edwin Hodges. The ass slapped him on the shoulder.

"I'm going with Farooq's colt."

"Ah. Nice horse. But my money is on that filly, Karma's Revenge! What a great name. Well, looks like they're taking the ponies to the gate. Excuse me."

"Certainly," Quentin replied. He gave Ayda a nod of his head. It was time.

As he set down his empty glass and prepared to make his way to the door, his eyes followed Ayda's.

A . K . A L E X A N D E R

Two men.
Coming into the Prestige Box.
One of them Jack Jennings.

CHAPTER

75

Sheikh Mahfuz Farooq had been escorted to a private set of elevators that opened into a three-thousand-square-foot private box overlooking the track. At that same moment, the horses were on the track, making their way to the gate. The box was set apart from the rest of the grandstand, giving it the best view of the track. This was where all the high rollers were located. Everyone who was anyone—politicians, film stars, assorted billionaires—hobnobbed in the Infinity's Prestige Box.

Senators from California, Nevada, Washington, and New York were in attendance. Governors from Nevada, Arizona, and Colorado were also there. Edwin Hodges topped the billionaire list, and so did many of the investors and the horse owners in the box.

There was a bar, luxury seating, dining tables, big-screen TV monitors, and beautifully framed photos of each horse running, as well as photos of the jockeys and owners. No expense had been spared.

The couple hundred movers and shakers appeared to be enjoying themselves, and many of them greeted Farooq respectfully. However, none of the niceties could ease the knot in his stomach. He couldn't shake the feeling since he had left Whiskey—that feeling that something was not quite right. It was what Americans called the jitters. He told himself that it was because of what he planned to do after the race—tell the Americans what had been going on and how he had been involved.

For the first time in decades, Farooq walked to the bar. There were things that he wanted to do one last time. He knew that his colt, Whiskey Sour, was near the starting gate with the other contenders. He looked back for a moment as the television camera scanned his large chestnut boy, prancing, dancing, glistening, ready to run. "Whiskey sour, please." He nodded at the bartender who, if Farooq could have lived another life, a *true life*, one without shackles, Farooq would have admitted was attractive. He would have seduced the man and taken him home. Maybe Farooq could have fallen in love with the man. In another life. In a life where being homosexual would not bring shame upon him or his family.

It was insane that he had given in to Naqeeb's terrible demands throughout the years simply because he was afraid to live that truth. But he had no choice. Naqeeb had discovered the truth about Farooq and Wallid, Naqeeb's younger brother. Naqeeb had murdered his own brother for his transgressions and evil ways. He would not give Farooq the same kind of grace. He reminded him on a constant basis how their culture would perceive him. What their religion dictated. Farooq accepted all that Naqeeb Waqqas had told him, complied with all that he had instructed him to do in order to keep his family from shame. In order to remain alive. He had accepted that his status would have never allowed him to be who and what he was supposed to be. Who and what he really was.

In this life he had been bound by family, loyalty, religion, and the fear of shame and destroying all that he loved. He loved his wife and he most certainly loved his children, even the son so willing to join with others who were nothing but true evil.

Farooq had been held hostage and he was finished. The truth had to come out.

He searched for Ayda, who had texted him saying that she was already in the box. That was odd. He spotted her standing next to one of the other investors, Bradley Quentin, as two other men who looked intent and as if they didn't belong there at all approached.

Farooq began to head toward them when one of his bodyguards stopped him and whispered in his ear. The bodyguard had followed orders from his true master—Naqeeb Waqqas. "Laugherty has been drugging the horse with dermorphin to mask an injury. I had to tell you. Your colt has a tendon injury. He could die out there."

CHAPTER
76

Jack knew that Bradley had recognized him the moment he and Paul entered the Prestige Box. Bradley caught Jack's eye when he was only a few feet away. The man had done a good job changing his look. No longer a man with buzz-cut blond hair and blue eyes, he now had longer, darker hair, graying around the edges, and he obviously wore colored contacts that made his eyes brown. His cheekbones looked higher and more pronounced than Jack recalled; still, he had no doubt this was the man he'd known as Darren Bradley.

"Excuse me, gentlemen, this is a private affair," Bradley said.

"Darren, it's been a while," Jack replied.

"I...have no idea what you're talking about."

Paul held up a photo of Ivy. "Recognize this man?"

"No. What is this about?" Bradley asked.

Jack noticed Sheikh Farooq's daughter standing close by. He also took note that Bradley flashed her a quick look. Did Bradley know her?

The sheikh's daughter turned to walk away. Jack grabbed her by the arm. "Miss Farooq, do you know this man?" Jack asked.

"This is ridiculous! I demand to know who you are and what you want," Bradley said. "Let Miss Farooq go."

"No, I don't know him," she replied. "I've only met a few people here today."

Most of the people in the room had taken their seats to watch the race, only a few of them aware of the dustup.

"I think we should allow these people who have donated so generously the opportunity to watch the race in peace," Bradley said. "Let Miss Farooq go. Why don't we take the elevator down to a more private area? You obviously have something pressing you need to discuss with me."

The sheikh's daughter struggled to free herself from Jack's hold. "Let me go! We have to get out of here *now*," she pleaded, looking right at Bradley.

"Why, Miss Farooq? Why do you need to leave now?" Jack asked.

"I just find your questions of Mr. Quentin and me ridiculous." She turned as if looking to catch her father's attention.

She turned, but the sheikh was not looking at her. One of his personal bodyguards was whispering in his ear.

The sheikh suddenly bolted out the doors. As he did, Jack looked at Paul, and in that moment of inattention was caught off guard when Bradley shoved him hard onto the ground. Bradley grabbed the sheikh's daughter and ran for the entrance.

CHAPTER
77

Holly hurried down the corridor, her weapon drawn. She could hear cheering in the stands above her. She spotted a paramedic loitering around his ambulance. She knew it was Ivy and screamed his name. He turned toward her as he shut the rear ambulance doors.

Wild-eyed and confused, Ivy quickly looked from side to side.

Holding the gun on him, Holly yelled, "There's nowhere to hide, Ivy! You can stop this!"

He bolted around to the driver's side and climbed into the ambulance. Holly didn't want to fire. She didn't want to kill this man, not yet. If Jack and Paul weren't able to get to Bradley, bringing Ivy in alive might be the only way to find him.

She raced toward the ambulance. As she ran she took the walkie-talkie off her hip and shouted into it, "Ted Ivy is on the south side of the building in an ambulance. I'm going after him!"

She heard Alex's voice: "Stand down, Detective. Backup is on the way!"

She didn't respond. She continued running down the drive. The lights on the ambulance turned on and she knew that Ivy intended to head out onto the track. She surged forward to catch the handle on the back of the vehicle and grabbed hold. The doors swung open, and that's when she saw it. That was the moment that reality hit.

A bomb. Ivy wasn't only targeting the sheikh.

CHAPTER
78

Farooq did not think, did not ask questions, when his bodyguard had told him Whiskey had been drugged. His glass slid from his hands and crashed to the floor as he ran for a staircase, ignoring the elevator. The sheikh charged down the flight of stairs, running wildly toward the track, some of his other people trying to catch up. He screamed at the top of his lungs, "Stop the race!"

The tenth horse had been loaded into the starting gate. "Stop the race!" He continued running, his men unable to keep up. He knew what would happen if the race wasn't stopped. He knew now that he should have trusted his instinct when he looked into his horse's eyes. Whiskey had been masking pain in those eyes. He had tried to tell him.

"Stop the race!"

Bystanders got in the way, but the sheikh kept running.

The final horse was loaded into the gate. Tears streamed down Farooq's face. Gasping for breath, he paused on the sideline with spectators in fancy hats. The woman next to him smiled and held up her drink. He started to sob.

The gates opened.

The horses were off.

Waqqas's sniper had him in his crosshairs. But the sniper was not the only one following the sheikh's movements.

As Farooq stood watching and praying that nothing would happen to his most beloved possession out on the track, a woman dove at him and knocked him to the ground. The whine of a bullet whizzed by. Lying on the ground stunned, Farooq heard voices over a radio. "Sniper down. Repeat. Sniper down." The woman whispered in his ear. "Are you okay, Your Highness?"

"I think so," he replied breathlessly.

"Good, we need to move quickly. We need to get you to safety."

CHAPTER

79

Holly leaped inside the ambulance as Ivy sped out toward the track. Her head struck a side panel as he made the sharp right turn. *"Ivy!"* she shouted as she fell.

She struggled to pull herself back up. Out of breath, her mind desperate to determine the next move, she was tossed around again as Ivy picked up speed.

Ivy and Bradley didn't intend to just assassinate Sheikh Farooq.

They intended to kill more than one.

They intended to kill every mover and shaker in the Prestige Box.

Bradley planned to make a statement. His apocalyptic vision would begin right here at the Infinity.

She looked at the bomb in front of her, strapped securely to the gurney. She had no idea how to disengage an explosive device. None whatsoever.

But first things first. She had to take Ivy out.

"Ivy!" she screamed. *"Don't do this!"*

The ambulance slowed. "Fuck you, bitch! Do you know what they do to these animals? Look at all these goddamn people! They don't care!"

"I know what they do, Ted, but murder isn't the way to make it right. And this isn't about the horses for Bradley! He's setting you up! Stop!"

He accelerated again. The back doors to the ambulance swung wide and she could see in the distance that the horses were out of the starting gate. The timer on the bomb had started clicking down: three minutes left. Her mind raced at a clip as rapid as the hooves hitting the turf behind her. But she had no time to think rationally. What she had to do was think in terms of survival—and not necessarily her own.

Holly thrust her Glock through the small window between herself and Ivy. "You have one last chance to make this right."

"Fuck you!" he screamed again.

Holly aimed at the back of his head and fired. Blood and brains splattered everywhere. The ambulance slowed as Ivy died instantly.

She looked at the timer again: two minutes and fifteen seconds. With strength fueled by adrenaline she jumped from the rear doors even as the ambulance still rolled along, and raced to the driver's side door. Opening it, she pushed Ivy's body over to the passenger seat and got behind the wheel. She glanced in the rearview mirror, seeing the horses pounding down the track. She had to get the ambulance off the track, away from the animals, away from people. The horses would be on her within seconds. There was no time to think. There was no time to feel.

She knew what had to be done. In that split second, she understood why Jack had made the choices he had, because in that split second she had to make a choice to allow many, many others to perish—humans and animals—or to take the risk of losing her own life.

She twisted the wheel hard to the left and accelerated. She didn't know what else to do. Chloe's sweet face flashed through her mind, then Maddie, Megan, Brendan...Jack. Tears welled in her eyes, but this was the only way. There were over 200,000 people on hand, and she had no idea of the magnitude of the blast.

She prayed her family would understand, as she now understood Jack's motives from ten years ago. Her heart raced, her mind blurred, but in those last few seconds, Holly felt a calmness go through her, and she knew her decision was the right one.

Holly could not allow a catastrophic tragedy to happen.

CHAPTER

80

As they came out of the starting gate, the beating of O'Leary's heart matched the pounding of the filly's hooves. He didn't trust Perez to not play dirty no matter how big the stakes. Perez was pissed and hateful. Bad combination.

Besides, O'Leary knew enough about Karma that hanging back, waiting, watching the positions of the other horses solidify was the right move. The horse was only in second gear and she had at least three more to turn on.

As the colt pulled out in front by two lengths, O'Leary began to put on the gas.

O'Leary blinked hard as Karma broke through to the front. *What in God's name?!* The filly was thundering along at a clip so fast it was as if they were truly flying. But they weren't. That ambulance in front of them was. Holy shit! The horses kept running. The jockeys collectively knew that to try and pull up at that moment could be catastrophic. Karma, focused, did not seem to notice what was going on in front of her and to the left.

The filly kept on running.

CHAPTER
81

The horses were running their hearts out on the track as Bradley ran with the sheikh's daughter to the glass doors. Jack regained his balance and Paul was right on his heels.

Jack pulled his gun from his holster, aimed for Bradley's backside and fired. Bradley fell into one side of the double glass doors, shattering it, a bullet now lodged in his spine.

Paul was next to Bradley within seconds and bent down feeling for a pulse.

Screams rang out in the box. The sheikh's daughter dropped to her knees next to Bradley. Tears streaming down her face, she glared up at Jack. "What have you done?"

Jack didn't respond.

"My God, I loved him," she said, just loud enough for Jack to hear. "I loved him."

"Thready, but he has a pulse. Get him an ambulance," Paul said.

Jack called in for help as Alex rushed into the box with another agent, who took note of the chaos. "Jesus! What the hell happened here?"

"Doing our job," Jack said. "You?"

Alex nodded. "Someone took a shot at Farooq," he said. "But Samantha saved him. He's in protective custody now. We took the sniper out."

As Alex related this information, the people in the room let out another gasp. "Oh my God! What the hell?" someone yelled.

Jack looked out the window as an ambulance careened across the track, went through the rail and was catapulted off the berm.

"Oh no!" Alex said.

"What?" Jack yelled.

"Detective Jennings! I think she's in that ambulance!"

CHAPTER

82

The colt closed in from behind the filly as she pulled out in front. Whiskey worked hard to catch the filly. Perez wanted this! He wanted to tell Elena Purdue and that asshole O'Leary to go to hell. Then he saw it. He tensed, and as he did, so did the colt. It was that one slight shift. That was all it took.

An ambulance had gone off the inside rail.

The filly was just passing where the ambulance sailed through the air. She kept running.

Whiskey pushed on, but Perez knew in that second that the colt was off, and he began to pull back. His career would be on the line, and likely lost, if he drove the horse too hard. And so he pulled back as chaos ensued around them. Horses passed them by.

The sounds from the grandstand came to his ears now. It was a mixture of cheering and a collective gasp. Oh no. Had the colt broken his leg and Perez not realized?

As Whiskey slowed to a canter and then down to a trot, he jumped off.

Thankfully, he could see there was no break, but there was swelling, and although it wasn't as horrible as it could have been, Perez knew that the colt's racing career was over.

The Infinity belonged to the filly. Karma's Revenge was taking it to the finish line at least five lengths ahead of any other horse.

CHAPTER

83

Karma's Revenge crossed the finish line and Jack watched in horror as a burst of water exploded from the lake. It was a much bigger splash than should have resulted from the vehicle landing in the water. Jack knew instinctively that a bomb had gone off. *Holly.*

He turned to Paul. "I have to go!"

He headed down a stairwell and out onto the track. He passed onlookers and was pushed back by a security guard. "My wife is out there!" he screamed. The man tried to hold him off.

Sam ran up to him. "Jack! No! You'll blow everything!"

He turned to her, tears in his eyes. "She's my wife."

"No. No, she isn't." She shook her head. "And she's been spotted already. Help is on the way. We'll keep you updated."

"I have to know, Sam. I have to know if she'll be all right."

Sam shrugged. "I'll get you out there."

She contacted another agent, and soon an ambulance pulled up nearby. She flashed a badge at the security guard. They climbed into the back of the vehicle, which sped out to the scene.

Jack jumped out and ran to her. Her lifeless body lay on the side of the berm. "Holly! Please! *Holly!*" He took her pulse. He didn't feel anything. He began mouth-to-mouth.

Another ambulance pulled up, and the EMTs got out.

"I can't get a pulse," Jack yelled.

One of the paramedics radioed in for Life Flight.

Jack continued to work on Holly.

She took a small breath. And then another, stronger breath.

"Oh my God!" he said. "Thank God."

Sam placed a hand on his shoulder. "We have to go."

Jack stood. The EMTs grouped around her as Jack climbed back inside the ambulance that had brought them there. He could hear the blades of the Life Flight helicopter in the distance.

"You have to let her go, Jack. You have to let the past go. She'll be fine. I'm sure of it, but she has a new life and so do you," Sam said. She took his hand. "So do you."

They pulled away, and Jack knew that he would never see his wife again.

CHAPTER

84

Elena sprinted for the Winner's Circle. A lot had just happened, and whatever the hell that spectacle was out in the center of the track didn't matter at the moment. What mattered was that her filly had just won the most prestigious race in the history of racing. On top of it she would be able to call Leann and tell her that no way was Golden Hearts going under. In fact, they were going to expand their rescue center.

She made it to the circle. O'Leary was beaming atop Karma. The glorious mare was slick with sweat. She proudly pranced from side to side as camera flashes went off all around them.

Elena heard O'Leary say, "I've never ridden any horse like her. She's amazing and cool in the head. I don't know what the hell happened out there, but she didn't skip a beat. Focused and determined. That's this filly." He reached across her neck and wrapped his arms around her, then patted her on either side of the neck. The commissioner approached and laid a blanket of red roses across her.

Elena caught O'Leary's eye. He swung a leg over and jumped off the mare. He threw his arms around her. "She is amazing. Like you." He beamed. He reached to unzip the pocket of his breeches and got down on one knee. The cameras went crazy. "Elena Purdue, I lost you once because I was foolish. I never want to live a day without you. Ever again. I love you with all of my heart and soul. I love who you are as a woman, a friend, in business, and with the animals you work with. You shine with a light that no one can match, and I hope you will say yes to me, because my world hasn't ever been right without you in it." He took a breath. "Will you marry me, Elena?"

She grasped his hands, her own hands shaking, tears of joy streaming down her face. She nodded. "Yes, O'Leary. I will marry you."

He leaped up and kissed her hard as millions of viewers on television witnessed the proposal.

It had been quite a day in the world of horse racing.

CHAPTER
85

"Horse sense is the thing a horse has
which keeps it from betting on people."
—W. C. Fields

A horse can be told she's a winner, draped in roses, and immortalized in pictures, but she probably doesn't really understand.

What a horse does seem to understand is kindness, good feed, and an open field. Those are the rewards for the horse.

CHAPTER

86

When Holly opened her eyes, the first thing she noticed was a large bouquet of red roses. What the...? And then the memory came rushing back. The ambulance, Ted Ivy, the racetrack, the pond, the crash and explosion.

As the ambulance hit the water and began sinking, Holly had clambered to get out as quickly as she could. She had taken a chance that the explosives would not have the same destructive capacity once in the water. She also knew that she only had seconds to escape.

She had tried to push open the driver's side door of the ambulance. Ted's body fell on top of her. His weight and the water flooding in caused panic to speed up every beat of her heart.

Holly had squirmed under Ted and pushed her way through. The driver's door was stuck as the vehicle continued to roll farther onto its side. She had maneuvered both of her feet and with every ounce of strength she could muster she kicked at the passenger door. The door opened and water flowed in. She held her breath and worked her way out. As she did, the bomb went off. She had flown straight out of the water. That was all she remembered.

"Jack?" she said softly. *Where was he?*

"No, honey. It's me." It was Brendan, and he sounded confused. "Shh. It's okay. You had a pretty hard blow to the head. You're lucky to be here, love."

Everything hurt, hurt bad all over. She focused on Brendan at her side. Tears were in his eyes. "We are lucky to have you."

He took her hand, and she squeezed his. He sat back down in a chair next to her. "Oh God, Holly, we are so lucky."

A nurse came in. "Oh, look who is awake. Wonderful. How do you feel?"

"Like hell," Holly muttered.

"I'm sure you do. You are quite the hero, Detective. The talk of the town, the country, the world."

"I am?"

"You saved a lot of people. It appears to have been some type of terrorist plot. But I'm certain you know that already. That Ivy guy was a crazy anarchist wanting to make some kind of statement. They say he was driving that ambulance straight for the tunnel under the Prestige Box." She shook her head. "Absolutely crazy! But thanks to you, that didn't happen."

Holly's brain tried to keep up with the nurse's words. Some of it was true. Some of it was not. Where was Bradley? Where was Jack? She looked at Brendan, who said, "I think she's tired. Maybe we should let her rest."

The nurse nodded. "Of course. I just came to change her meds."

She switched out the IV bag. Another nurse entered the room. "If you don't mind, I need to change the dressing on her backside."

Holly's butt hurt like hell. "What...?" she asked.

"Glass shard. The doctors removed it. You also have some broken ribs," the second nurse replied.

"I can feel them."

"And you have a broken leg."

"I would hate to see what my face looks like. It hurts, too."

"You have some cuts and bruises, but you'll heal."

The first nurse left the room.

"You are beautiful," Brendan said.

Holly struggled to sit up. There was something about the nurse that seemed familiar.

"Want to give us a minute?" the nurse asked Brendan.

"Sure. I'll get some coffee and be right back. You go back to resting, love. I'll be here when you wake."

Holly grimaced as she turned her head to the side and spotted a few more bouquets. She also saw a small potted plant.

A plumeria.

Jack.

Her heart sank.

Brendan.

With the door closed, the nurse came closer and leaned over Holly.

"Sam?"

She nodded.

"What's going on?" Holly asked.

"I need to brief you, and we need to be quick."

"Jack? Where is he?"

"He's gone, Holly. He's on his way to Washington. He knows of your status."

"My status?!"

"Listen, you're both different now. You need to live your life and forget you ever saw him. What you need to do is revel in the fact that you are a hero. You took out someone who murdered four people in cold blood and planned to murder a whole lot more."

"I don't understand. What happened to Bradley?"

"He's in custody at a government hospital. He may or may not live. Jack took him down."

"Aren't you going to let the American people—the world— know who was behind all of this?" Holly struggled to ask.

Sam shrugged. "No. That would not be a good plan. Bradley once worked for us. He worked high up for us. If it came out what he was planning to do, I don't think it would reflect well on our government. Do you?"

"I don't think lies reflect well," Holly said. She swallowed hard. Her throat burned. She remembered Jack and making love to Jack. And now he was gone again. As deceitful as the government that employed him. He had betrayed her once again, and she had betrayed a man who truly loved her. That all-encompassing guilt and self-hatred held onto her. "What will you tell a public who believed that Bradley Quentin was a good guy? A financier? Someone who designed state-of-the-art security systems?"

Sam bent closer to her and lowered her voice. "Here's a really interesting thing about the American people...they are really gullible. You don't need to worry about Bradley's story. It will be bought and sold by the media. Go live your life, Holly, and let all of this disappear. What the people don't know cannot hurt them. Be smart. You continue being one of the good guys, and so will we. We just work on different levels. Separately."

Holly nodded and closed her eyes, reading between the lines. Sam left the room. Jack was gone again, fighting for the government. The good guys? She wasn't sure any longer who was good and who was bad. She wasn't even sure about herself.

Brendan came back in. She may not have known who all the good guys were any longer. She had doubts about the man she once called *husband*.

But she knew one good guy was still left standing in this world. And she was looking at him.

CHAPTER

87

Three weeks later

Edwin Hodges saw that Marvin Tieg's documentary did air, with the addition of what had taken place at the Infinity.

Holly watched.

The show made her question a lot of things.

She remembered the conversation she'd had with Brendan before she left for the Infinity as she sat on the couch petting their new kitten, Piper. The conversation regarding humans and the good, the bad, the ugly.

She'd learned a lot about horse racing in a short amount of time and her verdict on the sport was still out. She had discovered the good, the bad, and the ugly within that world.

Hodges had gone ahead and included Scott Christiansen and his Equine Health Systems in the documentary. The short segment showcased the passion and will on Christiansen's part to better the life of the horse. Holly wondered if the people who owned, trained, and ran racehorses would consider the option to better support the animals' legs. She didn't know.

The other good she'd found on the track were people like Elena and Leann Purdue and Pete O'Leary. After Elena returned home from Vegas, Leann had flown out to see her sister and heal, if she could, from all she had been through.

Leann had invited Holly and her family out to Elena's place in Ramona. The family had met the now very famous Karma's Revenge, who was enjoying her time off the track in a green pasture with an old friend.

"This is Badger," Elena told them. "He was born here and then sold off as a yearling. I'd heard that his owner recently passed away, so I decided to get him back. Think I've made her happy." Elena pointed to the horses standing side by side, grazing, and occasionally nuzzling each other.

Pete O'Leary was a nice man who, Holly discovered, was writing a book about Ivy and the incidents that took place. He'd even interviewed Holly, who could not be as truthful as she wanted to be. The truth in its entirety would never be disclosed.

As Brendan, the girls, and the rest of them watched the horses enjoy the lazy afternoon, Leann asked, "That agent you were working with from the FBI. Twinnings?"

Holly crossed her arms. She had not mentioned him to Brendan. "Yes."

"Have you heard from him? You guys seemed to work well together. Efficient."

"No." Holly shook her head. "He's with the government. I didn't know him until he was brought on the case. It's very doubtful that I'll ever work with him again."

"Oh."

Brendan was watching her. He took her hand. "She's going to take some time off so we can plan that wedding."

"That's right," she agreed.

The good. People like Leann, Elena, O'Leary, and Scott Christiansen.

The bad.

People like Perez, who was under investigation by the racing commission for misconduct. It had come to light that Perez had been behind the drugging of Cayman's Cult last year—definitely not Rafael Torres. Perez, along with Tieg, had helped set up the facility where the dermorphin was being made in Guadalajara.

Laugherty, too.

The truth about the fire, the drugs given to Farooq's colt—everything was coming out, and Laugherty was likely going to jail for a long time.

The bad.

The ugly.

The ugly—the real ugly that Holly had discovered was the apathy across the nation for what went on with some of the horses on the track. The racinos, the money before the animals, numerous unnecessary deaths at such young ages. A seediness that was truly ugly.

She thought about herself as she got up and turned the TV off. She'd recorded the documentary. Her family was now in bed, but she had not been able to sleep.

Earlier in the evening, Brendan had shown her the koi pond he'd finished. Next to it he had planted the plumeria. The one that Jack had left.

Now she wondered…Brendan had said she was nothing but good. Holly knew, even as she prepared to marry Brendan, that she did have some bad in her, and she did have some ugly. And as she climbed into bed with the man soon to be her husband, she couldn't help wondering what the other man she'd once called husband was doing at that moment.

She kissed the sleeping Brendan on the cheek, knowing that the good in her had made the right decision.

Brendan was the right choice.

ACKNOWLEDGMENTS

First, I want to acknowledge and thank all the readers who e-mailed me and commented that they wanted more of Holly Jennings. I never expected to write another Holly thriller, and now I can't wait to give readers more. So, thank you!

I have to acknowledge my dear friend Terri Rocovich. Terri is one of the most educated horse women I have ever had the privilege to know and call friend. She grew up on the tracks, breezed horses, and if I don't have the answer, I go to Terri. She does an amazing job with my own horses and I am indebted to her for her support, friendship, and wealth of knowledge that she shares freely and honestly.

I want to thank Corine Selders, DVM, who is also a friend and always willing to help advise me when writing medical information concerning our equine partners.

Monty Crist deserves a big thank you from me. Without his support and understanding over this past year, I don't think I would have been able to write this book.

My gratitude goes out to two of the best friends anyone could have—Jessica Park and Andrew E. Kaufman. Thank You, for seeing me through some dark days.

I have to thank Nicholas Newman of Lexington, Kentucky, who took my daughter and me on a tour through gorgeous Thoroughbred country. I think my dad was in on that and made certain we met.

Thank you to my dear friend Seyamack Kouretchian who helped me come up with a plot twist that I hope no one saw coming.

I also want to thank twenty of the most supportive, talented women writers in the world. I am blessed to be a part of something amazing. They know who they are.

Huge thanks to Anita Kemper who is an angel on Earth and my aunt is always my first reader, and always tells me the truth.

I need to acknowledge my family. My husband, John, who picks up the slack when I am writing, grills a mean steak, and always has a glass of wine waiting for me at the end of the day; my sons, Alex and Anthony, who inspire me every day; my daughter, Kaitlin, who is a talented equestrian, and who understands when Mom needs to be writing. Kait, you put a smile on my face every single day and just for that alone, you need to be acknowledged. This is all for you guys.

Many thanks to the team at Thomas & Mercer. You are all a joy to work with! I feel blessed to be a part of the family.

Finally, I have to give a huge thank you, to my mom. She is the one who has supported my passion for horses since I was a little girl, and now helps support her granddaughter. My parents built a company that gives back every day to horses. It has not been an easy year with losing my dad, who was always my biggest fan, but together Mom and I have muddled through. She is the one who reminded me that I needed to get "that book written." My dad would have expected me to stay the course, and so I did.

I love you always, Daddy.

ABOUT THE AUTHOR

A. K. Alexander dreamed of being a writer since the age of nine, earning a degree in journalism from the University of Southern California before tackling fiction. Today she is the author of almost two dozen books—women's fiction, paranormal novels, mysteries, and thrillers—including her recently reissued debut novel, *Covert Reich*. A lifelong equestrian, she helps to run her family business manufacturing sports-medicine products for horses. She is a native of San Diego, California, and still lives there today with her family, which includes three kids, nine horses, four dogs, and a cat.